"[FATAL TRUTH is] a riveting cop story, as only a real cop could tell it. I couldn't put it down."

Edgar award-winning author
William Heffernan

"WHAT THE HELL?"

I wiped some of the fog from the windshield and saw them. Squeaky. And someone chasing him with a gun.

I recognized the man tearing after the hype. I'd known him for years. Abernathy. Narcotics Detail.

Sometimes with the adrenaline racing you never hear the shot. I heard this one.

I grabbed my radio. Threw open the door. I keyed the mike to call for an ambulance and a supervisor.

Abernathy shoved his foot into Squeaky's side, rolled him over, and shot him in the chest.

I watched as Abernathy looked in my direction.

And pointed his weapon at me.

Other Kate Gillespie mysteries
by Robin Burcell

EVERY MOVE SHE MAKES

ROBIN BURCELL

FATAL TRUTH

AVON BOOKS
An Imprint of Harper Collins*Publishers*

AVON BOOKS
An Imprint of HarperCollins*Publishers*
10 East 53rd Street
New York, New York 10022-5299

ISBN: 0-06-106123-9
www.avonmystery.com

First Avon Books paperback printing: August 2002

Printed in the U.S.A.

10 9 8 7 6 5 4 3 2 1

To all the officers, men and women, of San Francisco PD, a department steeped in rich history. May God keep you safe.

PREFACE

I believe in the innate goodness of people, and of police officers nationwide. True there have been scandals, the bad apples that have come to light, even more so in this day of mass media. But the reality is that the percentage is small in comparison to the numbers of officers who work in this country today.

To that end, I would say not to judge a department or other officers by the corrupt few who have slipped past the safeguards our courts and society have erected. Judge each on their merit, using honesty and objectivity, not anger.

I say this because I chose to write about a situation that could essentially happen in any department, perhaps has happened somewhere—a situation, we pray, will never happen anywhere. It is purely a product of my imagination, which I have chosen to weave into *my* fictional world of San Francisco PD.

A portion of the author's royalties will be donated to COPS, in memory of the men and women who have given their lives in the line of duty. COPS provides resources to assist in the rebuilding of the lives of surviving families of law enforcement officers killed in the line of duty.

ACKNOWLEDGMENTS

I owe many people a debt of gratitude, and am sure to forget a few, so my apologies in advance. Any factual errors were mine. This work is purely a piece of fiction, and meant to be entertaining, nothing more.

To Lt. John R. Hennessey, SFPD, formerly of the Homicide detail until his promotion. Many thanks for bringing me up to speed on the intricacies of the department, and for calming my fears on my plot points. I imagine I owe you a lunch or two by now.

To Sgt. Rick Leslie, Stockton PD, for information regarding firearms and officer-involved shootings.

To my agent, Jane Chelius, who came into my life and made the topsy-turvy world of writing a bit steadier.

To Jennifer Sawyer Fisher, my editor. Many thanks for not giving up on me when I seemed to disappear from the face of the earth.

Many thanks to Marty Weybret, *Lodi News Sentinel,* for his generous donation to the Lodi Boys' and Girls' Club. May you be pleased with your role in this mystery.

As usual, to all my favorite mocha places: Cottage Bakery, Mocha My Day, and House of Coffees. I couldn't have stayed awake to patrol the streets on those early mornings without you.

To the Golden Ox, for letting me use your name in my last book, even though *that* establishment could never compare, especially when it comes to the wonderful food you serve.

To my neighbors the Welches, Bill for rescuing my computer from viruses (and from me) on many occasions, and to Marsha for being a good sport by allowing me to drag her husband away when I needed him.

To Susan Crosby for always being there when I pick up the phone to say: What if . . . ?

To my sister, Alwyn. Belated thanks for your help in *Every Move She Makes*.

To my beautiful daughter, Cara, who played secretary for me in the middle of nowhere on Interstate 5 when inspiration suddenly hit.

To my husband, Gary, who played Mr. Mom for me when inspiration wasn't so sudden, and for buying me my own personal espresso maker so that I didn't have to drag all the kids out on my day off to get a mocha.

FATAL TRUTH

1

The ring of the phone jarred me from a sound sleep and I reached for it, not wanting to see the time. It was still dark out, I'd started my vacation, and the only news that could come at this hour was not good.

"Gillespie?"

"Yes," I said, eyeing the clock, its orange face reminding me of a full moon. Two-ten.

"Rocky Markowski. We need you down here."

So much for my week of leisure. "What's up?"

"Stabbing. Blue versus red this time. Got about fifteen witnesses that need to be interviewed. It was you or Zim. I sorta begged the LT."

"My lucky day." Not that I blamed him. Zim was not a well-liked member of the Homicide detail. "Give me about forty minutes. Kevin's staying with me for a few days," I said, referring to my late brother's thirteen-year-old son. "I need to get my landlord up here to watch him."

"Sure. One other thing . . ."

His tone told me I wasn't going to like what followed. "Yeah?"

"It was Nita Gonzalez."

I closed my eyes. Nita's death made the fifth gang killing in as many days. Another victim of a senseless war.

"Yeah," he said, reading into my silence. "See ya in a few."

My landlord, Jack, lived downstairs with his wife. I called him, dressed in jeans and a sweater, dragged a brush through my shoulder-length brown hair, and then hurried to wake Kevin, who was asleep on the couch. "You need to go to Jack's," I told him, tousling his dark curls. He was past the kissing age, at least in his opinion. "I have to go in to work."

"Okay," he said, then rolled over. We'd done this routine before. Numerous times. I'd helped my aunt raise Kevin ever since my brother, Sean, had overdosed twelve years ago. Sean's was a death I had yet to reconcile, perhaps because he had always been a clean-cut, all-American kid. The poster child for wholesome. And he was a Narcotics officer at SFPD at the time. His death by heroin had devastated my father, so much so that when social services had discovered Kevin's existence—we knew nothing about him—my father had refused to acknowledge the child.

My aunt, on the other hand, took one look at Kevin, said in that no-nonsense way of hers, "He's a Gillespie, all right," and immediately set about raising him as one. His drug-addicted mother fled to avoid prosecution for my brother's overdose, and I enrolled in the police academy, trying to make up for my father's loss—right the wrongs that had taken my brother's life. My goal was to save the world—for Kevin.

How naïve I was back then, I thought, tucking my weapon into my waistband and zipping up my coat.

I passed Jack on the steps. The grandfather Kevin never had, he was dressed in striped pajamas and a green robe. "Take your time, Kate," he said. "I'll get him to school if you're not back."

"Thanks." My car was parked in the driveway behind Jack's. I figured I'd stop for a caffeine fix somewhere between my Berkeley Hills apartment and the Hall of Justice in San Francisco. The Bay Bridge was almost deserted heading into the city, and I found that I couldn't quit thinking about Nita. In addition to my duties as a Homicide inspector, I helped on occasion with the police Explorer post, a division of the Boy Scouts that allowed kids to learn about police work. The Gang Task Force brought Nita to me, hoping to get her off the streets and involved in something worthwhile. She'd told me she wanted to be a cop. And now she was dead.

The Homicide detail was on the fourth floor of the Hall of Justice—we referred to it simply as the Hall—and when I got there, Rocky was waiting for me at his desk. Appearances were deceiving, and had he not been wearing a shoulder holster along with a badge clipped to the belt of his tan Dockers, I doubt anyone would guess his occupation as a cop. At five-five, he stood as tall as my forehead. His brown hair was cut in a flat-top, a style that seemed at odds with his thick mustache. Round face and round gut gave testament to his love of food.

"Where'd it happen?" I asked.

"In an alley about a block away from the shooting last night. A bunch of kids were walking home from a party. Nita Gonzalez was with them. Wrong place, wrong time sort of thing is what it looks like to me," he said, grabbing his keys and overcoat. "I'll drive."

When we arrived, Rocky showed his star to a uniformed officer on the perimeter. He moved a barricade and let us into the alley lit with flashing red, blue, and amber lights from two patrol cars. On one side of the alley was a small white building that read "City Sausage and Meat Company," and on the other side, behind a neat whitewashed fence, was a house I'd been to numerous times on patrol. I was well familiar with the octogenarian owner, Harriet Maze, as was every officer in the department. Better known as Crazy Mazy, she reported a crime about every other week and was about as credible as a tabloid magazine. There was a bit of truth in everything she said, but it was lost in the mire of her imagination. "She a witness?" I asked, dreading his answer.

"The RP," Rocky said.

Reporting party. Great. "You talk to her yet?"

"Figured we'd save her for last."

"For last or for me?"

"Did I forget to mention that Andrews wants you to be the lead investigator on this?"

"Guess that tiny detail slipped your memory."

"It happened over there," Rocky said, pointing about dead center of Mazy's property. Yellow crime scene tape was strung across the alley from her fence to the bumper of a refrigerated truck belonging to the sausage company. Rocky lifted the tape and I stepped under. A crime scene investigator snapped photos of a dark stain on the asphalt.

I'd seen enough. More than enough for a lifetime. "Where are the witnesses?"

"All over. Patrol got most of the names. There's a few waiting at the Hall, and some are at home. Their parents came and got 'em."

"Suspects?"

"No one in custody. Crazy Mazy copied a plate number from a blue Monte Carlo, but they haven't found it yet."

I looked over at her house. There was a light burning in the back, and I figured we might as well get that interview over with. "Let's go talk to her," I said.

She lived in a white Victorian with yellow trim, a fortune of property and no apparent heirs. We walked around to the front and as we ascended the porch steps, the door opened a crack, Mrs. Maze undoubtedly peeking out at us. I pulled out my gold star. "I'm Inspector Gillespie," I said. "And this is my partner, Inspector Markowski."

The door opened farther, revealing a petite woman, her face a network of interlocking wrinkles and her long white hair swept into a spinster bun. Dressed in a pink housecoat, she held a flashlight in one hand, its weak beam the only light.

"Shhh," she said, putting her finger over her lips. "They're back there."

"Who?" I asked.

"The spies. Hurry. Before they leave."

She motioned us inside, shut the door behind us, then pointed the beam down the hallway, the dim light bouncing off hundreds of tiny glittering eyes. Harriet Maze had a teddy bear collection that filled up every crevice, shelf, and seat cushion in her house, leaving very little space to walk. In the dark, the eyes seemed to follow us, an eerie sensation. No wonder the woman thought she was being spied on.

She led us into her kitchen, on past the white-enameled oven. A faint scent of something sweet and citrus filled the air. Switching off her flashlight, she pointed out the window toward the alley. "There," she said triumphantly. "Do you see them? The spies?"

Rocky cleared his throat, and I took a deep breath. This was our main witness? "Those are officers, ma'am. Crime scene investigators who are out there because you reported a stabbing."

"Of course they are," she snapped. "I'm not talking about them. I'm talking about the spies inside that building where they make the sausage. *They* know I'm on to them." She gave me an accusing look, then paused. "Don't you have a brother on the force? You look just like him. Dark eyes, dark hair. I know I told *him* about this. *He* would have believed me. Such a nice young man," she added, shaking her head.

Rocky and I exchanged glances, and I figured he thought the same thing I did. Alzheimer's. Even so, I was touched that Mrs. Maze seemed to remember Sean so kindly, despite that he'd been dead these past twelve years.

"About the stabbing?" I reminded her. "You saw kids back there?"

"Kids. Hmmph." She patted a stack of political flyers on the yellow Formica table. "Democrats is more like it. They're after these."

"The kids?" Rocky and I asked simultaneously.

"The spies. Who do you think? They want these campaign secrets. They've moved their headquarters to that sausage plant right there." She pointed to City Sausage and Meat through her window. "They park that darned truck back there on purpose, leave it running all the time. You can hear it now." As if on cue, the truck's refrigeration unit kicked on. Nothing like adding fuel to her fire. She nodded sharply. "There, you see! They'll stop at nothing to win. I'm afraid to leave my house for fear they'll break in. Especially after what happened the other night."

"What was that?" I asked, resigning myself to the fact that she was never going to give us the information we came for.

"They were robbed. I was in the kitchen grating lemon peels for my lemon squares, when I thought I saw someone climbing in their window. Well, let me tell you," she said, narrowing her eyes and planting her hands on her hips. "Those hoodlums, it just makes me sick the way they throw bottles at my back fence whenever they walk in my alley."

"Hoodlums?" Rocky asked her.

"Yes. You know the ones. They dress in those football jackets and black baggy pants. Well, I went out to tell them that I was fed up with their nonsense and that I was calling the police. I was frightened near to death when I saw someone climbing in their window."

"Whose window?" I asked, thinking that at last she was back on track with the gang activity.

"The sausage place. They got away before I could call the police, and I just know they'll blame it on the Republicans, and quite possibly come after me."

"The hoodlum boys?" I asked.

"Heavens, no," came her exasperated reply. "The Democrats. They'll think I'm on to them, that I was the one to break into their headquarters."

"I can see why you'd be concerned," Rocky said, "what with elections coming up in the next few months."

I wanted to kick him. Instead I tried to guide Mrs. Maze back to the homicide. "You reported to the officer that you saw the stabbing."

"And that's exactly what I've been telling you," she said, shaking her finger at me.

"I need a unit to clear," came a dispatcher's voice on Rocky's radio. "Vehicle four-five-nine in progress."

That was as close to divine intervention as I could get. We were about a block away from the location given by the dispatcher, so I volunteered our services, hoping it might be related to the homicide in the alley. Maybe one of the suspects was hiding while he waited for the cops to clear the area. I smiled apologetically to Mrs. Maze and grabbed Rocky's radio. "Someone's trying to break into a car. We have to go."

"Oh." Suddenly she looked lonely and very much her age. "Well, let me pack you some cookies for the road."

"Only wish we had time," I said, as she picked up a plate filled with lemon squares.

Rocky grabbed two, and to be polite, I took one myself. "Thanks," I said, handing her my card as we left. "Call if you think of anything else you've forgotten."

This time I drove.

"She's wacko," Rocky said. "But she makes a mean cookie. You shoulda let her give us more for the road."

"And cheat you out of a possible arrest stat? Not a chance."

Rocky called in our arrival. I shut off the headlights as we rolled to a stop.

"Should be right up the street," he said.

"Let's get out here. Move in on foot."

The coastal fog was patchy, and there was a faint smell of brine in the air. We exited our vehicle, quietly shutting the doors. At the corner we sidled up to a townhouse and peeked through the hedge to the street beyond. I saw a slight movement, a dim light coming from the interior of the fourth car parked on an incline to our left.

"There," I whispered as I pointed. "Inside the white Toyota."

We drew our weapons, kept close to the houses, made our way to the vehicle. Rocky's chest heaved from the exertion of running low up the hill. Nevertheless, flashlight in hand, he moved around to the driver's side, while I took the passenger side, noting the door was slightly ajar. Whoever was inside ducked.

"Police," Rocky called out, aiming the beam of his Streamlight as well as his weapon into the window.

The figure inside shot up, bumped his head on the dash, and stumbled from the door, landing in the gutter.

"Hands up," I shouted.

"Hey man, it ain't what you think," the burglar said in a high-pitched whine that I recognized instantly. Squeaky Kincaid, a snitch I'd used for information in the past and, unfortunately, like gum on the bottom of my shoe, hadn't been able to shake since. He sat up, his sunken cheeks and sallow complexion contrasting sharply against his black clothes. "I was just trying to get warm."

"Really," Rocky said, moving around to my side. "Thought maybe you were wearing them gloves because you didn't want to leave prints. Now get your hands behind your back like a good little dope addict, and we won't rough you up too much."

"I didn't steal nothing. The car was unlocked."

That I didn't doubt, about the car being unlocked. Squeaky usually went after easy prey. I holstered my weapon, then took out my cuffs. Rocky covered him. "You got any needles on you, Squeaky?" I asked. "Or do you want to know what'll happen to you if I get stuck?"

"Got one in my right sock."

"Good boy."

I patted him down, found a pocket full of quarters, the needle in his sock, but nothing else. My guess was the change in his pocket came from the car. Parking being at a premium in the city, there was no guarantee that the victim's car was parked in front of the victim's house. "Run the twenty-eight, Markowski."

He radioed in the license plate. The registered owner, a Marsha Welch, lived three houses up, and was adamant that she always left her car unlocked—so no one would be tempted to break in. Although she thought the loose change from her car's ashtray was missing, she wasn't willing to sign a complaint.

We kept that bit of information from Squeaky. Better to let him think he was being taken in—the proverbial ace in the hole, I thought, watching him shivering against the front fender of the victim's car. He was still handcuffed and no doubt contemplating how he was going to get his next fix from jail.

"What'dya think?" Rocky asked loud enough for Squeaky to hear.

"I think his PO will be mighty interested to know what he stores in his sock." I secured the syringe into a plastic bio-hazard tube. "What're you looking at, Squeaky. Six months? A year?"

"Lemme work it off." He looked at me, his eyes pleading like a puppy's. "Tomorrow or the next day. I'm working on something big. Soon as my sister gets here with her car. Got it all scoped out."

"I'll be holding my breath," I said. I fished out my handcuff key and unlocked his cuffs. "If the temptation to take the chill off in anyone else's car strikes you tonight, stifle it with the thought of how much fun it is to swallow methadone instead of fixing a nice shot of heroin. You catch my meaning?"

"I'm outta here. I swear I'll call you."

The following afternoon I'd pretty much dismissed him from my mind, wanting to find Nita's killer and then return to my vacation. I was almost finished with my paperwork when Gypsy, the Homicide detail's secretary, walked in with a report in her hand. Built like a centerfold, she ran the office with all the efficiency of a captain running a ship.

"I know it's late," she said, "but the lieutenant wanted me to get this to you right away. Interrupted burglary, possible gang ties related to your last homicide. Victim's in the hospital, not expected to live."

So much for the remainder of my vacation. My phone rang and I answered it while scanning the report. "Gillespie, Homicide."

"It's me. Squeaky."

I nearly dropped the phone at the sight of the victim's name written in the investigating officer's neat block printing: "Maze, Harriet."

Crazy Mazy.

I stared in disbelief, then shook myself, as I realized Squeaky was waiting for me to acknowledge him. "What is it?" I asked curtly.

I cradled the phone on my shoulder, turned to the body of the report, and scanned it. Someone found her in the alley near her fence. There was some gang graffiti sprayed on the fence boards, and the officer made a note that it might have something to do with the gang stabbing in the alley, quite possibly a retaliation because she had called the police.

I listened with half an ear while Squeaky talked about some burglary he'd committed not too far from where we found him, unfortunately without enough details to do me any good. If he was confessing to me, he must have gotten caught in the act.

"Did you hear me, Inspector?" he whined in his usual nervous, high-pitched voice.

"Hmm? Yeah," I said, unable to believe we'd stood in Mrs. Maze's kitchen just the night before. "Is there a point to all this? Like, what you stole? Where you were? Anything I can use?"

"I've got to talk to you right away. And not on the phone. Something big's going down in about five days."

"Can't. I get off in twenty minutes. I've got plans for the night."

Suddenly he burst out crying.

I pulled the phone from my ear for a couple seconds, wondering how I'd ever had the misfortune of hooking up with the likes of Squeaky Kincaid. For whatever reason over the years, he had latched on to me like I was his personal cop. He'd often said I was the only one he could trust, no matter how many times I'd encouraged him to call Narcotics with the information he wanted to sell for drug money.

Several seconds later he still hadn't calmed down. Tempted to hang up on him, I asked, "You okay?"

"They're gonna kill me," he sobbed. "I saw them and they're gonna kill me."

"Who?"

"Foust. I got something he wants."

"Foust? Jesus. Can you at least give me an address? Tell me what you've got?"

"Not over the phone . . . Oh, God. Please . . . you have to help me. It's not just Foust. They're right there. All around you. Like I told you the other night, this is big, man. Bigger than you and me." I could hear him sniffling, but my mind barely registered it. Antonio Foust was on the FBI's Ten Most Wanted List. He'd made a couple of attempts on my life, was suspected of killing two other cops, and I definitely wanted him arrested.

"You need me to pick you up?" I asked. Squeaky didn't drive.

"My sister's in town. She'll give me a ride. It's gotta be tonight."

I thought about Kevin, waiting for me in my apartment. He'd had what I assumed was a normal pre-puberty-driven argument with my aunt, which was why I was letting him spend the week. And while he was old enough to be left alone for a few hours at a time, it didn't mean I liked doing it. Then again, as unreliable as Squeaky was, whatever he had to offer up on Foust couldn't take that much time. "Tonight, then," I said.

"No one's listening, are they?" he asked.

Rocky walked in just then and I waved Harriet's report at him. He took it and I saw his eyes widen as he read the name. "No," I said into the phone. "No one's listening."

"Okay. In the alley past the old print shop at eight-thirty."

"Eight-thirty." I glanced out the window toward the Bay Bridge and saw that traffic for the on ramp was at a standstill. Which meant I wouldn't make it home in time for dinner. Kevin would have to eat at Jack's. "I'll be there."

"Alone. And don't tell anyone. Please," he begged.

"Look—" I started, but he'd hung up on me.

I replaced the phone on the cradle. Rocky, I noticed, was still reading the report, his expression hard. I flipped through my phone list, found the number for ICU at the hospital, and called it. "Can you give me the status of Harriet Maze? She was brought in early this morning," I told the woman who answered.

"Hold on, Inspector." I heard a rustle of papers and some muffled talking. "She's hanging in there."

"Any chance of an interview?" I had to ask, as heartless as it sounded. My priority was to find her attacker. The hospital's was to save her life, and I would defer to their wishes.

"No. If anything changes, we'll let you know."

"Thanks."

I hung up, feeling deflated. Crazy Mazy. Lemon cookies.

And she had remembered my brother as an officer after all these years.

"What do you suppose happened?" Rocky asked, handing the report back to me.

"I don't know. But I intend to find out." If she died, I couldn't let her be just one more statistic. I knew every cop who worked that area would feel the same way. We might hate getting called to her house, but she was part of the culture, part of the beat. Ours alone. For now, all I could do was wait. I glanced up at the clock. Fifteen minutes before the end of my shift and then it was homeward bound. No, correct that. Meeting with Squeaky. I looked out the window and saw it had started raining. Hoping it wasn't an omen, I asked Rocky, "What are you doing tonight?"

"Nothing. My mother-in-law's coming over."

"Good. Then you won't mind coming out with me for a contact."

"What'dya got?"

"Squeaky's dropping the dime on something big tonight. He says he can give me something on Foust. Whether it's legit, I don't know. He wouldn't give details."

"Yeah. Sure," he said, when I told him where. "Give me a good excuse to get out of the house. How about I meet you about a block from the rendezvous, say, ten minutes early?"

"Perfect."

I called Kevin and then my landlord, Jack, letting them know I'd be tied up for a few hours. For dinner I ended up buying a bag of tortilla chips from the vending machine and spent the remainder of the evening looking up reports on Harriet Maze that might have some connection. I would have had better luck printing the case numbers and throwing a dart, she'd called the police so many times—never mind that trying to discern fact from fiction in her reports was nearly impossible. When it was time to hook up with Rocky, I checked my weapon, shoved it in my shoulder holster, grabbed a radio, then pulled on my jacket, managing to make it to my car without getting drenched.

The rain sounded like rice bouncing off my windshield—and reminded me of my wedding a couple of years ago, a six-month disaster. I drove for fifteen minutes, finally easing my car into the narrow alley about a block away from where Squeaky had directed me to, and where Rocky had said he'd meet me. I switched off my headlights, parking about a third of the way in beside a vacant warehouse, battle-scarred with shattered windows and boarded doorways. At the far end of the alley the lifeless glow from a street lamp slashed across the wet pavement like a stroke in an oil painting.

I killed my engine, then rolled down the window about an inch. And waited. Rain sluiced through the opening. I shivered, but not from the cold. Rocky never arrived. It was ten minutes past the time he'd said he'd meet me and so I called him. When he didn't answer, I left my cell phone number on his pager. I was there on my own. Against department policy. Without backup.

Only me and God.

And maybe out there my damned informant—waiting somewhere—not that I intended on meeting him without Rocky.

Glancing at my watch, I wondered what Squeaky could possibly give me for my trouble. He was known for his tall tales.

My cell phone rang and I picked it up. It was Markowski. "Where the hell are you?" I asked.

"My kid got sick. Had to take her to MEH," he said, referring to San Francisco General Hospital's emergency. "I couldn't get ahold of Shipley, so I called Zim. He told me he'd cover you. Isn't he there?"

"No, he isn't," I said, keeping my anger at bay. "I wish you'd called me earlier."

"I meant to. I'm sorry. I didn't plan this. What're you gonna do?"

"Leave," I said. I couldn't depend on Zim. "Hope your kid's better," I added, then disconnected.

As I tossed the phone onto the seat, the far end of the alley lit up from the headlights of a car that had yet to turn the corner. But instead of the car, I saw a man barreling toward me as though running from the light source. Lit from behind, only his silhouette was visible, until I switched on my own headlights.

"What the hell?" I wiped some of the fog from the windshield. Squeaky. And someone chasing after him.

My hand froze midair.

The man tearing after the hype held a gun.

I recognized him. Abernathy. Narcotics detail.

Sometimes with the adrenaline racing you never hear the shot.

I heard this one.

Saw the addict's empty hands.

His body lurched forward.

Crumpled to the wet pavement.

I grabbed my radio. Threw open the door. Apparently Squeaky's ability to stay one step ahead of the law just ran out.

I keyed the mike to call for an ambulance and a supervisor. SOP for officer-involved shooting.

Abernathy shoved his foot into Squeaky's side and rolled him over. Shot him in the chest.

I saw them. They're gonna kill me.

Squeaky's words.

I hadn't believed him. He'd lied before. Anything to get money for heroin.

I watched as Abernathy, whom I'd known for years, looked in my direction.

And pointed his weapon at me.

I never had time to go for my gun.

Bullets hit metal.

"Son of a—"

I slammed the gearshift in reverse. Stabbed at the gas pedal. Tires screeched. Slick pavement. More shots.

"Go, car. Dammit, go!"

Trash cans clattered off fenders. Free of the alley, I never stopped. Never remembered shutting my door. Only shoving the gearshift into drive. Metal ground against metal.

Gas pedal floored. Down the street, up a hill and down another. On past warehouses. Past towering high-rises. Past Chinatown. Sidewalks deserted. Rain.

What the hell had Squeaky told me when he'd called this afternoon?

My right wheel hit a pothole, jerking the car. I gripped the steering wheel more tightly and cursed. My hands stung from adrenaline.

All I could see was Squeaky's body. The muzzle blast from each shot. I couldn't think. Nausea gripped me. Refused to let go.

On the outskirts of Chinatown, I pulled my car to the side of the road, threw the door open, leaned out. Dry heaves racked my gut. I tried to take a deep breath.

I glanced skyward, letting the rain cleanse my face. When I closed my eyes, I couldn't erase the sight of Squeaky's body, lying there while the rain beat down. An image burned in my head, one of blood running through puddles of water.

Not over the phone . . . you have to help me. It's not just Foust. They're right there. All around you. Like I told you, this is big, man. Bigger than you and me.

Brakes squealed. The familiar sound of a radio car. I forced my mind to alertness. Slammed my door, ducked down, killed the lights. The patrol car turned down my street. It grew closer. A spotlight reflected off a nearby building. It swept over my car, flooding the interior with light.

Instinct and pure fear held me still.

I should flag it down. Call for help. I told myself its presence could be coincidence. The officers could be on routine patrol. But what if they weren't? What if they were looking for me?

Squeaky had alluded to something that was too big for me. Why else would a Narcotics officer try to murder a potential witness to the homicide of a heroin addict?

And what recourse did I have? I glanced at the dashboard clock. Eleven minutes had elapsed. And with each of those minutes came a deeper problem. It was my duty to report what I'd seen. Immediately. The time lapse was inexcusable. Precious minutes wasted. Minutes that needed to be accounted for. Explanations as to why I was letting a police cruiser go by without notifying them of what happened.

But something kept me there, riveted to my car seat—not picking up the radio, though time bled away.

The sound of fear in Squeaky's voice.

One particular word he had used.

Several times, in fact.

They're.

As in *They're gonna kill me.* And *They're all around you.*

They're.

As in Abernathy wasn't the only one.

2

A deep-seated instinct told me that I couldn't just march into the department and announce what I'd seen. Then just march out.

I had to think. Think.

Abernathy. There was no doubt his attempt to kill me was for one purpose only. A cop doesn't turn a gun on someone without identifying himself. Unless he feels he's in danger and there's no time. Or he wants to eliminate a potential witness.

A witness to murder.

The question was, had he seen me? He had to have seen my car when I pulled out.

But had he seen *me*?

Could he identify me? Go after me?

Kevin.

Dear God. He was at my apartment. Alone.

I punched in my home number, letting the phone ring while I slid up to check the street in both directions. Clear. My answering machine came on. I called out for my nephew to pick up the phone. When he didn't I called Jack's number, figuring he must still be downstairs. And got no answer there, either. I panicked, driving way over the speed limit en route to the Bay Bridge. Maybe that was why I didn't notice the cop car behind me. Not until it red-lighted me. I pulled over, fighting my growing alarm as he angled his spotlight into my rearview mirror, blinding me momentarily.

From my open window I heard his approaching footsteps, and with each step my heart rate increased. *I'm being silly,* I told myself. *I was speeding, nothing more. I can't suspect every cop because of what happened—because one cop murdered Squeaky and tried to murder me.*

All too soon, he was at my window. CHP, I realized on seeing the tan uniform a second before he aimed his flashlight at me.

"May I see your driver's license and registration, please?"

I gave a slight nod, not trusting myself to speak. I found my license, gave it to him, and was dismayed to see how much my hand shook.

His radio crackled, and he paused to turn it up. I heard a static-filled dispatch of, ". . . you to clear code three."

"Your lucky day," the officer told me, handing me my license without seeming to look at it. "Slow it down, okay?"

"Thanks," I said, but he was already running back to his car. Once there he hit the siren and made a U-turn, heading back to the city.

I sat there for a second, calming my nerves, then drove off at a reasonable speed until his lights were no longer visible in my rearview mirror. Then I hit the gas, praying that there were no more cops between me and home.

Traffic wasn't too heavy and I dodged cars while I tried to call my supervisor, Lieutenant Andrews. His answering machine came on. What was I supposed to say? LT, it's Gillespie. Just thought you should know someone from Narcotics tried to kill me?

Hardly. I disconnected and called Mike Torrance, the lieutenant in charge of Management Control, the politically correct term for Internal Affairs. We'd worked a past homicide together, almost had our own internal affair, and I trusted him. But there was no answer, not even a recorder. I knew his pager number, so I called that. I didn't know who else to call and worried about Kevin and Jack not answering the phone. After leaving my cell phone number on Torrance's pager, I called home again.

By the time I reached Berkeley, I'd convinced myself that he was down at the landlord's. That had to be it. Why then weren't they answering their phone? I'd called enough times; my phone battery was near dead. The steep street I lived on was crowded with parked cars. I could have pulled into my landlord's driveway, but that niggling fear kept me from doing so. I parked around the corner, walked down the hill, my hand in my jacket pocket, gripped tightly around the butt of my gun.

I cut across my neighbor's front lawn. Leaves, wet from the rain, slicked the grass, and I had to watch my step as I sidled around the hedge down the side yard. My landlord's light was on and I heard the TV as I edged by to the back of the house, a two-story built in the 1920s. I paused by their window, peered through the hedge into their TV room, but couldn't see in. Couldn't tell if Kevin was there or not. I stopped before I came to the end of the hedge, just a few feet from the stairs that led up to my porch, the entrance to my apartment. I drew my weapon, held it at close quarters, took a breath. Peeked through the space in the branches.

Saw a shadow by my door.

I moved through the hedge, approached the steps, keeping my aim steady. "Show me your hands," I called out.

The tall man stepped from beneath the eaves, his hands in the pockets of his tan raincoat. I had no idea who he was, wasn't watching his face. "I said, show me your hands."

Slowly he pulled both hands out of his pockets, holding them out as he took a step forward. "Nice of you to make it." It was Sam Scolari. Ex-cop. My ex-partner. He'd quit the PD a few months ago after his wife was murdered, and was now a PI. "You mind not aiming that thing at me?" he asked.

"What are you doing here?"

"Waiting for you." He gave a pointed look at my gun and raised his brows. Tall, gray-haired, he had a lined face that made him look older than his fifty-something years. "Maybe we should try this another night?"

"No," I said quickly, glancing up at my darkened apartment. With everything that had happened, I'd completely forgotten he was coming over tonight. He didn't want to be alone on his wedding anniversary. "No, tonight's good. I just need to find Kevin."

"Him and the old man took off when I got here. Said they were going to a movie."

Relief. Momentary. I glanced toward Jack's back door. To where I saw the blue reflection from his TV. He left it on all the time. Normal. That was good. "How long ago was that?"

"Fifteen. Twenty."

"You've been here that long?"

"I'm a patient man. Now you gonna stand there at the bottom or you gonna come up, invite me in, and tell me why you almost put a few new buttonholes in my raincoat?"

I stuck my semi-auto in my waistband, then dug my house key out of my pocket. Dinky, my landlord's oversized orange tabby, flew past me, anxious to get in, out of the wet. At the top, Scolari moved aside while I tried to unlock the door, the cat meowing at my feet. My hand shook.

"What the hell's going on?" he asked, taking the key from me, easily opening the door. Without waiting for my answer, he ushered me in, flicked on the light, and pushed me in the chair. "Christ Almighty, you're as white as a ghost. What happened?"

"Squeaky Kincaid. Someone murdered him." I met his gaze, gauged his reaction.

Scolari said nothing. I knew he was thinking the same thing every other officer, ex or otherwise, would be thinking had they known Squeaky—so what?

"It was Abernathy. He killed Squeaky and then he tried to kill me."

Scolari stared at me for a long second, then started opening the cupboards, painted white to match the hexagonal tiles on the counter. "You got anything to drink? Something strong?" He found the liquor in a cabinet by the sink, eyed the bottles, me, then pulled out the whiskey. He poured a couple of shots into two glasses he found in the dish drainer. I hated whiskey.

"Drink."

"I don't want any." I buried my head in my hands, trying to blot out the images that came when I closed my eyes.

"Look, Gillespie. Whatever the hell happened, happened. Now take a sip, let it burn, and get past it. And tell me what the hell is going on."

I took a sip, only because it made sense. I needed the jolt, the bitterness, something to make me move past this feeling of shock. I left the rest untouched, watching while he drained his glass.

"Go ahead," he said when he finished. "Tell me."

The cat jumped on my lap and I stroked his wet fur. I spoke, starting from the beginning, from the moment we caught Squeaky breaking into that lady's car, to the phone call I got from him about Foust, and then tonight. The murder.

"Why?" he asked, his voice raspy, soft. He cleared his throat. "You sure Abernathy didn't mistake you for a suspect? Think you were lying in wait? A danger to him?"

"I wanted it to be that. Thought so up until the moment he shoved Squeaky with his foot. And shot him again. The moment he became aware of my presence. He just started shooting at me—" I stared into my glass at the amber, foul-tasting liquid. "He never gave me a chance."

"You think he saw you?"

"I don't know. My headlights were on. I pulled out of there without thinking, but I was pretty low. Kept down."

"What car you in?"

"The blue Taurus."

"Could be anyone's. There's gotta be a million of them in the city."

He was right about that. There had to be several dozen just like it in the Hall of Justice parking garage.

"Where the hell was your backup?"

"Good question. Rocky was supposed to meet me, but never showed. He called and said Zimmerman was covering for him. Zim never showed."

"You talk to either of them since?"

"No." I was angry. Zim left me hanging. "I sure as hell plan to."

"Well, don't do anything yet. We gotta think about this."

I got up and paced the kitchen. "I've got to call Andrews. Let him know." I strode into the living room and picked up the phone. Before I could finish dialing, Scolari grabbed the phone and stopped me.

"You crazy? How the hell do you know he's safe?"

"How the hell do I know *you're* not in it? You were conveniently located on my porch the moment I got here."

"Yeah, I set this up a week in advance for an alibi."

We stood like that for several seconds, both holding the phone, staring at each other. His blue gaze never wavered.

"I'm sorry. But I have a hard time believing Andrews would be involved."

"So do I," he said. "But you gotta go on what you know. And what you don't know is whose phone is safe and whose isn't. And then you gotta know that whoever you're gonna tell doesn't tell the wrong person. Because if Squeaky said what I think you're saying he did, then you tell the wrong person, and you're dead. *Capice?*"

"You're thinking that 'bigger than you and me' means rank?"

"I sure as hell hope not. But do you want to take a chance?"

I let him have the phone, then sank to the couch. "Maybe it's only Abernathy."

"You and me both know that in a department that size, a vein of corruption can run deep."

"Yeah, but that's something you read about happening somewhere else. Some other city. LA. New York."

"And now San Francisco," he said.

I leaned my head back, closing my eyes. I had to think about this logically. "He said something was going down in about five days."

"Any idea what?"

"Not a clue."

"Anyone you absolutely trust?"

"Torrance," I said. "Mike Torrance." We'd worked together on the homicide of Scolari's wife, but in the past several months we hadn't exchanged two words, both going our separate ways once the case was solved.

"Call him."

I laughed. "Already tried."

"When's he gonna be back?"

"He didn't leave me his itinerary."

"Bit touchy about him," he said in response to my curt tone.

It took someone trying to kill me before I had the guts to finally call Torrance. And then when I had, I'd expected him to return my page immediately. I was disappointed that he hadn't. "He's just hard to read."

"And yet you still trust him?"

I looked Scolari dead on. "Absolutely."

"Okay. We wait for him to get back to you."

"And then what? In the meantime my career, if not my life, goes down the tubes? If someone saw me, I'm in danger. My family's in danger. I've got a nephew due back, an aunt. What am I supposed to do about them?"

"Keep 'em away from here and you."

"That'll go over well with Kevin's shrink. She already thinks I'm a bad influence."

"The kid's seeing a shrink?"

"A shrink who thinks all Kevin's problems are my fault, because I gave Kevin a watered-down version of how his father died and completely lied to him about his mother. I told him his father *accidentally* overdosed."

"So you told a little white lie?"

"Yeah, well I also told him his mother died in childbirth. How was I supposed to know he'd come across the damned news clippings my aunt had hidden in her closet? He's been having nightmares ever since."

"What a way to find out."

"Yeah. Nothing like reading about how your father died from an overdose that was allegedly supplied by your mother the drug dealer, who skipped town and abandoned you." I glanced into the kitchen, eyeing the remaining whiskey in my glass. How tempting. Instead I turned to Scolari. "Do you realize that every time I go to work, Kevin's thinking that something's gonna happen to me and I won't come back? I know that's why he and my aunt aren't getting along right now."

"So the kid's having a bit of a tough time. It'll pass."

"Pass? Jesus Christ. I'm still screwed up over my brother's death and that was twelve years ago. Do you realize that Kevin's goddamned shrink had the nerve to tell me I'm in complete denial because I still can't believe that the brother I admired the whole time I was growing up became some cop on the take and a heroin addict to boot?"

"It happens."

"Not to Sean," I yelled. I closed my eyes, surprised to feel tears welling up after all these years. "Sorry."

"No, you're not. And I don't expect you to be. I liked Sean. I was the one who was sorry. I figured he had something the others didn't."

"You did?" His statement surprised me. I was aware he'd known my brother, but not enough to offer that.

"He was a good kid. But you gotta face it, Kate. If what happened to him was any indication that the good can take a wrong turn, then what happened tonight proves it." He headed to the kitchen. I followed. "Things go wrong," he continued. "Things you don't expect. A divorce, money problems, women . . ."

His voice faded off, and I wondered if he was thinking about his dead wife. The things that went wrong with his marriage before she was murdered.

He picked up the whiskey bottle, poured himself another shot, and took a drink. "Think about Abernathy," he said, glass in hand. "You think he was dirty when he came on? What is he? Sixteen-, seventeen-year veteran? He had stars in his eyes, too. I remember them. I was there when he graduated from his academy class. Right there with your brother. And he was good, just like your brother was. Wasn't on the street longer than what, three, four years tops. Then off to Narcotics detail."

The phone rang, jarring my nerves. I met Scolari's gaze.

"You gonna get it?"

"Yeah." I answered it, not sure who I wanted it to be on the other end.

"You paged?"

"Yes." I covered the mouthpiece. "It's Torrance," I told Scolari. To Torrance I said, "I need to talk to you. In person."

"Now's not a good time."

"It can't wait."

Hesitation. I heard Greek music in the background, and recalled the restaurant he'd taken me to one evening. I wondered if he was on a date.

"Where?" he finally asked.

"Where?" I mouthed to Scolari.

He shrugged, then whispered, "Murphy's Law."

"Murphy's Law," I told Torrance.

"Sure."

I hung up. Scolari finished off his drink, then wiped his mouth with the back of his hand. "Put something dry on."

"I'm fine."

"You look like a drowned rat."

I probably did. I started toward my bedroom, but stopped, turning to him. "How are things with you?"

He didn't look at me for a long time, just stared at the bottle he held. The cheap whiskey. "Today we would've been married twenty years."

He fingered the bottle and finally put it down. "You better get moving. I have a feeling it's gonna be a long night."

Part of me wanted to comfort Scolari to help him get past the thoughts that haunted him, but I had ghosts of my own. Instead I went to my room, pulled off my damp clothes, then threw on some jeans, a sweater, hiking boots. I came out and called my landlord's apartment, leaving a message on his answering machine to let him know I was going to be later than I thought, and could he please take Kevin to my aunt's after they returned? After that, I grabbed a coat and my gun. We took Scolari's vehicle, a new black Ford pickup with more gadgets on it than the cockpit of a plane. The rain had stopped, but the streets were wet.

We pulled onto University, heading toward I–80. Scolari rolled down his window, then lit up a cigarette. I tried not to think about what had happened and instead concentrated on the taillights in front of us, following the red line they made down the hill to the freeway. Beyond that was the blackness of the bay, shot with white lights from the bridge and the city skyline. On any other night I might think it beautiful. Tonight I didn't care. I wondered about my brother, and if what had set him on the road of darkness was similar to what had happened to Abernathy.

By the time we reached the city I finally got up the courage to ask Scolari. "What do you think happened to Sean?"

He was smoking his third cigarette and stubbed it out in the ashtray. "Hard to say. If I had to guess, I'd say your brother fell hard for someone he was working with or met undercover. Informant, something like that. They probably had a coupla drinks, hit the sack. One thing led to another."

"I'd always figured she was a hooker."

"Not to rain on your parade while you're waxin' maudlin here, but we got a helluva lot more important things to be thinking about right now. Like how to get to Murphy's Law with the roads all jammed."

I forced my attention out the window and noticed we were just a few blocks from where Squeaky was shot. Scolari's pickup gave me a view above the traffic. I saw the flashing red and blue three-sixties of a patrol car up ahead. A uniform diverted all vehicles to the right, away from several barricades that were connected by yellow crime scene tape. We were about eight cars back. A group of men, some suited and some uniformed, stood on one corner, apparently in deep discussion.

"You think someone already reported your shooting?" he asked.

"Location's wrong. It was a few blocks east of here." Very big city blocks.

"Well, something happened. There's Lieutenant Majors."

Majors ran the Night Owls, the Night Investigations unit, which usually meant some sort of fatality.

"Motors," Scolari said. Two motor officers stood in the middle of the street, their white helmets reflecting the red and blue three-sixties of the radio cars. One held a roller-tape, the other wrote something in a small notebook.

I let out a breath, realizing I'd envisioned all sorts of crazy things. Like Abernathy moving the body. Setting up a new scene. Making it look like he was innocent. "An accident," I said, as though that explained everything, when in fact it explained nothing. Nothing relating to my incident. "Drive on up. Let's see what's there."

"I was thinking the same thing myself," he said. We neared the uniformed officer directing traffic. Scolari rolled down his window, nodded to the officer, and showed him the ID that identified him as a retired inspector sergeant. "Evening," he said. "Accident up ahead?"

The officer, his face pale and drawn, gave Scolari's ID a glance. "Hit-and-run," he said before he looked into the window and saw me. "Oh, hi, Inspector. Were you called out to the scene?"

I didn't know the officer, but that in itself wasn't unusual in a department this size. "No. What's going on?"

He swallowed, looking away for a moment as though to compose himself. When he finally turned back, he said, "Abernathy from Narcotics. He's dead."

3

I don't know what I expected to hear. I'd imagined any number of things.

Abernathy's death was not one of them.

"How?" I heard myself say, as if from a long way off.

"We're not sure. Looks like a hit-and-run."

Scolari was still beside me. He gripped the steering wheel, his knuckles white. He didn't look at me, just stared straight ahead.

"Is there somewhere we can park?" I asked the officer.

"Yeah. Over there," he said, pointing to a dry cleaner on our right. Three cars were parked there, all unmarkeds.

"Thanks."

Scolari signaled and pulled into the lot. "Now what?" he asked.

"I better check it out." The officer might think it odd if I didn't get out, at least, to inquire into the particulars of a fellow officer's death.

He rolled up the window, looking at me. "Yeah. The uniform knew you."

"You coming?"

"Sure. I been around long enough. No one'll think twice."

We got out and headed across the street, the officer stopping traffic for us. The group on the corner looked up as we approached. I scanned their faces—all appeared taut, concerned—and I recognized a few from Night Owls, a couple from Narcotics, and the watch commander from patrol. "Jamison's not here," I said under my breath, referring to Abernathy's partner.

"Yeah. I'm noticing that. Not that it tells us anything."

As in whether Jamison was involved. Had it been my partner, I would have been here come hell or high water. "IA isn't here, either," I said. Which meant that Abernathy was not suspected of any wrongdoing. Nor was any other cop. Yet.

We neared. The Narcotics lieutenant stepped forward, wearing jeans, long-sleeved T-shirt, and a down vest, standard fare for his detail. "Gillespie," he said, putting his hand on my shoulder. He looked grieved.

"Lieutenant Mattocks." I reached up, clasping my hand on his. He'd been my boss when I worked Narcotics. "We just heard."

Beside me, Scolari shook hands with those he knew, appearing appropriately concerned, the retired officer hearing about the death of a current officer. "Anyone know what happened?" he asked. "When?"

Lieutenant Mattocks nodded toward the markers about twenty feet away in the street, the number one lane. Fast lane. "Far as we can tell, he was crossing the street from the northwest corner when he was struck. Passing motorist called nine-one-one from the pay phone at that garage about twenty-one-hundred hours."

Nine P.M. About fifteen minutes after he'd shot Squeaky. I looked toward the northwest corner, saw an old gas station converted to a repair garage, closed for the night, pay phone mounted by the door. Beside the garage was a video store, windows barred. Also closed.

"Witness?" I asked.

"None that we can find, yet. Now we got Hit and Run investigating," he said, nodding toward the motor officers from the Hit and Run detail. They still stood in the street, taking measurements.

"You guys know what case he was working on?" Scolari asked.

Lieutenant Mattocks and one of the Narcotics officers exchanged glances.

"Don't know," Mattocks said.

Which meant nothing.

"I can't believe it," I said to no one in particular.

Scolari put his arm around my shoulder. "Come on, Kate. We better let them get back to work. This time of night, you guys were probably already knee-deep in calls." It was a statement thrown out to sea, like a worm on a hook.

"Until this," Mattocks said, "not a thing."

No report of any shooting.

Scolari offered condolences, said the good-byes, call if they needed anything. I switched from autopilot to instant replay, going over everything in my mind, the shooting, how long it would take to get from point A, Squeaky Kincaid's murder scene, to point B, the hit-and-run scene. I gave it eight minutes, tops. And that was at a brisk walk. I didn't see Abernathy running there. No, he'd just chased after the hype. Was probably tired. And running would bring attention. He couldn't do that. Not after being involved in a shooting. Not if he intended to cover it up.

No, I saw him walking. Fast, but calm. Not to the cellular in his car, pocket, or wherever. To a secure line. A landline. The phone booth. Something he knew couldn't be copied by any secondary listening devices. The question was, whom did he call? His partner, George Jamison, came to mind.

We left the accident scene, driving in silence past the Hall to the front of Murphy's Law, a cop bar.

I wished Scolari had picked someplace else. Someplace less public. I told him so.

"Actually, it works out for the best," he said. "You gotta be seen, act normal."

"Normal for me isn't hanging out at the bar."

"It is if you're going out with me."

"Come again?"

"As far as anyone's concerned, and until we know who we can tell, you were with me all night. You got it?"

"You barely tolerated me when we were partners."

"Yeah, me and the rest of the Homicide detail. But as far as they know, you solved my wife's murder, and I've seen the error of my ways. And regardless of what those idiots you work with think now, and what I thought then, a guy's allowed to change his mind. I was wrong about you. Back then, I figured you got the job by sleeping with the captain."

"Funny, I'd heard it was the captain's wife." She was a lieutenant, and rumors abounded about her power in the department.

"Yeah," he said gruffly. "I heard that one, too. But I was giving you credit for having taste. Now come on, we got a show to do."

He called it on the money. A show. Or a bad dream. That's what it felt like, the moment we walked into Murphy's Law. Dark, smoky despite the laws that banned cigarettes, it was filled to capacity with off-duty officers, and a few on-duty officers as well. A yellow and red neon beer sign flickered over the bar, but no one seemed to notice the wavering light.

We received nods, handshakes, pats on the back, and our share of stares as we walked in, no doubt several wondering what we were doing there together. In the year I'd worked with Scolari, I don't think we went out for a drink once. Questions were thrown at us from all sides. Had we heard about Abernathy? Did we know if they had a suspect? Was he on duty? Off duty?

Mostly Scolari answered, while I looked suitably depressed, receiving condolences from those who figured that since I'd worked with Narcotics, I must've worked closely with Abernathy. I didn't see anyone from Narcotics there, which was just as well, so I said little, except a few appropriate comments while Scolari bought us a couple beers. I looked around for Torrance, saw him seated at a booth deep in conversation with a petite brunette, the sort that would look good even in uniform, though I couldn't say I'd ever seen her in one. I didn't even know if she was a cop.

Scolari eyed me, eyed them, noticed Torrance hadn't seen us. "Who's she?"

"Who knows?" Torrance had told me once that he didn't date inside the department. Her presence made me wonder if she was the reason he hadn't wanted to meet with me.

We took a position at the end of the bar, giving us a view of both the front and the rear exits. Scolari stood, while I sat on a barstool I commandeered the moment it was vacated by an officer en route to the head. Torrance glanced our way, saw me, so I figured I'd let him make the first move.

"Yo, Scolari. Been a while."

Bryan "Bear" Berkowitz. Completely bald, he stood a good three inches taller than Scolari, weighed maybe a hundred pounds more. Legend had it that an officer tried to give him the moniker of Baldy, and ended up taking a job as a security guard for Wal-Mart—lucky he even got that, by the time Bear finished with him.

"Bear," Scolari said and nodded. "Buy ya a drink?"

"Nah, I gotta drive up to Santa Rosa tonight. Just came by after I heard what happened to Abernathy to see if the story's true."

Scolari tapped a cigarette from the pack and stuck it in his mouth. "What story's that?"

"That he wasn't on duty, and they're thinkin' his widow ain't gonna get a fair shake."

"You're shittin' me? Hey, Murphy, you got a light?"

The bartender tossed a pack of matches our way. "Ain't no smokin' in here, Sam."

"Yeah, yeah." Scolari flipped the book open and struck a match. A hint of sulfur drifted my way, then dissipated under the heavier tobacco odor. "Where'd you hear this from?"

"From some of the guys on my shift. They're thinkin' that the department oughta just say he was workin' even if he wasn't."

Scolari watched the smoke drift up from his cigarette. "How do they know he wasn't on duty?"

"That's what one of the guys heard at the scene when his LT showed up."

"Yeah, well, I wouldn't put too much store in what you hear tonight. A lot of rumors'll be floatin' around, some true, some not. Let 'em finish their investigation before you lose your cool, eh, Bear?"

"Yeah, sure, Scolari. Good seein' you again. You, too, Gillespie."

"See ya," I said. He lumbered toward the front, then took a seat by his shift partners near the door. "What'dya make of that?"

"Just what I told him," Scolari replied, draping his arm about my shoulder. "Watch out for rumors."

"I normally do." Torrance's comment startled me. I turned, taking in his tall form, dark hair, dark eyes. He wore a brown leather bomber jacket and faded jeans. His gaze lit on Scolari's arm as he said to me, "You wanted to talk?"

"You looked busy," I said, nodding to the woman he left behind. "Figured you might not want to be interrupted."

"I have a free moment." A slight smile lit his face. "Meet me out back in a few minutes."

Torrance returned to his table, and Scolari and I made small talk about anything nonpolice that came to mind. Several minutes later, I watched a couple female officers amble down the hallway in the direction of the ladies' room. "Time for the head," I said.

Scolari glanced at the women. "Good idea."

Lifting my bottle, I took a swig of beer, then started in that direction. The ladies' room was at the end of a dark, narrow hallway past the pay phone, and between the men's room and the alley entrance. About midway down, the men's door opened and someone stepped out, the light to his back.

George Jamison. Abernathy's partner.

As I gave him space to walk past, I saw Abernathy's face in the glare of my headlights.

His gun. Pointed at me.

Whom had Abernathy called? Jamison?

The thought fresh in my mind, I looked right at Jamison. My throat went dry.

I needed to say something. Anything. His partner had just been killed. But I couldn't move. Couldn't speak.

A warm presence behind me, a hand on my shoulder broke the spell. "Excuse me," came Torrance's voice through the rush in my head. "I need to use the men's room."

Torrance worked his way around me casually and superficially, as any man of brief acquaintance might were he trying to move past in such close quarters. Then he did the same around Jamison, displacing him from the men's room door.

I took a breath. "I'm sorry," I told Jamison. "I've just been out of it since I heard. I can't believe he's gone."

Jamison looked down the hall toward the bar. "Yeah. I know. I'm sitting here getting drunk and it still doesn't change anything."

"I'm sorry," I said again.

He nodded, then moved on, losing himself in a sea of well-wishers, all offering words of comfort and support.

I slipped into the ladies' room. It was empty. The two women must have gone out the back after all. I stood there, willing my nerves to calm. Was Jamison involved?

After several minutes, what I intended to be a sufficient amount of time, I washed my hands, exited. Scolari was on the pay phone, blocking my path. "Torrance went out the back, waiting for you."

"Where's Jamison?"

"Left out the front door."

"I didn't even see him come in."

"Me either. Better go talk with Torrance. I'll watch, make sure no one interrupts you."

I pushed open the back door. Torrance waited beneath the overhang, out of the rain. A single light, maybe all of forty watts, cast little more than a pale glow a few feet around us. I leaned against the door, looking out to the alley beyond, thinking it not unlike the area where the shooting took place. I shivered.

"You're cold," Torrance said. He took off his jacket and draped it around my shoulders, his fingers lingering at the collar. It was warm from his body heat and smelled faintly of leather and spicy aftershave. "How've you been?"

His question, uttered so softly, tore at me. I offered up something close to a smile. "I'm fine. Now."

"Now?" There was an edge to his voice, something that told me he had switched to IA mode. "Meaning what?"

"Abernathy tried to kill me tonight."

He said nothing and I looked away, pretending interest in the soft rain pelting around us.

He touched my chin, turning me toward him. For what seemed an eternity, he just looked at me. This time I saw a brief glimpse of anger reflected in his gaze, an anger I knew was not directed at me. "What happened?" he asked.

I told him about the call from Squeaky, about my wait, Abernathy's appearance, the shooting, the aftermath.

"What the hell were you doing there by yourself?"

"Rocky had an emergency. Zim was supposed to come. I don't know what happened. Afterward I called Andrews; he wasn't home. I called you, then paged you."

"You must have been on the line. I tried calling. Your cell phone was busy."

"I was trying to find my nephew, Kevin. Scolari told me he went to the movies with my neighbor."

"Where was Scolari when all this went down?"

"Waiting for me at my apartment."

"What for?"

I wondered if that was an IA question or a personal one. "He didn't want to be alone on his wedding anniversary. I'd forgotten he was coming over tonight. When you called me, he was already there. We headed back to the city to meet you, discovered Abernathy was killed when we got caught in the traffic jam. After talking with the CO at the scene, I figure he was killed maybe fifteen minutes after the shooting."

The door cracked open. Scolari leaned out, casual, tossing his cigarette. "Company. Big time. Jamison again. I'll head him off. Go buy him another beer." The door slid shut.

"What now?" I asked.

"Are you comfortable going home?"

I wanted to say no, to let him offer an alternative suggestion. Like stay with him. But I didn't. Couldn't. "My nephew's at a movie. As long as I know that he makes it home to my aunt's, I'll be fine."

"Then what?"

"Scolari drove me. He can stay at my place, or I can stay at his."

He looked away. "Let's do one thing, first. Show me where the informant was killed," he said, meeting my gaze once more. "Wait for me on the southwest corner of the intersection. Away from the alley. I don't want you in there until I get there."

"What about your friend?"

A look of amusement flickered in his eyes, making me wish I hadn't brought her up. "She's the understanding sort," he said as he held open the door.

"How convenient." I edged past him, regretting my words the moment I said them. We had no ties to each other. No promises. Still, he gave no indication he heard me, and I was grateful. I gave him back his jacket, and he returned to his table and the woman. He leaned down and whispered something in her ear. She stood. He helped her into her raincoat, and they left.

Scolari met up with me at the bar a couple minutes later. I saw no sign of Jamison. Scolari said he was at the table behind Bear's. He kept his arm about me in case anyone was watching. Act normal. Right.

"What'd Torrance say?" he asked, once we were in the truck.

"Not a lot."

"Figures."

"He wants to meet us around the corner from the crime scene."

"Who's the girl?"

"Didn't say."

"You two don't have anything going?"

"Nothing."

"Hmm. Woulda guessed otherwise."

"Woulda guessed wrong."

We drove to the scene, avoiding the main streets, still backed up from the hit-and-run investigation. Torrance showed a few minutes later. Alone. He slid into the pickup beside me on the bench seat.

I refrained from asking him where his friend was, or rather where he left her. I didn't want to know the answer. Didn't want to know if he planned on picking her up when he was through. I nodded toward the entrance of the alley a half block from where we sat in Scolari's truck. "That's where I drove in. Abernathy came in from the other side."

"What is it?" Torrance asked. "About two, three blocks from the hit-and-run?"

I nodded. "He could have driven there. Or walked. I don't know."

"Why?" Torrance asked.

"I think he called someone," I said. "There's a pay phone on the corner near the accident scene."

"Speculation on the call?" Torrance asked.

"Tell someone what happened on a secure line. Maybe tell them I witnessed it."

"Hell, for all you know," Scolari said, pulling forward, "he died with his dirty little secret. Killed by a drunk driver. Sort of fitting."

I wanted to believe that. Tried to believe it. Up until the moment we pulled into the alley.

And saw that Squeaky's body was gone.

4

The alley was deserted; we made sure of that after driving around the block several times. Finally we pulled in to retrace my path.

"I was here," I said. "Parked by this Dumpster."

Scolari pulled his Glock from beneath the seat, shoved it in his waistband. "Where was Abernathy?"

"About there." I pointed through the rain-splattered windshield toward the center of the alley maybe thirty yards in front of us. Nothing but wet pavement.

"All right," Torrance said. "Let's get out and look."

We checked the Dumpster for a body, found it empty, then walked the distance, watching the ground for evidence, yet keeping an eye on our surroundings. For a few moments it felt like old times, like Scolari and I were working just another case. But Torrance's presence reminded me otherwise.

Scolari had a mini Streamlight and scanned the ground with the beam. I didn't know what I expected to see. Blood. Bits of flesh. Something that would prove I hadn't imagined the whole thing.

"Raining hard?" Torrance asked.

"Hard enough," I said. Hard enough to dilute any blood, assuming the body was pulled out in a reasonable amount of time.

We looked over every inch, broadening the search in case I was off, hoping to find a bullet casing. Anything.

We found nothing.

The rain had stopped. I looked down the alley, at the backs of businesses that were shut up tight after five. No one would be around to call about shots fired. No one would notice if someone dragged a body away. Or straightened up the trash cans I'd knocked over.

Someone went over the alley with a fine-tooth comb. The question was who? Not Abernathy. He was dead ten or fifteen minutes later.

I glanced at Torrance, and saw he was still focused on the alley. "What's on your mind?" I asked him.

"I'm wondering about Abernathy's accident."

"Could be just that," Scolari said. "A hit-and-run."

"Or," Torrance interjected, "he was a liability."

"Meaning what?" Scolari asked.

I answered, for the simple reason it was precisely what I had been thinking myself. "Meaning he called someone, told them there was a witness that got away. A witness that might ID him."

"An unidentified witness," Scolari said. "Which is why they got rid of Squeaky's body. To discredit the witness, cover up the crime."

"Could be anything," Torrance said. "Regardless, I'm not comfortable standing here."

He was right. We got into Scolari's truck and drove Torrance to his vehicle. From there we followed him down the street, up a hill, and to the right. Finally he pulled into the parking lot of a grocery store, closed for the night. Scolari nosed his pickup in beside Torrance's vehicle in the opposite direction, mirror-to-mirror so they faced each other through their windows.

"What now?" Scolari asked Torrance.

"I've called Captain Lombard," he said. "He wants to meet Gillespie in the field. Since you weren't directly involved, I didn't feel the need to mention your presence for this meeting."

"Thanks," Scolari said. "Being retired has its perks after all. But maybe I better drop Gillespie off at the scene myself, to keep up the appearance that we been out all night." Torrance agreed.

As we drove back to the hit-and-run scene, Scolari gave me a pat on my shoulder. "Anything I can do for you in the meantime?"

Kevin and Jack would undoubtedly be back soon if not already, and I had no idea how long my night would last. "Can you check on my nephew? Make sure Jack got my message and that Kevin gets home to my aunt's?"

"Sure thing."

I called my aunt, giving only a vague explanation about an emergency at work as to why Kevin was not going to be staying with me. No sense worrying her about something she didn't need to know. Next I called Jack and got his wife. He and Kevin went for ice cream after the movie. By the time I finished both calls, Torrance was pulling into the same dry cleaner lot behind us. I got out of Scolari's pickup and waved at him as he drove off, then met up with Torrance beside his car.

I saw Captain Lombard standing on the sidewalk, speaking to one of the motor officers about the accident scene. Mid-fifties, Lombard was tall, thin, with white hair and a mustache that covered his top lip. As Torrance and I approached, Lombard held up a finger, indicating he would be a moment longer. We waited on the corner a short distance away, and I shivered in part from the temperature and in part from the memory of what I had witnessed.

Torrance offered me his jacket, but I shook my head no, picturing how it would look to the number of cops standing around. I'd worked too hard to gain even a modicum of respect in this place to have something like that misinterpreted.

"You okay?" he asked.

"Fine," I said as Lombard joined us.

"Let's step away," Lombard said. "I'd rather not be overheard."

We returned to the parking lot, and I leaned against the warm front fender of Torrance's car while I explained what I'd seen. My stomach knotted at the memory. Captain Lombard stood shoulder to shoulder with Torrance, listening intently, his gaze focused on the pavement while I spoke. When I finished, he remained silent for several seconds.

"Jesus Christ," he finally said. He looked at Torrance. "What's your opinion on this?"

"Two assumptions," Torrance replied. "One, they saw Gillespie and are after her. The other is that they don't know she's the witness. It fits with what happened, why Abernathy was killed. Why the informant's body was moved. Either way, she's at risk."

"Okay," Lombard said. "Taking your first theory. They saw her. You're thinking something like witness protection? What's the chance they're going to take her out when all she saw was Abernathy? Why else kill him?"

I didn't like the way they were playing with my life, my freedom. I knew what it was like to have a constant bodyguard. And, depending on the bodyguard, for the most part I didn't like it. "I'm aware of the danger."

"Are you?" Lombard asked.

"Yes. If they saw me, they know I'm talking to you

anyway. But realistically, I can't believe whoever is behind this is going to just gun me down. Not with Abernathy dead. After all, he's the only one I know who is actually involved in whatever this is."

"The informant," Lombard said. "Who knew you were meeting him?"

"Markowski."

"And if he tells someone?"

"He already has. He couldn't make it and called Zimmerman. Zim never showed. I haven't had a chance to find out why."

"I don't like it," Lombard said. He pulled his pager from his belt and pressed a button. It lit up, glowing green. I was not privy to what he read. He returned it to his belt, then patted his left suit coat pocket as though looking for something. "We received a report that someone in the Narcotics detail was being set up."

"How?"

"I don't know. The investigation isn't even six hours old. Something that was supposed to go down in the next four or five days."

"That's what Squeaky told me," I said.

"Yeah, well, after what you allegedly witnessed, I'm beginning to believe the report was real." He checked his other pocket. "Where the hell is my phone?" He glanced back at the group of men he'd just left. "Dammit."

"I can assure you that what I witnessed was not alleged," I told him.

"We have no body, Gillespie. And the only other witness is dead."

"Are you saying you don't believe me?" I tried to contain my anger but failed.

"What I am saying," he replied, his tone authoritative, brooking no argument, "is that until I know exactly what is going on, I think you need to be on AL."

"Administrative leave?" Lombard's words hit me like a fist to my stomach. Vacation was one thing, forced leave quite another. "You can't do that."

He said nothing.

"Tell me you're not serious."

"It's protocol in an officer-involved shooting, and until I get a full report, you don't have a choice. In the meantime, I'm ordering you not to tell anyone. That includes Andrews."

I didn't stop to ask why I couldn't inform my supervisor. I was more concerned with being removed from the detail. "But I didn't do the shooting."

"You were involved, Gillespie. And I already have one dead officer. I don't want another. Now if you'll excuse me, I need to find my phone to make a call."

Torrance offered his phone, but Lombard refused. They moved off, exchanging a few words in private. I got into Torrance's car and waited, not willing to reveal more of my anger.

On the way back to my apartment, I fumed in silence. Torrance said, "It's for the best," but I ignored him and he didn't try any further conversation.

Traffic was light; it took us about twenty minutes to get to my place. Torrance walked me up and we stood there on the porch while I read a note that Scolari had left on my door, saying he was driving Kevin home and would return shortly.

"You want to make sure your apartment's clear?" Torrance asked when I finished.

Since Abernathy was dead, I didn't figure it was all that necessary. But I didn't answer, and he took that as a yes. I unlocked the door and allowed him entry. We checked the first three rooms, but when we came to the bathroom, I stood back, letting him go in alone. It was too small for both of us, I told myself. In reality, it was too intimate. A few months ago he'd been my pseudo-bodyguard while we hunted down Scolari's wife's killer. Torrance had kissed me in that room— okay, it was a little more than a kiss. I recalled each moment in vivid detail. The way his lips touched mine as he lifted me to the edge of the sink, the paradox of the cold porcelain through the silk of my dress and the heat of him against me . . .

He gave me a searching look, and I drew my thoughts from the past, wanting to ask him who the woman was that he'd been sitting with at the bar.

"You think you'll be okay by yourself until Scolari gets here?" he asked.

"I'll be fine."

Now as he exited, I wondered if he even remembered that night—up until the moment he said, "That's still my favorite room."

I met his gaze and saw what I could only describe as a wicked sparkle. I couldn't help myself. "Definitely a multipurpose room," I said.

We returned to the kitchen, and suddenly my entire apartment seemed too small. I didn't know if I should be grateful that Scolari was en route, or dismayed. "Thanks for the ride home."

"Good night, Kate."

He slung his coat over his shoulder and I watched him leave.

That night I went to bed thinking about Torrance, wondering what might have happened between us had we worked for different agencies.

But we didn't.

Which meant that I would never know.

The phone rang at seven-forty in the morning. I picked up on the third ring. "Hello?"

"Gillespie? Lieutenant Andrews. I need you down here ASAP."

"Something I should know about?" I asked, wondering what Lombard and Torrance had set into motion.

"I'll let you know as soon as you get here."

"I'm on my way," I said, but he'd hung up. I guessed that meant my stint on AL was over. So, apparently, was my vacation.

I showered, dressed, informed Scolari of the latest, and left him to lock up. Outside, the night's rain had washed the world clean, and as I walked up the hill to my car, I breathed in the fresh air. Cirrus clouds floated overhead in a blue sky, promising more inclement weather. For now, I enjoyed the sun, the brisk morning.

My car was right where I'd left it, not that I expected anything different. I suppose I'd imagined IA coming during the night, towing it off to examine it for signs of the shooting I'd *allegedly* witnessed. I circled my car, searching for proof that I was more than an alleged victim. Abernathy shot at me, hit my car. There was a dent on the left front fender, probably from the trash can I hit. No bullet holes that I could see. Strange. Maybe it was the sound of a round hitting the Dumpster? I'd check it out later. For now I needed a latte, a bagel, and a miracle to get me to work at a decent hour. I got the first two. Traffic over the bridge was a nightmare.

When I entered Homicide, Gypsy greeted me with a nod. "Morning, Kate," she said, a quick glance up from her word processor. "The lieutenant is waiting for you."

I went directly to his office, knocked on the door.

"Come in." He looked up, his brown gaze sweeping over me before returning to his paperwork. His tie was loosened, and the crisp white of his dress shirt contrasted sharply against his dark skin. "Shut the door. Have a seat."

I did, waiting.

He put down his report, and looked me squarely in the eye. "I'm assuming you're aware that you're here because of Abernathy."

"I'd guessed as much."

"Then there's no need to go into lengthy explanations, other than to tell you I've been in a meeting all morning with Lombard."

I said nothing, imagined everything.

"He's asked that you handle Abernathy's homicide."

Everything but that.

5

Investigating the homicide of the man who tried to murder me was not something that I anticipated. Nor was it something I thought I could do without some prejudice. There was a clear conflict-of-interest problem, yet I was prevented from pointing that out, because I'd been ordered by Captain Lombard to say nothing about the case. "Don't you think Shipley would be better for this?" I suggested.

"Why is that?" he asked, but before I could answer, someone knocked at the door and opened it.

Abernathy's partner, Jamison—the last person I expected to see here. The last person I wanted to see here. He didn't move from the doorway, just stood there, clad in jeans and a black T-shirt with a marijuana leaf on the front, his brown hair pulled back in its usual ponytail. "You got a moment?" he asked Andrews.

"Yeah. Give me a couple." Andrews turned to me. "Why Shipley?"

Jamison hovered over me, eyeing me. I ignored him, tried to at least, while I formulated an answer. "It's just that under the circumstances, I figured you'd want a more experienced Homicide inspector. His widow might take offense."

"I doubt it," Andrews said. "What do you think, Jamison?"

"I think she'll have other things on her mind."

"I agree. Any other objections, Gillespie?"

"No, sir." I felt Jamison's gaze on me still. "I'll get started on it right away."

"Jamison will assist you any way that he can."

"Great." I left. Jamison remained, closing the door after me. I returned to my desk, sat and prayed that Jamison wasn't involved.

He could be innocent. But he and Abernathy were close. Closer than many. Abernathy's widow was Jamison's sister. Jamison had been Abernathy's best man. I didn't think that someone with ties like Jamison's would be completely ignorant of Abernathy's actions. Now I was supposed to let the man help me investigate his partner's death? Could my day get any worse?

Apparently so. In walked Zimmerman, tall, gray-haired, ruddy-faced. He carried his navy sport coat over his shoulder, so that all the world could see his shoulder holster and the growing sweat stains at the armpits of his light blue shirt. He took one look at me and said, "Where the hell were you?"

"Exactly where I was supposed to be." I glanced at the lieutenant's door, saw it was still closed, Jamison tucked safely inside. I didn't need him wandering out right now to hear this. "Where the hell were you?"

"I was right here, waiting."

"You were here?"

"Just like Rocky said. You never showed."

Rocky wasn't there to defend himself and as far as I was concerned, it was for the best. Until I knew who to trust, I might as well let Zim think we got our wires crossed. "Apparently there was a mix-up. I was waiting downstairs."

"No shit?"

"No shit."

"Too bad we weren't out there. Maybe we coulda done something to help."

"Yeah. I've been assigned his homicide. Jamison's in with Andrews right now."

Zim's phone rang. He picked it up and started talking with someone about the murder case of a male prostitute.

Jamison walked out of Andrews's office right about then. "You need anything? Any information?" he asked me.

"You know what he was working on last night?"

"Haven't got a clue. I was out to dinner with my wife. Wasn't even aware he was going to work."

"If you find anything, let me know."

"Sure." He left. I took my first solid breath, wondering when life would get back to normal.

I called my ex-husband, Reid Bettencourt, a DA's investigator. We were on friendly terms. At least as far as our professional lives were concerned. "You busy?" I asked. "I need a little inside info."

"I thought you were on vacation."

"I'm investigating Abernathy's homicide. I was wondering if you could see what your office has on file. The last cases he was working. Anything special."

"Like what?"

"CIs, that sort of thing." CI stood for confidential informant, particularly one whose name is sealed in court documents to protect his identity during search warrants or court cases. I wondered if Squeaky Kincaid had worked for him, but didn't feel comfortable just throwing his name out. Not yet.

"I can check," Reid said. "Might take me a bit to get back to you. I have to go to San Jose to interview a witness. Wouldn't it be easier if you just checked with Narcotics?"

Well, yes, if I knew whom to trust there. "One of their own has just been killed, Reid. I figured if you did it, it would give them a break."

"Right. I'll get started on it as soon as I get back."

"Thanks."

I hung up, staring absently out the window. I'd have to ask everyone in Narcotics some pertinent questions if I didn't want to arouse suspicion. The basics would do. Did he have any enemies? How was he getting along with his wife? That sort of thing. Like being in IA, digging around without letting anyone know what you were really up to. The thought brought Torrance to mind. I wondered what he was doing, what he'd found out.

My phone rang, and I figured it was probably him.

"Gillespie, Homicide."

"Kate, dear, I hate to bother you at work after reading about that officer who was killed. I know you must be busy."

"You're not bothering me, Aunt Molly," I said.

"I've just gotten off the phone with Dr. Higgins." Higgins was the school psychologist who saw Kevin on a regular basis outside school. I had yet to be impressed by anything she said about Kevin.

"And what was her prognosis this time?" I asked.

"You know he's been asking about his mother lately. Well, Dr. Higgins thinks his underlying problems have to do with the way he was abandoned by his mother."

"Now there's a profound statement."

"Really, Kate."

"He's like any other kid his age. Normal," I said. "He just has a few more skeletons in his family closet."

"She thinks it would be best if we found his mother."

"His mother's a two-bit drug dealer who is better off being lost. Very lost."

"Well, Dr. Higgins thinks he should know what happened to her. That it'll bring some closure to his life, and help him move on."

"A better shrink will help, is what I think."

Rocky walked in just then, and I wanted to corner him to find out exactly what he'd told Zim about where to meet me.

"I agree with her, Kate," my aunt continued.

"Okay," I said, waving at Rocky. He headed my way. "What is it you want me to do, Aunt Molly?"

"I want you to find her."

Distracted, I covered the mouthpiece. "You got a minute?" I asked Rocky. He nodded. Then to my aunt, I said, "Please tell me you're kidding?"

"There's some old papers here . . . she sent them to me right after Sean died."

I took that to mean she was serious. From everything I'd heard about my brother's case, the woman wasn't worth finding. Assuming she wasn't dead. "I don't know—"

"Please. We don't have to tell Kevin yet. But what if Dr. Higgins is right? And this is what he needs?"

I wanted to tell her that I was working a homicide and didn't have time for Dr. Higgins's theatrics. But this was my aunt and she was doing it for my nephew. "All right. I'll look into it. But I can't promise anything."

"Thank you, Kate. I know you won't regret this."

I was already regretting it, but wasn't about to tell her.

"About last night," Rocky said as I cradled the phone. "I didn't mean to leave you hanging."

I wanted to lay into him, but saw the circles under his eyes. "You have Scolari's new office number?" I said instead, even though I had it in my file.

"Yeah. Why?"

"My aunt needs a little PI work done."

He gave me the number, and I called Scolari and informed him of who it was my aunt wanted found.

There was a long silence. "Jesus, Kate. Why the hell do you want to do that?"

"I don't. My aunt does. Some psychoanalysis bullshit. Just call her, do it, okay?"

"This over the table or under?"

"However you want it."

"I'll see what I can do."

I needed to speak with Torrance about Abernathy's case, but not on the phone. Grabbing my coffee, I headed to his office. He was at his desk when I got there, typing on his laptop. I knocked even though the door was open. He looked up, saw me, and said, "I get the feeling you're not here to discuss bathroom fixtures?"

"Sharp, Torrance," I said, closing the door after me. "I like that in a man."

"What's on your mind?" he asked, hitting the sleep on the laptop and banking the humor in his eyes.

"Conflict of interest."

He waited.

"I've been assigned the Abernathy homicide."

"I know."

"You know?"

"Lombard told me about it this morning."

"And?"

"I told him you'd do a fine job."

"Well, thanks for your vote of confidence, but doesn't anyone see a little bit of a problem, here? The guy tried to kill me."

"And you'd be happier on the sidelines doing nothing?"

"Of course not."

"I didn't think so," he said, ignoring his ringing telephone. "Which is why, when Lombard suggested it, I agreed with him."

"Regardless of the conflict of interest?"

"You're missing the point, Gillespie," he said, glancing out his window to the adjoining office. I followed his gaze and saw Sergeant Kent Mathis, one of his IA/Management Control inspectors, sitting at his desk, motioning for Torrance to answer the phone. "Hold on," he told me, picking up his extension. "What is it?" he asked quietly, then listened intently to whatever was being told to him. "No. You better leave right away." He hung up, then returned his attention to me. He said nothing for several seconds and I wondered what he was thinking, if it was about me and if it had to do with business. Or not.

"You were saying?" I prodded.

"About the Abernathy case. I know it's a conflict—"

"To say the least."

"But I have a couple reasons of my own for wanting you as the assigned inspector."

"And they are?"

"If you are investigating it, you'll be the first to know if something's not right."

"Meaning what?"

"Meaning that you and I both feel that Abernathy's

case is related to the murder of that informant. Naturally your investigation would parallel the first homicide without bringing undue attention to it—or you. Which also means that if someone knows you're the witness in the alley, you have a better chance of finding that out if you're assigned to the case."

"That can work both ways."

"It can. But would you want to take a chance that you missed the signs?"

I sipped at my coffee while I considered his words. He was dead on. I wouldn't chance it. "No."

"I didn't think so. Neither did Lombard. But the danger is real."

"Trust me. I know, firsthand." I tossed my empty cup in his trash. He went back to his computer. I started to leave, then hesitated. "What was the other reason you wanted me assigned to the case?"

He picked up a pencil from his desk, looking at it before meeting my gaze, his expression serious. In the seconds of silence that followed, I could hear his secretary typing away at her keyboard.

"Do you really want to know?" he asked, his voice quiet, daring, the sparkle in his eye giving him away.

"Definitely not."

"The better to watch you, Inspector."

"Great. I'm working with the Big Bad Wolf." I turned to leave and caught his reflection in his office window, the dark gaze that followed me, the smile that made me appreciate a man with a sense of humor. But as I left, I wondered at his words. Watch me? How? I wondered. As in IA/Management Control watch me? Or watch over me?

I was determined to put Torrance from my mind, and the best way to do that was to concentrate on the case. But there were too many unanswered questions in Abernathy's hit-and-run file, and I knew I'd somehow need to learn what he might have been working on—if he was working officially—the night he was killed. I checked my calendar to see if anything significant was occurring in the next few days, but nothing stood out. I decided to drive over to the Narcotics office, which was housed away from the Hall.

When I got there the only person in the office was the secretary, and she was talking on the phone. This could be a good thing—if I only knew where to look for the answers.

As I swept past, I waved and said, "Came for some paperwork."

She gave a nod, not really paying attention, just as I'd hoped.

Several desks filled the room, each partitioned off, allowing the investigators some privacy and the illusion of their own space. Abernathy and Jamison's desks were in the far corner at right angles to each other.

I sat in Abernathy's chair, wondering who had been the last person there, trying to imagine myself in Abernathy's position. It had been a while since I'd worked out of this office. Everything looked normal. There were a few case files on top of his desk, spread out as though he might return to work on them.

That was the odd thing about this, the normalcy of his desk. I'd felt it before when other officers had been killed. Walking past their offices, lockers, whatever. These places always seemed a little more quiet, a little more reverent, and still so very much like the officer could walk in, pick up where he left off.

But there was nothing reverent about Abernathy's

death. Nothing at all. And the quiet of this place bothered me.

I didn't know if he had acted alone, or with someone. Even more disturbing was, if there was someone else involved, what that person might think should I be discovered here at this moment. Not wanting to find out, I got to work right away, starting with the files on his desktop. I opened each, careful not to disturb the order or placement on the desk, then set about checking his desk drawers. They were all locked, so I ran my hand beneath the top drawer. A number of officers hid their spare key there, in case they lost the other.

Bingo.

I pulled the key free and tried it in each of Abernathy's locks. It slid in, but wouldn't turn. Frustrated, I leaned back in his chair, tapping the key to my chin, looking around the room. There were a number of desks. I did the only thing I could, turned and started with the closest, Jamison's. The key slid easily into the top drawer. The tumblers clicked and unlocked, making me very curious as to why Abernathy had a key to Jamison's desk taped beneath his. I supposed it could all be very innocent. Here, take my key in case I forget mine. But it didn't seem likely.

I pulled open the drawer. Standard fare, pencils, pens, a memo pad. A manila folder beneath your basic Saturday night special—a twenty-two caliber, cheap piece of crap that no cop worth his weight would carry.

Interesting. I supposed it could be a piece of evidence Jamison had picked up somewhere, hadn't yet booked. Or it was a throwaway gun. Something that couldn't be traced, something that Saturday night specials are known for. Two scenarios came to mind. The use-it-toss-it scenario, favored by drug dealers and gangbangers after a hit or a drive-by shooting. Or the plant-it-lose-it scenario, favored by bad cops after a shooting of an unarmed subject. A subject such as Squeaky.

What if I hadn't been there? Would Jamison have brought this to Abernathy? Planted it on Squeaky to make the shooting appear legitimate?

Cognizant of prints, I didn't touch the weapon, instead copied the serial number on a piece of notepaper. The only other thing of interest in there was the manila folder. I was able to partially open it without disturbing anything. A tip on a shipment of cocaine due in at one of the piers. Jamison's notes showed that Abernathy had passed on the tip to all the appropriate agencies, including DEA and the Coast Guard. No apparent cover-up there. Even so, I decided to jot down the contact names: Stilwell and Rosenkrantz—no first names. I was interrupted when I heard voices out in the secretary's office. I shut the drawer, locked it, and taped the key beneath Abernathy's desk just as my ex-husband, Reid Bettencourt, stepped around the partition. He was dressed in a tan designer suit—silk, I thought, that went with his blond good looks, but not his DA investigator budget. He eyed me withdrawing my hand but said nothing at first, just raised his brows—which was just as well, since Jamison was on his heels.

Jamison stopped short at the sight of me sitting in Abernathy's chair.

"Kate," Reid said in a way that could only be interpreted as *What the hell are you doing here?*

This was one of those times when ad-libbing skills came in real handy. Unfortunately mine at the moment sucked. "Hi," I said, directing myself to Jamison. "I was hoping you'd show."

Jamison waited for me to continue.

I stood, feeling even more uncomfortable. "I need to ask everyone here if they knew what Abernathy was working on that night or if he had planned to meet someone. I just can't seem to find anybody." Sounded good. Normal behavior, nothing out of the ordinary, except maybe why I was sitting at his desk.

Jamison glanced at Reid, who met his gaze with an expression I found highly curious. Something I'd have to corner Reid on later.

"No one knows," Jamison said. "We've asked everyone over and over."

Why was it that no one knew? Especially his partner? Or was he just not telling me? After all, there was that file in his drawer. "I guess what I'm really looking for is if your partner was . . . involved in anything dangerous?"

"All their cases are dangerous," my ex said. *Thanks, Reid, for your analysis.*

"I mean cases out of the ordinary."

Jamison eyed his desk. "You're thinking it's connected to the hit-and-run?"

"I have no idea," I said. For a millisecond my conscience got to me, made me think he suspected I'd seen the file. "But it would be stupid to assume it was just an accident, maybe miss a lead, don't you think?"

"I'll look through the cases," Jamison replied. "See if I can come up with anything."

Although curious as to why he wouldn't mention the cocaine case, I didn't bring it up. I was not about to tip my hand. "I'll let you know if I come up with anything else," I said, then left with a casual wave.

"See ya," Jamison said.

I glanced back and saw Reid staring thoughtfully after me. Why was he here and not in San Jose as he'd told me? Something else I'd have to check out later.

In the parking lot I saw Captain Lombard pulling his black Crown Victoria into a space. He didn't appear to see me yet, and I kept a steady walk toward my own car parked farther down.

"Gillespie," I heard him call out.

"Captain Lombard," I said, turning with a smile. "What brings you here?"

"I was about to ask you the same."

Translation: He wasn't telling shit, but wanted a full report from me.

"Just came to see if Jamison could offer any insight."

"And did you find out anything?"

I noticed he did not ask me if Jamison had mentioned anything. I decided to play my hand close—maybe because Scolari's words seemed to echo in my head. *In a department this size, a vein of corruption can run deep.*

"Jamison didn't have a lot to say," I told the captain.

He gave a slight nod, then said, "Well, keep up the good work," then walked off in the direction of the building.

How very like a supervisor to throw out a compliment like that. I'd told him essentially nothing, and it was still "Keep up the good work."

"I'll do that," I said to myself.

As I headed to my car, though, I had the unpleasant sensation of being watched. It wasn't until I unlocked my car and got in that I realized Lombard stood watching my every step from the shadows of the doorway. I drove off, his gaze on me even as I pulled out of the lot.

Maybe I was being paranoid. Ask any cop if they trust their supervisors, and you'll get a resounding no from the majority of them. It's a simple fact of police life. So I tucked the incident away, and when I got to my office, I decided to review the Abernathy hit-and-run again in hopes I'd missed something. There wasn't much in the report that differed from what I'd learned at the scene last night. The only witness was the anonymous woman who called 911 initially to report the crime. Apparently she drove up on the accident just after it happened, and saw very little except a dark-colored sedan leaving the area. She called from the pay phone on the corner.

If I harbored any hope of learning who killed Abernathy and what connection Abernathy's death had to the shooting I'd witnessed, there was only one action I could take.

Return to the scene of the crime.

6

They say the suspect always returns to the scene. While not always true, it does happen in some cases, and as I parked my car, I wondered if the killer was out there watching me. Normally I'd have taken Markowski with me, but since all I intended to do was have a look around, question a few merchants, I didn't see the need.

During daylight the intersection looked entirely different, bustling with traffic and pedestrians, the surrounding businesses open. I parked in the same dry cleaner lot as the night before, but this time there were no other cops, nothing but the residue of burned flares in the roadway that gave any indication that something out of the ordinary had occurred here.

I walked over to where I'd seen the motor officers taking their measurements, stopping at the curb. A car honked as it drove past, the driver perhaps thinking I meant to step off in front of it. Across the street was Silva's Repair Garage and the pay phone. I made a mental note to have the records checked to see what calls were placed prior to the 911 call. If my theory proved correct, Abernathy had come here specifically to use that phone.

And yet he was killed on the opposite side of the street. Why? Why did he cross over?

There was a video store next to the garage. It had been closed last night. Even so, whoever worked in there looked out on this corner day in and day out. Perhaps they could offer something. Anything.

I strolled to the corner, waited for traffic to clear, and crossed. The phone booth was situated on the street side of the garage, and I went there first to copy the number and address for future reference. I looked around the asphalt parking lot and the sidewalk, but saw only oil drippings, old gum, and cigarette butts, nothing that appeared evidentiary. I moved on to the video store.

Posters of films long past their prime covered the walls. The shelves were filled with well-worn VHS tape covers, some faded to a near blue cast from exposure to the sun. There were no customers, and the cashier, a thin woman in her late forties, sat on a stool behind the counter watching a game show that required the contestants to guess the prices of retail items. Her hair, overprocessed blond with dark brown roots, was pulled back into a ponytail and tied with a red ribbon that matched her red sweater. She didn't look up at me, or acknowledge my presence in any way.

"Three-ninety-eight," she called out. The item appeared to be a large jar of pickles.

"Excuse me," I said.

She held up her finger indicating she wanted me to wait a moment. The announcer asked the contestant for his price and he covered his mouth while he contemplated. "Two-fifty."

"Three-ninety-nine," the announcer said, while the audience voiced their disappointment.

"Ha!" the woman in red said, then turned to me. Her face was pretty, but the bright blue eye shadow she wore detracted from her looks. "What can I do for you?"

I showed her my star. "Inspector Gillespie, Homicide. I'm here about the hit-and-run last night."

"Yeah, I saw it on the news this morning."

"It happened sometime after nine."

"I closed at nine, but didn't see anything, because I went out the back. Sorry," she said, her attention slipping from me to the TV. It was then I noticed a video monitor beside it, picking up the street outside, cars darting past. I looked out the window.

And saw where Abernathy had been killed.

Please let it be on video. Turning back to the woman, I pointed to the surveillance monitor and asked, "You keep a tape in that thing?"

"Ha! You'd think so, considering we been robbed five times, now. But the owner won't pay to have it fixed. I mostly just use it to check out who's coming and going."

Figures. It'd be too damned easy to have the whole thing on film. "You happen to know of anyone who hangs out in this area on a regular basis?"

"Sorry," she said, not paying me the least attention. "Four-fifty," she shouted at the set.

"Thanks," I said, leaving.

As I stepped out the door, she said, "You might try DeLucci's market a couple doors down. They have a regular clientele."

"Thanks."

I hadn't noticed DeLucci's last night, a mom-and-pop market, but then I'd been in a mild state of shock. I could see a few bins of fruit out front that on closer inspection looked more like castoffs from the bigger chain markets. There was a sign on the door that said they closed at nine as well. Inside the dimly lit store the clerk shrugged his shoulders at my questions and was of no help. I stepped out into the bright sunlight, nearly running into a bearded man who smelled as if he hadn't seen a shower in weeks, if not months. He was about my height, five-seven, stocky in build. He wore a green knit cap pulled down past his ears, even though the weather was mild. I couldn't tell how old he was. He looked like he might be in his late fifties, but he had the face of an alcoholic who'd lived hard on the streets, seeing enough for several lifetimes.

"Excuse me," he said, his eyes downcast as he stepped aside for me to pass.

"No problem."

He went inside and I waited on the dirty sidewalk for him to emerge. He did, his purchase being a small bottle concealed in a crumpled brown paper sack.

"You mind answering a few questions?" I asked when he started to walk off in the opposite direction.

He stopped but still wouldn't meet my gaze.

"I'm Inspector Gillespie," I said, showing him my star. "Do you live around here?"

"Here and there," he said, staring at the sidewalk.

"Last night where were you staying?" I asked as the wind shifted, bringing with it his distinct unwashed odor.

He nodded toward the intersection where Abernathy was killed. "Around the corner," he said, then shuffled past me.

He took off at a brisk pace and I followed. At the garage he turned right, crossed the street, disappeared between two buildings. The space was too narrow for an alley, but too wide for a catwalk. About ten feet in, it stopped abruptly, dead-ending into a solid wall that probably at one time continued through to the other side of the block.

Abernathy would have had to walk past there, either on this side or the other side of the street after he fled the alley. The space faced north, no sunlight making it between the tall buildings. When I stepped in, I was assaulted by the strong smell of urine. Trash cans lined the right side and I saw a large cardboard shelter that he undoubtedly called home for the time being, at least until the property owners discovered him and forced him to move on.

I didn't enter, instead called out. "Hello?"

Leaning to one side, I could see him sitting beneath his shelter, watching me. "Can I have a word with you?"

He scooted out, then hesitantly walked toward me, saying nothing.

"A man was killed last night," I said as he approached. "He probably walked past here right before it happened."

He looked in the direction of the gas station behind me, something flickering in his eyes before he looked back to the ground.

"You saw something, didn't you?"

He said nothing.

"You have any identification?" I wasn't about to let him disappear without knowing who he was.

"I don't have any warrants," he said, pulling out a California ID card as though he was used to the routine.

His name was William Dellwood, and when I copied his birth date into my notebook, I was surprised to see that he was much younger than I thought. Forty-two years old. When I gave back his ID, he turned away in silent dismissal.

"He was an officer," I said.

Dellwood paused but still wouldn't look at me.

"I saw him," he said in a surprisingly soft-spoken voice. "He walked past here just before I left. Used the phone on the corner. Tall guy, long brown hair."

"That's him," I said.

"Yeah. That's when a car pulled up on the other side of the street and he crossed like that's who he was waiting for."

"What makes you think that?"

He shrugged. "Maybe because I saw the driver roll down his window. Couldn't see into the car, though. Happened too fast."

I glanced toward the street, trying to imagine the scene. "How long did he talk to the driver?"

"Never did. He was crossing the street when he got hit."

I pictured Abernathy heading across the wet asphalt, the other car coming around the corner, maybe not seeing him until it was too late. "An accident?" I wondered aloud.

"Maybe." He still wouldn't look at me. "Pulled out his gun just before he got run over. Like he knew the car was after him."

"Did he fire?"

"Could have. Sounded like it."

"Did you happen to see the driver who hit him?"

For the first time, he looked up at me, his blue eyes bright and piercing. Then he quickly looked away.

"Don't know," he said, shifting from foot to foot. "It was dark."

He was holding something back, and I wondered if he'd seen the driver. Could identify him. Other than that, everything Dellwood had said fit with what happened that night. And made it sound as if Abernathy was set up. Someone waited until he stepped into the street to take him out. If Abernathy drew his weapon, he'd suspected as much. The question is, who was he going to shoot? The person who ran him down, or the person he was intending to speak with on the other side of the street? And if Abernathy was set up, it meant that whoever killed Abernathy wouldn't fail to do away with me—or anyone else who stood in their way. Suddenly I grew very afraid for the man before me, and I didn't know how to convey my concerns to him without revealing too much of the investigation.

"Mr. Dellwood," I said, "have you told anyone else about this?"

He shook his head, small short jerks.

"If someone comes around asking about this homicide, unless it's me or a lieutenant named Mike Torrance," I said, "don't tell them that you saw anything."

He twisted the paper bag around his bottle, but said nothing.

"There's a mission," I said. "I can take you there. Get you a place to stay, some help."

He held up his brown-bagged bottle. "Got everything I need right here."

Digging out my business card, I handed it to him. "If you remember anything else—or need anything, call. Collect or otherwise."

He took the card without committing himself, without meeting my gaze, then walked back to his private corner of the world. I started off in my own direction, wishing I knew what he was holding back.

7

I returned to the Hall, unable to relegate William Dellwood to the recesses of the Witnesses-interviewed section in my mind. Normally I wouldn't have any trouble just sitting down, typing up a statement, turning it in, and then being done with it.

My conscience wouldn't allow it.

He had witnessed a murder, chosen to tell me, and was content to hide in his bottle.

His bottle wasn't bulletproof.

I told myself that I could be wrong. He could be wrong. He was an alcoholic, probably drunk when it happened. Hell, the entire thing could have been coincidence. A hit-and-run not even connected to Squeaky's murder.

Coincidence . . .

That Dellwood seemed to withhold something from me when I asked if he'd seen the driver? Or that once again—according to Squeaky's call, at least—Antonio Foust's name was linked to a murder? The fleeting thought that Foust had gotten to Dellwood first gave me pause. But I quickly dismissed it. Foust didn't give warnings. He eliminated the problem. Which meant that Foust didn't know of Dellwood's existence. Yet.

At my desk, I called the Pacific Bell security department, gave them the number and address of the phone booth, and then our required clearance code. I was told they would forward to me as soon as possible any outgoing calls from that phone booth for the time period given.

"Gillespie?"

Lieutenant Andrews stood in the doorway of his office.

I hung up the phone. "Yes, sir?"

"The DA's on the line. He wants to know if you've gotten the autopsy on the Braxton case. He'd like to know the results."

"Got it right here," I said, flipping through my case files. I'd forgotten all about it with everything that had taken place in the last few days, and it served to remind me that life goes on. "Interesting results."

"I take it it wasn't a suicide?"

"Definitely not," I said, pulling out the autopsy report. Tom Braxton was a real-estate developer who made millions from his projects. A little over a week ago, he'd been found in his bed with a single bullet wound to his right temple. His wife, who stood to inherit his entire fortune, reported it as a suicide. I read the cause of death aloud. "Asphyxiation prior to the gunshot."

"Any suspects besides his wife and business partners?"

"From what I understand, he didn't lack for enemies."

"I'd like to see a detailed list of suspects. Have Markowski get that to me by tomorrow. I also want him to take over the Nita Gonzalez case."

"Markowski?"

"Lombard wants you assigned solely to Abernathy's homicide. If you have any other pressing cases, I want them ASAP for reassignment."

"Yes, sir," I said, returning the autopsy report to the folder, then tossing it on Rocky's desk. He wouldn't mind, but I had a feeling some of the other guys might. Excluding Nita's stabbing and Abernathy's homicide, I had about nine active cases, three of which I considered cold cases that could wait.

One, however, was the Maze file, and I thought about Harriet lying there in her hospital bed, all alone. I worried that if I gave that case up, someone like Zimmerman would get it. I didn't want to entrust Harriet to the likes of Zim. Or anyone else. Picking up the other five files, I carried those into Andrews's office, leaving her folder behind. If he asked me about it, I'd be truthful. If he didn't, then so be it.

I dropped the stack of case files on his desk.

He fanned them out, giving the names at the top of each a cursory glance. "How's it going on the Abernathy case," he said as I started to leave.

"I have a couple leads. Nothing solid as yet."

Andrews gave a slight nod. I was almost out the door when he said, "Gillespie?"

"Yes, sir?"

"Lombard was adamant. I better not see any overtime come in on the Maze case. Is that clear?"

Translation: I better not get caught working it on duty. Off duty, I was on my own.

"Yes, sir."

I returned to my desk, just as Gypsy poked her head in the other door that divided her office from ours. "Kate? Lieutenant Torrance has been trying to reach you."

"Thanks," I said, and picked up the phone. "You called?" I asked when he answered.

"I have something I think you should see."

"I'll be right there."

Grabbing the two cases I was left with, I stuffed them into my briefcase, then headed to his office. I wanted to talk to him about what I'd discovered.

"Come in," he said when I knocked on his door. "Have a seat." He indicated two chairs on the opposite side of his desk.

I chose the one farthest from him, pulling my briefcase onto my lap, only to have him move to the front of his desk and sit on the edge, stretching his long legs out before him.

"I don't bite," he said.

Not wanting him to think I was affected in any way by his presence, I set the briefcase down beside me, then gave him a casual "Are you sure?"

"Not in public," he replied with a slight smile.

My gaze lit on his mouth, particularly his even, white teeth. The room grew very warm as my imagination took flight. It was an effort to look away. "You wanted to see me?"

"I ran across this today. I thought you should see it." He handed me a report, his tone all business, and I wondered how he could switch gears so easily. Or maybe he was never on that other gear, and it was only me.

Taking the case, I quickly read it. And read it again. It finally occurred to me what I was looking at—the name was a bit different from what I was used to. A missing person's report on a Timothy Kincaid, AKA Squeaky.

"His girlfriend reported him missing?" I asked, although that was precisely what the report said.

"Apparently."

"Then this proves that he's dead."

"No. It proves that he is missing. We still have to find a body."

"They obviously dumped it," I said, excited that something had finally surfaced on what I'd witnessed. Once his body was found, it was only a matter of time before everything else came to light—undoubtedly the very reason his body was moved. Ballistics would prove that Abernathy's gun killed him and the rest would fall into place.

But there was still Abernathy's homicide. Which reminded me of Dellwood.

"I found a witness to the hit-and-run," I said, then told Torrance about what the homeless man had related. "He can't—or won't—identify anyone, but it's clear from what he told me that our theory about Abernathy being taken out was correct. And there may have been more than one person involved, assuming the car that stopped did so to set him up for the impact. On top of that, Abernathy and Jamison may have been working a high-profile cocaine trafficking case." I told him about the hidden key and the case file I'd seen, as well as the twenty-two.

Torrance stood and looked out his office window at the other IA inspectors. When he turned back to me, his expression was troubled. Another rare glimpse into a man I barely knew.

"It's not too late to pull out," he said.

"I knew going into this that it was dangerous."

"It would be different if we knew who he was involved with."

"Didn't we just have a conversation about you realizing that my investigation would keep me at the forefront for a purpose?"

He glanced at the report I held. "What do you intend to do?"

"Go talk to her, of course."

I stood, needing to put distance between us. As I left, he said, "Kate?"

Stopping, I faced him. He said nothing. The look in his eye told me he was about to throw out one of his usual double entendres. But Sergeant Mathis walked in and Torrance's expression turned purely professional. "Be careful."

I'm not sure exactly when I realized I'd left my briefcase in his office, but I knew with a certainty that the room was far too charged for me to go back in there and get it. I decided to retrieve it sometime when he wasn't there. I wasn't scared. Just being pragmatic. And my pragmatic side told me I had more important things to do at the moment, such as determining what Reid had been doing in Jamison's company when Reid said he was going to San Jose. I called his office to find out if he was back, found out he was, then took the stairs to his floor.

The DA's office is the law enforcement arm for the district attorney, and the investigators, Reid being one of them, worked at the direction of the DA. Sometimes their cases were a continuation of those started by SFPD, and other times they worked cases that we never touched. Sometimes when elections came around, sensationalism ruled the day, and they worked cases that made the biggest splash.

A multimillion-dollar cocaine case could make a very big splash.

Reid's desk was in the center of the investigators' office. He saw me approach, didn't look too pleased, then headed me off and quickly escorted me to the hallway.

"What are you doing here, Kate?"

"You were going to check on that CI thing for me in Narcotics?"

"I told you I had to go to San Jose."

"Well, if you *had* gone to San Jose, I might not be here. Now what were you and Jamison so chummy about?"

"Nothing that concerns you," he said, looking up and down the hallway as though to ensure we weren't being overheard or seen.

"Something wrong?"

His expression turned wary. "I'm meeting Beth for lunch." Beth, known to the viewing public as Beth Skyler, Channel Two News, was his current girlfriend, someone he started dating when he was trying to fix our marriage.

I glanced at my watch. It was nearly two-thirty, a bit late for lunch. "You wouldn't want to keep her waiting," I said. "But before you go, I would like to know what it was that Abernathy and Jamison were working on."

"I can't tell you."

"What do you mean you can't?"

"One, because I haven't found out yet. Two, because what little I do know is that if the DA finds out I've been discussing this with you, my ass is in a sling."

"What the hell are you talking about?"

"All I know is that it's about drugs and lots of them. The DA's been in hush-hush meetings with Lombard all last week. Some big shipment's due in sometime soon and they think someone on the inside is involved."

"Someone as in a cop?"

"Or cops."

"The night Abernathy was killed, Lombard mentioned that someone in Narcotics was being set up."

"I don't know anything about that, but—"

The door opened and a couple deputy DAs walked out, eyeing us. Reid stiffened, then said loudly, "Like I told you before, Kate, you want another penny from me, go talk to your lawyer." When they were out of earshot, he added, "I need to go."

"Does that mean I don't get that three K you owe me?"

He glanced toward the attorneys. "Think of it this way. As long as I never pay you back, we'll always have a cover when I'm passing info on."

"How lucky can I get?"

I left to check on the missing person's case after Reid's promise—close to meaningless, in my opinion—that he'd call if he learned anything else. And if he did call, I would have to consider it a bonus. Reid followed no one's agenda but his own—in his world, the only person who counted was himself.

My car was in the parking garage, and I had to pass the morgue to get there. The hard heels of my shoes echoed across the empty causeway of the north terrace, and as I glanced in the glass door, I thought of Scolari's wife, a pathologist there before she'd been murdered a couple months ago.

I wondered if I would ever be able to enter that place again without thinking about her.

Scolari couldn't.

He'd loved working Homicide, but after that, it had put him too close to where she'd worked day in and day out. His PI business was new, not yet flourishing, and I was glad I could send some business his way. Even so, I wasn't sure I wanted him to succeed with the assignment. Finding Kevin's mother was about as high on my priority list as cleaning out the drain trap in my shower.

Squeaky's girlfriend, Amanda Sue Ryan, lived in a small apartment, one of several situated above a bar in the Tenderloin District. The door was painted mint green, at least the last coat. The cracked and peeling paint revealed a white layer, and below that the gray of old wood. A few flakes drifted to the floor when I knocked, and I heard a shuffling inside before the door opened.

"Amanda Ryan?" I asked, holding out my star.

"Amanda Sue," she corrected, then opened the door wider. She was maybe an inch or two shorter than I. Her body and face were emaciated with too much drug use, her brown hair stringy and unwashed. She looked fifty—in drug years that put her around twenty-five—and wore too much makeup: eyeliner, clumped mascara, blusher too heavy, all of it smeared, probably left over from the night before, and none of it able to erase the hard edges of her current lifestyle. She had a baby propped on one hip, its face dirty, nose running. Another child, maybe three, hid behind her leg, peeking out at me with startlingly beautiful brown eyes and shoulder-length blond hair. I figured the kid for a girl until the woman said, "Johnny, go get Mama's smokes."

The child gave me a shy look, then darted into the back of the apartment, returning a few seconds later with his mother's cigarettes and lighter. The young in training, I thought as Amanda Sue lit up, then exhaled a stream of smoke, stepping aside to let me enter. She lived in a two-room apartment. There was a stained twin mattress on the floor in one corner where, judging from the one-eyed teddy bear, empty baby bottle, and torn blue blanket, the kids probably slept. There was no refrigerator, and the scarred linoleum floor was littered with trash and filthy clothes. The door to the back bedroom was open, and it didn't look much better.

"You find Squeaky yet?" she asked, the cigarette hanging from her mouth.

"No. I wanted to ask you a few questions."

"Go for it." She hefted the baby higher on her hip, rocking it to the beat of a Rolling Stones song heard clearly through the floorboards from the bar downstairs.

I pulled my notebook from my pocket and flipped it open. "I know you went into all this with the officer you spoke with last night, but can you tell me why you think he's missing?"

" 'Cause he ain't here, that's why." Looking mildly annoyed, she took a long drag and blew the smoke to one side, away from the baby.

"Has he ever left before?"

"Yeah."

"Look, Ms. Ryan—"

"Amanda Sue."

"—if you want our help, you're going to have to try a bit harder."

"Sorry," she said, looking anything but. "It's just that I'm tired. I was up all night."

I bet you were, I thought, seriously doubting it had anything to do with her kids and everything to do with the bar she lived over. "You work?"

"Sometimes."

"What do you do?"

She looked at me for several long seconds as if contemplating the gravity of my words. "Turn a trick here and there."

I glanced at the kids, wondering if she brought the men into her apartment while they were there, and who watched them when she went out to hook.

"I got a roommate who helps baby-sit," she said, apparently guessing my thoughts. She undoubtedly knew the routine, knew that I'd have CPS over here to grab her kids before she could step out again. I made a mental note to call them anyway. Couldn't hurt.

"About Squeaky," I said. "Did he give any indication where he was going or who he intended to meet the last time you saw him?"

"Not really. I assumed he was going to get me my money."

"Why?"

"He owed me big time. When he couldn't get a fix, I'd help him out, turn an extra trick, ya know? He probably owed me a couple thousand. He said he was going to pay me back by yesterday."

Could Squeaky have stolen some money to pay her back? Was that why Abernathy had been after him? Because he'd been ripped off? I'd seen Abernathy lose his temper before and imagined that if he'd found out some two-bit hype had ripped him off, he might not take it too calmly. But then that brought up the question of what was Abernathy doing with that much money? Unless it was drug-buy money and Squeaky was working for him.

I wrote down "drug $" in my notebook, and wondered if anyone in Narcotics had reported a theft of the money they used for their undercover buys.

"Any idea where Squeaky was planning on getting this money?" I asked.

"I got my ideas." The baby started crying, and, cigarette still hanging from her mouth, she looked around, saw a pacifier about a foot away on the grimy floor. Using her foot to scoop it closer, she bent down, picked it up, and stuck it in the baby's mouth.

I stared at the baby, who contentedly sucked away, and pictured my nephew and his mother—the woman the psychologist insisted I find—in similar circumstances. I couldn't help but wonder if had my brother not died, and Child Protective Services not taken Kevin in, would he have grown up in surroundings like this? Hating Kevin's mother, and trying hard not to transfer those feelings to the woman before me, I held my tongue and tried to listen to what she had to say.

"I think he had something on the mayor," she repeated.

Her words surprised me. "The mayor?"

"None other."

"What makes you say that?"

" 'Cause it's election year, and Squeaky told me he had something on someone big, which meant big bucks. Thousands and thousands, he said. He promised me he was gonna bring home the bacon and now he's gone."

"And you think the mayor did something to him?"

"That or Squeaky tried to run off with the money. Hard to say with him. All I know is I want you to find him and get me the money he owes me."

Tempted to tell her I wasn't a bill collection service and, by the way, Squeaky was dead, I kept my mouth shut. She had nothing else to offer, and I left her. I wanted to get back to the Hall to notify Child Protective Services.

But then I pictured the dirty pacifier and her kicking it over with her foot. I saw my nephew Kevin as a helpless infant.

Why the hell wait? I called CPS from the car.

8

It was almost four and I'd seen more despair and poverty in the past couple days than I cared to. Too much more was bound to send me into a tailspin of depression, and I couldn't figure out why. After all, it wasn't as if I weren't used to seeing that sort of stuff. I'd been a cop for over a decade. I was tough. Cynical.

And needed a heavy dose of caffeine.

I made a beeline for the nearest Starbucks, ordered a double latte, then headed back to the Hall. As soon as I walked into Homicide, Gypsy caught me. "Lombard's looking for you," she said. "I think he wants an update on the Abernathy hit-and-run."

"Thanks."

So much for a relaxing moment with my coffee.

I left it on my desk, then headed for Lombard's office. His secretary sent me straight in.

Lombard, dressed in a gray pin-striped suit with power red tie, was speaking on the phone.

He nodded at me and I took a seat, waiting for him to finish the call. I gathered it had something to do with Abernathy's funeral arrangements. Lombard confirmed this when he finally hung up and said, "We're trying to find out what sort of service his widow wants."

I said nothing.

He gave me a noncommittal shrug. "For obvious reasons, we can't deny him an honorable funeral. Not without giving away our investigation."

"You wanted to see me?" I said, keeping my thoughts about that to myself.

"I was wondering if you'd discovered anything new."

"A few things."

He got up, closed the door, then returned to his desk. "Shoot."

"First of all, I've found a witness who saw the entire thing."

"You're kidding."

Without mentioning his name, I told him what William Dellwood had related to me.

"You're saying this guy saw Abernathy draw his weapon just before he was killed? That would mean he was murdered. Or he thought he was about to be."

"Or he was about to murder someone and they got to him first," I said, thinking of my own experience in the alley with Abernathy. "At least from my witness's point of view."

"And who is this witness?"

I hesitated.

"You do have his name?"

"Of course. It's just that I feel sort of responsible for him. Frankly, I'm worried that if it gets out—"

"Understood. His name?"

"William Dellwood."

"And how did this Dellwood come to witness this?"

"He lives in the area."

"Where?"

"Between businesses." Lombard eyed me, waiting. "He's homeless."

"Our key witness is some homeless guy?"

"And an alcoholic."

"Jesus Christ. That'll go over well."

"I'm hoping it will be kept confidential for the time being."

"I can just see the media getting ahold of this."

"I'm more worried about somebody in the department."

He rubbed at his chin. "You said you had something else?"

I wanted a confirmation from him that Dellwood's name wasn't getting out, but decided to take it slow. "I spoke with Squeaky's girlfriend. She thinks the mayor's office is dirty, and that Squeaky was going to drop the dime on them."

"Blackmail?"

"I guess so."

"Abernathy working for the mayor? That's a bit far-fetched."

"Stranger things have happened. I have another theory, if you care to hear it." I told him about the drug-buy money, thinking that Squeaky might have ripped off Abernathy and gotten killed for it.

"Check into it," he said.

Yeah. I was going to march right into Narcotics and say, *Oh, by the way, did anyone steal any of your drug-buy money, and do you think Abernathy murdered the guy who took it? In cold blood?*

"In the meantime," Lombard continued, "I'll have someone make some discreet inquiries into the mayor's office. See if anything pans out."

"About Dellwood."

"What about him?"

"I think he might be in danger if it gets out that he's a witness."

"I'll take that into consideration. Right now, your safety's my first concern. I don't like the way this is developing. I've seen this sort of thing before back when I worked IA and—" He stopped suddenly, his pale blue eyes narrowing. "Have you told Torrance?"

"Earlier."

"In the future you're to report to me and only me."

"Yes, sir." I left, feeling uneasy at his order, and if truth be told, angry over the funeral arrangements. I looked at my watch and saw it was almost five. In my office I grabbed my purse, dumped my coffee, which had grown cold, then took off before anyone else had a chance to stop me. In the parking garage I was unlocking my car when I heard Torrance call out my name.

Turning, I waited for him to catch up to me.

His stride was sure, fast. He carried a briefcase—mine, I realized when he neared.

"You left this in my office."

"Thanks." I took the briefcase from him and leaned against my car.

"You okay?"

"Picture perfect," I said, as a couple of uniformed officers walked past. Torrance and I both nodded at them, neither of us moving. "Lombard's in there planning an elaborate funeral for the man who tried to murder me and in the same breath orders me to report only to him. Other than that, nothing going on with me that a little mindless sex wouldn't cure. That or a fifth of whiskey."

"You hate whiskey."

"You catch on quick, Lieutenant," I said, tossing my briefcase in through the open door and onto the backseat. The garage would be teeming within minutes, the nine-to-fivers in a rush to get home. Safety in numbers. I got into my car and started it, very much aware of him watching me. Rolling down my window, and feeling secure with a door between us, I said, "Good night, Torrance."

"Kate—" he said as I backed out.

I didn't wait to hear what he had to say. I hightailed it out of the parking garage, thinking about Lombard's parting order. It was far better to lose myself and my temper in the crawling mass of cars on the Bay Bridge. A traffic officer directed my lane to the on ramp. After passing the last turnoff, traffic came to a standstill. The sky was heavy with clouds, dark, threatening a downpour if their color was any indication. My cellular rang and I answered it, hoping it was Torrance. It was my aunt.

"Have you called Kevin's psychologist?"

"No, Aunt Molly."

"Well, I told her you would, and she's waiting at her office to hear from you."

Undoubtedly charging us by the minute, too. "What's her number," I said in resignation.

She gave it to me.

I called the number. "Dr. Higgins? Kate Gillespie."

"Hello. Your aunt told me you had some hesitations over locating Kevin's mother."

"Some."

"Do you mind if I ask what those are?"

"Besides that, as far as I'm concerned, she's doing us all a favor by staying out of our lives?"

The silence that followed told me she didn't care for my answer. "Do you mind if I ask what happened to your own mother?"

Her question caught me off guard—never mind that

I didn't want to answer it. "What does that have to do with anything?"

"Just that if you have some unresolved issues involving your own mother, I want to make sure those aren't transferred to Kevin. He has enough problems of his own."

"Look," I said. "I'm not paying you to psychoanalyze me—"

"Your aunt said your mother left when you were two. That you haven't seen her since."

"And I got over that a long time ago," I said, resisting the urge to toss the phone out the window. "Never mind that my mother wasn't a drug addict, and she didn't cause my father's death."

"Which means she didn't have an excuse . . ."

I pressed my lips together, angry that she had opened up a subject I had long considered closed. My mother didn't want to be married to a cop, and she didn't want to take care of kids.

Apparently neither did Kevin's.

Not wanting to examine the similarities, I said, "I don't even remember my mother."

"If I may be frank, wouldn't you like to know? What happened? Is she dead? Alive?"

I didn't answer. I wasn't sure I wanted to know.

"Kevin needs to find out," she continued. "Let him. Then he can put it to rest. Move on."

I didn't want to tell her that I'd hired Scolari to find the woman. If he located her, I was going to make sure she wouldn't endanger Kevin in any way. I'd already lost a brother because of her. I was not about to lose my nephew, too. "I'll consider it," I said.

"Do that, Miss Gillespie. Because I honestly feel that Kevin's well-being is tied up with his mother's history."

I refused to believe that my nephew's mental health somehow hinged on finding some drug-dealing, possibly murdering, two-bit addicted woman. I disconnected, my depression complete. Just when I thought my life couldn't become more complicated, my pager went off. Pulling it from my belt, I pressed the button, and hell if the message didn't throw me off balance. JUST TELL ME WHERE AND WHEN.

Mindless sex.

With Torrance.

Had I the guts, I would have called him right there and said, "Now." I could only thank the Lord that I was stuck in one-way bridge traffic surrounded by water on both sides with nowhere to turn around. Taking anything Torrance said or did as a positive sign that we might be able to have something together was ludicrous. We were completely out of synch. When I wanted him, he turned into someone with the morals and standards of a bronze statue—a damned good-looking one. When he was ready for me, I turned as flighty as a pigeon roosting on said statue.

Someone honked, letting me know that the car in front of me had moved three feet, and why on earth wasn't I moving with it. Easing my foot off the brake, I glanced in my rearview mirror, catching sight of the city behind me and a single ray of sun that had somehow pierced through the storm clouds even as the first drops of rain hit my windshield.

Clouds, dead gray and threatening, lurked on the horizon the next morning. Thunder rumbled in the distance. The sensation of being watched hit me as I drove to work. Ridiculous, I thought, as I parked in the Hall of Justice garage.

Reaching into my backseat, I hauled out my briefcase. When I reached my office I ran into Zim's partner, Shipley. Unlike Zim, Shipley took care with his appearance. He wore a navy blue suit, neatly pressed white shirt, and blue and red striped silk tie.

"How's it going on Abernathy's case?" Shipley asked.

"So far not much to go on." Was this what Torrance felt like, working IA? Having to keep up the pretense of not knowing much about the case to fellow officers?

"You need any help, let me know."

"Thanks," I said. "I will."

Gypsy nodded at me as I swept past, and it seemed odd not to have her hand me a pile of reports now that I was technically assigned to a single case. Andrews wasn't in yet; Zimmerman gave me a withering look, undoubtedly because he'd been saddled with a couple of my cases. Rocky strolled in a few minutes later, holding a half-eaten breakfast burrito.

"Mornin'," he said, brushing egg bits from his brown sport coat. "You hear we got a lead on Nita's killer? Arrested him last night. Got a full confession."

"You question him about the attack on Mazy?" I asked.

"Yeah. Got him to admit he and his friends tagged her fence, but he denied knowing anything about what happened to her."

"You believe him?"

"No reason not to."

"Which means we're back to square one on her case." Not a comforting thought.

"Don't worry," he said. "Something will turn up."

He finished off the burrito in two bites, then went straight for the coffeemaker, eyeing the empty pot. "Hell. No coffee?"

"Sorry," Gypsy called out from her office. The guys bribed her very well to have it made and stagnating for them by the time they came in. "I forgot to set it last night."

Rocky tossed his burrito wrapper in the trash, then set about making the coffee himself. "You get anywhere on Abernathy's hit-and-run yet?" he asked me.

"Hard to say."

"You need any help with anything?"

To say the least. "Not yet."

"If you do, just holler."

"Yeah," Zim said. "I'd like to catch the bastard that killed him."

Yeah, me too. But not for the same reasons. "Thanks, guys. I'll let you know."

I dropped my briefcase on my desk, pushed both latches, and noticed that the top file, Abernathy's hit-and-run, was not there. My chest tightened.

Think.

I locked my car last night.

It was locked this morning.

I pulled open my desk drawers, one by one. When I reached for the file drawer, I eyed the lock as it slid out. It shouldn't have opened. But it did. Had I forgotten to lock it last night?

I flipped through the remaining files in my drawer. It wasn't as if there were that many to go through. I'd given all but Mazy's case away. That, I'd stuck into the file with the other gang homicides, a note attached to the face to check with the Gang Task Force about a possible retaliation connection.

Where the hell had I put Abernathy's case?

Think.

Torrance.

I'd left my briefcase in his office.

Of course. I was beginning to get paranoid. I'd call him, find out if I'd left the file there, or if he'd taken it. My worry would be unfounded.

I called his extension. He wasn't in. I busied myself with paperwork, transcribing notes, but I couldn't shake the feeling that something was amiss. Had someone gone through my files?

"Ya look like you lost something," Rocky said, eyeing me as I stared at my briefcase.

"Abernathy's file."

"Lombard probably took it," Zim said. "He came in here looking for you about a half hour after you took off last night. Wanted to know if you took the file with you."

"Did he say why?" I asked.

"No. Just wanted to know where you kept your active cases."

"He went through my desk?" I asked, surprised.

Zim glanced at the coffee pot, nearly full. He grabbed his mug and stood. "I didn't stick around to find out," he said, walking over to the coffeemaker. "The wife had a pot roast cooking. Didn't want to be late."

He filled his mug and I returned to my paperwork trying to make sense of what he had told me. Had Captain Lombard gone through my desk? And if he had, was it any different than what I had done yesterday? Going through Jamison's desk? It felt different, I told myself. It *was* different. I was investigating a homicide. Jamison was a potential suspect. I ignored the fact that it was unethical, to say the least. And what if Lombard had gone through my desk? Okay, that too was unethical, and more than likely, the reality was that I was reading too much into it. He was merely looking for Abernathy's case file.

Which I still hadn't found.

I tried Torrance again. Still no answer. I dropped the phone in the cradle and it rang almost immediately. "Gillespie, Homicide."

"Inspector? Leon Perry. Pacific Bell security. I have those numbers you requested from the pay phone." I copied them into my notebook as he recited them. "Call if there's anything else you need," he said.

"I will."

"And I want you to know, I'm sorry to hear about your Narcotics officer. My condolences to your department."

I glanced out the window at nothing in particular. "Thanks."

I hung up, thinking about Scolari's words the night I told him about Abernathy killing Squeaky. *You sure he didn't mistake you for a suspect?*

What if I was wrong? What if he had thought precisely that?

No. Squeaky's hands were empty, and Abernathy shot him in the back.

Besides, who would hide the body if it were legitimate? And what the hell could be going down in a few days that would get Squeaky killed?

"You here, Gillespie?" Rocky asked, staring at me.

"Yeah. Just thinking," I said, drawing my attention back to the here and now. "Anything significant going down in the next three days? President visiting? Chief retiring?"

"Same shit, different day. Why?"

"No reason. Just wondering." I hated this. Hated that I couldn't discuss possibilities and suspicions of the case with my partner. The pretense of looking into this as if it were a simple hit-and-run was getting to me, and I tapped out my frustration with my pen on the desktop.

Rocky eyed the pen, then me. I ignored him.

"Too much caffeine?" Zim asked.

I ignored him, too. If I wanted to solve this, I had to get past the fact that Abernathy tried to kill me. It was clouding my judgment. No, what was clouding my judgment was the thought that someone else out there might try to pick up where Abernathy left off.

Get past it. No one's shooting at you.

But I eyed my open briefcase, unable to dismiss the thought that someone had been in it. I pulled out the contents, giving it a thorough look. Shoved in the middle was the file folder containing Abernathy's case. Had I overlooked it in my rush? Of course, that was it. I'd been in such a hurry that I'd apparently paid little attention to where I'd stuck the folder. Nothing more.

My imagination was getting the best of me, undoubtedly from a lack of sleep the past week. What I needed to do was get back on track. Prioritize.

Find the killer.

I glanced at the numbers from the pay phone that I'd scrawled in my notebook. There were three phone numbers appearing in the right time frame. Two seemed vaguely familiar, but didn't stand out. I called the first number. It rang several times, then picked up. Instantly I recognized the voice on the answering machine. "Hi, this is the Jamison residence. Please leave your name and number at the tone . . ."

I hung up, somewhat surprised, though I shouldn't have been. Jamison and Abernathy were close. Just because Abernathy called his partner, didn't make the man involved. Though it did make him a damned good suspect, I thought, looking at the second number and punching it in.

It rang once. "Rosenkrantz, DEA," a man answered.

"Oh, sorry. I think I hit the wrong number," I said, then disconnected. That was definitely one of the names in Jamison's drug file. Why, then, would Abernathy have called a DEA agent minutes before he was killed unless he was working on *that* case at the time? And what reason would Jamison have for pretending he knew nothing about the case?

I looked at the third number. The prefix belonged to a cellular. It rang twice.

"Hello," came a male voice, then away from the phone a muffled "Thanks, see you tomorrow."

My breath caught. My heart drilled against my chest.

"Hello?" he repeated. "Who is this?"

I slammed the phone down.

9

The brass-plated latches of my briefcase gleamed beneath the fluorescent lights.

I slapped the briefcase shut, secured the latches, then grabbed it and left the office with a hurried "Late for an appointment," when Rocky gave me a curious look.

Someone had gone through my desk. I was sure of it. Looking for what? Abernathy's file? It had been in my briefcase. Had someone gone through that as well? Where or when I had no idea. I'd left it in Torrance's office—not that I suspected him—but someone could easily have gone in there and seen it. But if that was the case, if it was a cop, they could go and pull the report from Records. Pretty simple. Why go through my stuff?

In the future you're to report to me and only me.

Oh, God. Don't let it be.

In the hallway I was hit by a rush of thoughts and couldn't clear my mind. I heard Squeaky, plain as day. *This is bigger than you and me.*

I didn't want it to be big. I wanted it to be simple. But simple did not fit with the number I had just called. Or the man who answered.

It was Captain Lombard's voice on that phone. Torrance's boss. The man Zim had seen at my desk, wanting to know where I kept my case files.

I needed to get out of the building to think. I glanced up and down the hallway. To my left, a uniformed officer walked in my direction. I immediately headed the other way, feeling as though someone had dropped me in the midst of some alien world where everyone looked the same but I had no idea if they were really who I thought they were. Like their eyes would glow green the moment my back was turned.

In the world of cops and robbers, you were supposed to know who the good guys were. I didn't know who anyone was anymore, or whom I could trust.

Torrance. I had to find Torrance.

I took the stairs to his office. His secretary, a dark-haired woman in her forties, said he'd just left. I asked her to send him a page.

"What do you want me to say?" she asked, bringing up the paging program on her computer.

"Tell him . . ." I thought about the parking garage, my mindless-sex comment, and his answering page. "Tell him, here and now."

"Here and now?"

I nodded. "That and his office number. He should get it."

She typed in the message, followed by my call sign and then his office number. I sat in one of the chairs near her desk. About two minutes later, the phone rang. "That's probably him," she said, handing me the line.

"Management Control," I answered.

"Why do I get the feeling that this is not about sex?"

"Because you know me too well?"

"What's wrong?"

I took a breath. "I just need a break," I said, cognizant that not only was his secretary listening, but also several IA inspectors sitting at their desks just outside her office.

"Lunch?"

"Thought you'd never ask."

"I'll be back in about twenty minutes."

"How about I wait in your office."

"Fine. I'll see you in a few."

Entering his office through his secretary's door, thereby avoiding his coworkers, I took a seat at his desk, setting my briefcase on the floor beside me, then stretched out my fingers, stiff from the death grip I'd had on the handle. Torrance's office was spotless, his desk immaculate, with his laptop centered and on, the time flashing across the black screen. Sleep mode. Eleven-eighteen it said, jumping from corner to corner.

I watched it change colors as it bounced, red, yellow, blue. Curious. Torrance wasn't the sort to leave his computer on where anyone could walk in, gain access. He was working a parallel case to mine. I doubted that anyone in his office, including his secretary, was privy to the case. And yet here was his computer, on.

My pager beeped. I read a message from Rocky. Scolari was trying to reach me and it was important.

I called the number Rocky had left. Scolari answered. "Hey, kid."

"What's up?"

"Found her. She goes by Cassandra White."

I said nothing.

"You want the number?"

Exhaling, I leaned back in the chair. "No."

"Yeah, well, you can thank me later. Got a pen?"

I grabbed a pencil from Torrance's desk. "Shoot."

He recited the number; I copied it on a memo pad. "Let me know how it goes," he said.

"Yeah, thanks." I disconnected, staring at the paper. They were just numbers. Why did it feel as though I were holding a paper with 666 emblazoned across the face of it?

Call her. Get it over with.

My fingers rested on the phone, refusing to move. This was stupid. It wasn't as if she could do anything, was it? Kevin was thirteen. He loved us. He wouldn't abandon us to go live with his mother.

Was that what I was afraid of? That he'd think the pasture was greener with some drug-addicted mother he never knew? That he'd leave us high and dry because of some stupid argument he'd had with Aunt Molly over God knew what?

I looked at the name I'd written. We were better than that. We were a family. But my fingers shook as I reached for the phone, keyed the number in. It rang. I chewed on the pencil eraser, waiting for her to answer, fighting the urge to hang up.

It wasn't as though one call could change our entire lives.

"Hello?"

Hang up. Do it.

"Hello?"

"Cassandra White?"

"Yes."

"This is Kate Gillespie of the San Francisco Police Department."

"Oh, God. What do you want?"

Her voice sounded as shaky as my hand. For some reason the thought had a calming effect. "I need to talk to you."

"Oh, my God."

"I know you don't know me, but I'm—"

"I know exactly who you are," she said, her voice stronger, surer. "And I don't want to talk to you or anyone else there. Do you understand?"

"Look—"

"No, you look," she said, her anger shocking me. "Leave me alone."

The phone disconnected. I glared at the receiver in my hand, then dropped it in the cradle, questions swirling through my head as I went over her gamut of emotions in so short a call.

I went back to gnawing on the pencil's eraser, told myself I was glad—she wanted nothing to do with us or Kevin, that much was obvious. I didn't stop to examine the reasons why. Plenty of opportunity for Dr. Higgins to do that. We paid her enough.

The time bounced across the laptop screen, nearly eleven-thirty-eight. I eyed the keyboard, wondering what secrets were just beyond my reach, what he might have been working on before he left in such a hurry. Once again it occurred to me that Torrance wasn't the type to leave his computer open, accessible to anyone. A person only need reach over with the pencil, stab at a key, and—

"Kate."

The pencil flew from my hand as I swiveled his chair around, hoping he hadn't noticed my intent. "Hi," I said, standing.

He retrieved the pencil from the floor, his gaze reminding me of obsidian, impenetrable. He looked from the computer to me as he dropped the pencil on his desk. "You ready for lunch?" he asked.

"Yes."

Grabbing my briefcase, I started for the door while he shut off the laptop. I had no idea if he suspected my intent, or rather my temptation. He mentioned nothing, and being an intelligent woman, I figured it best not to bring it up.

We strolled across Bryant Street to the deli. I suppose that somewhere in the back of my mind was the hope that this lunch had nothing to do with business. A silly thought, considering the number on the pay phone leading to Lombard's cell phone—something I couldn't mention at the moment, since we were surrounded by cops and attorneys and everyone else from the Hall trying to beat the lunch rush.

Torrance eyed me while I scanned the menu, and I wondered if he was thinking about the computer. "You want to go someplace a little quieter?" he asked.

"Sure."

He drove, while I stared thoughtfully out the window, unsure how to broach the subject of Lombard's possible involvement. "Something on your mind?" he asked as he pulled into a space near Demetrias, a Greek restaurant, one we'd been to before.

"To say the least." My stomach growled at that precise moment. Probably had something to do with my lack of food since dinner last night.

"Let's order first."

We sat in a corner, near the window, which offered a view of pedestrians and parked cars. A lone bicyclist opted to walk his ten-speed up the hill—a necessity, as steep as it was.

I thought about how and what I was going to tell him. I wasn't worried that Torrance might be close to Lombard. I didn't think Torrance was close to anyone in the department. It was more that Torrance was a facts-first sort of man. And just because Lombard answered the number I'd called, or gone through my desk, didn't mean he was involved in Abernathy's murder. Still, even though it placed him high on the suspicious list if not the downright suspect list, there could be a very logical explanation. What, I didn't know. I intended to find out.

A waitress, dark-haired, heavyset, brought us water. "Inspector Torrance," she said with a wink. "You need any menus, or you want the usual?"

"The usual is fine, Athena," he said. "But you might want to bring a menu just in case."

"What's the usual?" I asked.

"House salad," she replied. "Extra gyros, extra feta, extra olives."

"Sounds right up my alley," I said. "And an ice tea, twist of lemon."

"You got it." She bustled off toward the kitchen.

Once she was out of earshot, Torrance said, "If it's not mindless sex you wanted to see me about, what then?"

"If I told you I'd lied," I said, noting the look of humor in his eyes, "and that it really was the mindless sex I wanted, what would you do?"

Our gazes locked. The humor was still there in his, yet it was barbed with something darker. "I'd say to hell with lunch—"

"Mike?"

The lilting voice came from the kitchen area, the petite brunette I'd seen Torrance with the night of Abernathy's murder.

He smiled at her and stood.

She rushed over, wrapping her arms about his waist, looking up into his eyes. "I never got to thank you for the other night," she said.

He seemed slightly uncomfortable over her show of . . . whatever it was she was showing besides her cleavage. And even I couldn't miss that. I smiled, waiting for an introduction, figuring he couldn't very well get out of it this time, and at last I'd find out who this perfect little thing was.

"Chloe," he said, gently disentangling her arms from about him. "This is Inspector Kate Gillespie. Kate, Chloe Demetrias."

She held out a finely boned hand, each nail manicured to perfection. "How do you do?" she said.

"Fine thanks," I replied, shaking hands. Since I wasn't the jealous type, I didn't bore myself with comparisons. Why bother? She could give Miss America a run for her money.

"Let me cook you dinner some night," she told him, reminding me what it was to feel like a wallflower, something I hadn't experienced since, oh, the twelfth-grade prom. Not much younger than her, come to think of it.

"I'll call you."

"Okay." She stood on tiptoes and gave him a peck on the cheek, then gave me a "Nice to meet you. Gotta run, late for an afternoon class," before rushing toward the kitchen area.

"Where were we?" he asked.

Mindless sex. But the waitress arrived with our salads. "Work," I said instead once she left. "There's something I need to talk to you about."

"Likewise. You want to go first?" he asked.

Perhaps I should have said yes, but his expression had turned so businesslike, I grew curious as to why. "By all means, you go first."

"Is there a possibility that you left something out the night Abernathy was killed?"

"Then what are you saying?"

"I'm saying it appears that someone is doing a damned fine job to make it look like you might be involved. And if that's the case, your life is at risk."

"So tell me something I haven't already thought of."

He didn't look pleased with my response.

"Who knows about it?" I asked.

"The tip?"

I nodded.

"Other than the sergeant who took the call? No one but me."

"Who took it?"

"Kent Mathis."

Mathis worked in IA. Which meant the call was legitimate. It didn't say anything about the caller, however.

"What now?"

"I have a meeting with Captain Lombard after lunch. I'll let you know, then."

Talk about segues. "Just the person—"

I stopped when he pulled out his pager and read whatever message had just come his way. "Christ." He stood. "I've got to go," he said, digging for his wallet. He dropped a twenty on the table. "You mind taking a taxi?"

"No. What's up?"

"I'll let you know the moment I find out anything."

As if I expected him to tell me. I watched him walk out, then up the hill to his car, his jacket flying open in the wind, revealing the gold star on his belt and the gun at his side, a not so subtle reminder that there was more to this man than met the eye.

10

The waitress, Athena, bustled over a few moments later. "You want a couple of containers for your lunch?"

I looked down at our untouched salads, completely losing my appetite. "How about some baklava to go?"

"Sure." She returned with the pastry and I paid, then caught a bus instead of a cab—for the simple reason that the bus got there first. I ended up sitting next to some girl with so many body parts pierced, she would have set off the metal detector at the Hall from about a block away. An older woman across from me was reading a romance with a hunk on the cover, and I wished for the freedom of doing the same, escapism by literature. There was too much darkness in my life right now, and someone, my aunt I think, told me that romance novels all had happy endings. Fiction. Must be nice.

I got back to the Hall and was approaching the side door, when who should I run into but Jamison, clad in his usual T-shirt and jeans. He nodded at me and said, "How's it going?"

It was one of those moments when I could say, "Fine" and move on, or stop and force him to converse. There were so many things I wanted to ask him—so many things I couldn't, because I didn't know how involved he was, if at all.

I opted to stop. "You have a moment?"

He hesitated before answering, something I found strange for someone who shouldn't have anything to hide. But someone like Jamison working Narcotics had plenty to hide. The question was whether what he was keeping from me was relevant to the case.

Glancing over his shoulder toward the door, then back at me again, he finally answered.

"Something I can do for you?"

"I'm hoping." Now how to proceed? These opportunities never seemed to happen when you were ready for them. "You were going to get back to me on whether Abernathy was working any unusual cases," I said, even though this was beating the proverbial dead horse. Jamison had told me twice in no uncertain terms that he did not know.

He shrugged, noncommittal.

"I don't remember anything unusual. I can check."

I can check? Forget that thing I said about the dead horse. I couldn't believe he was being so casual about not recalling. Had it been my partner killed, possibly murdered, I'd have had a magnifying glass out on each of his cases. But he left me an opening and I took it.

"The reason I'm asking," I said, trying to come up with one, "is just that . . . Abernathy mentioned that he'd just gotten some tip on a drug shipment."

"Abernathy told you that?" he asked, his gaze narrowing.

Call it sudden inspiration. With Abernathy dead, Jamison couldn't verify the truth of what I said. "Yes."

"When?"

If I guessed wrong, it could blow everything.

"Maybe a day or two before he was killed? I remember him saying it was something he wasn't supposed to talk about, but that it was big. Ring any bells?"

"Yeah," he said, looking off to one side as though trying to recall the insignificant details of something that suddenly came back to him. "Now that you mention it, there was this cocaine case. I'll look up the details and get back to you."

"Thanks," I said, seriously doubting that he'd get back to me with anything. He had the case in his top drawer. Why the hell was he hiding his knowledge of the thing? "I appreciate it."

He left, and I headed to the fourth floor, fully expecting to see the Homicide detail deserted, everyone having left for lunch. Instead, several of the guys were standing around the television set in the lieutenant's office. "What's up?" I asked Rocky.

"You didn't see the news crew out front?"

"I didn't come in the front."

"They're making an announcement on Abernathy's murder. Suspect information or something." He spared me a glance. "Then again, you probably already know that, being that you're investigating it."

My insides did flip-flops as I leaned against the doorframe, opting for casual. I couldn't explain the feeling about this, but after my little conversation with Torrance at lunch, and his sudden departure, I expected the worst. I got that and more.

The camera zoomed in on a petite brunette newscaster on the Hall of Justice steps, wearing a red jacket with black velvet trim. I recognized her immediately. My ex-husband's girlfriend.

"This is Beth Skyler, Channel Two News, with an exclusive report on some late-breaking information concerning the hit-and-run of Narcotics Officer Lee Abernathy, who was killed earlier this week. Apparently the police department has just received an anonymous tip. The caller reported that Inspector Abernathy might have fired his weapon at the vehicle moments before he was killed."

The camera cut to a young man in the newsroom. "So the police are investigating this as a murder and not an accident?"

"Yes, Tom," she said, the focus on Skyler again. "At this time, they have few details they are willing to release. What they can tell us is that the suspect vehicle is described as a dark blue or black Ford, and may possibly have some sort of damage from gunfire. The mayor intends to give a press release when more details are available."

The camera panned the newsroom again, showing Tom. "In light of the journalist conference going on at the Moscone Center, I expect this will receive plenty of coverage . . ."

"Undoubtedly, Tom," Skyler said.

Had I not been leaning against something, I might have been in serious trouble. It was all I could do to act normal. No one else seemed to think anything odd about what they just heard. But then, no one else in the detail drove a dark blue Taurus. Not even Rocky reacted, and he shared my vehicle on occasion.

I could only hope that no one would suspect one of their own.

Then again, if enough hints were laid out, false or otherwise, everyone would. I wondered just how many parallel investigations were going on in this case. And of those, how many were looking for the real killer. And how many were looking for me.

Taking a breath, I forced my expression to remain neutral and tried to keep my anger at bay.

"Jesus," Rocky said, looking at me. "You knew that about Abernathy?" he asked me. "That it was out-and-out murder?"

Shipley and Zim both eyed me. Now would be a good time to think of something really slick. Like why a bit of information like that would come out on the news before it was released to them. How about, *Gee, someone's setting me up, and the vehicle they're looking for happens to be mine?*

Don't think so. But there was no need to lash out about something they had no control over— something I apparently had no control over.

The three of them watched me like hawks.

"Knew?" I said, trying to keep my voice calm. "I only just found out myself. How the hell was I supposed to know that it would end up on the news ten minutes later." That was as close to the truth as I was willing to get.

"How'd they find out?"

Rocky's question caught me off guard, more so than hearing my vehicle described on the news. I pictured Dellwood standing near his cardboard shelter, his whiskered face, his piercing blue eyes. "I don't know," I said, tossing the crumpled baklava bag on my desk. This was spinning out of control faster than I could deal with at the moment. "But I intend to find out."

I started from the room. Shipley's calm voice stopped me.

"You need a backup?"

"Not unless you think someone in Management Control is going to do me in."

I didn't wait to find out his opinion. I went straight to Torrance's office, figuring this needed to be done in person. His secretary said he was in with Lombard.

Thanking her, I said I'd be back later, then promptly exited and stood in the hallway next to Torrance's door just out of the secretary's line of vision. I could hear muffled voices, and wished I had a glass to prop against the wall and listen in—a thought I'm sure many an officer had after coming under the scrutiny of Management Control.

Two IA sergeants rounded the corner, saw me, and nodded. I smiled in greeting as they entered their office, not worried about what they thought since I was becoming a regular fixture in their domain. Though I was tempted to follow them in hopes of getting a better listening post, the sound of Lombard's voice raised in anger made me stay put.

"I'm the one in charge of this investigation," Lombard said. "Do I make myself clear?"

The door opened a crack, and I saw Lombard standing just inside. I stayed long enough to catch Torrance's quiet, "Yes, sir," then took off.

Apparently not fast enough. Lombard saw me and called out. "Gillespie. A minute of your time."

I turned, going for the casual I-was-just-walking-by look. "I'm sorry, you said something?"

"If you have a moment." He held open Torrance's office door, allowing me to enter, before indicating I should take a seat. There were two empty chairs. The one behind Torrance's desk, and the one next to that occupied by Torrance himself. Before I could even make up my mind, Lombard placed himself in the position of adversary by taking the chair behind the desk.

I glanced at Torrance. He might as well have been

sitting at a poker table for all I could tell from his expression.

"What can I do for you?" I asked Lombard as I sat.

"This case has taken a new twist, one I don't care for, which leads me to believe I have no alternative but to place you on AL."

I felt like someone had just dropped me in the frigid bay. I couldn't move, couldn't speak for several seconds.

Torrance said, "He thinks you're in danger, because your vehicle description was just plastered all over the media."

"Great," I said. "And just how the hell did the press learn of that so-called anonymous tip you received?"

There was a second of hesitation at my accusatory tone, and then Torrance gave a pointed look at Captain Lombard.

"You told the press?" I asked the captain. Coupled with what I knew about him, I was stunned. And angry.

He didn't answer and even appeared flustered.

"I can't believe you gave out a pertinent piece of the investigation to the press without regard as to how it would affect my investigation, never mind my life." Torrance tossed me a look of warning, and I reined in my temper for the simple reason that I wanted, needed, to be put back on this case whether Lombard wanted me there or not. "With all due respect, Captain, someone went to the trouble of calling in a suspect vehicle description that coincidentally or not happens to match mine. Now if it's a legit tip, which I'm not saying it is, then the killer is or was driving a vehicle of that description."

"Which is why the press should know."

"And if it is not legit, as in the killer wants you to think it's my vehicle and I'm involved, then we've just played into their hands and aired a false description to the entire city."

"All the more reason to take you off this case," he replied, pushing his chair from the desk to stand. He turned to look out the window, keeping his back to us as though he found the surrounding architecture fascinating. "If that doesn't make you realize the danger you're in, then I don't know what will."

"You think I don't know that they're playing for keeps?" I asked. "I watched a man get murdered, for God's sake. It seems I'm the only one who knows that Abernathy was a cold-blooded killer. Now the entire goddamned department has my vehicle description to think about every time they step out onto the street. Removing me from the case is only going to make it worse."

"My mind is made up, Gillespie. You're on AL as of now."

"You can't do that," I said, shooting from my chair.

"You'rc dismissed," he said, without turning around.

I forced myself to relax. Be calm. Think. My glance strayed to the phone.

Torrance raised a brow, almost imperceptible, as though he suspected I was about to play a different hand. "There is one thing . . . Zim said you went through my desk last night." A *slight* embellishment of the truth.

Lombard faced me. "I needed Abernathy's file. I figured it would save me a trip to Records. Your point, Inspector?"

"I received a call from Pac Bell security this morning." I paused letting that sink in. "I didn't get a chance to tell you, but Abernathy made a few calls from the pay phone just before he was killed."

"And?"

"The first was to his partner."

"Which means what?"

"I'm not sure. It's the last call he made that I found interesting. It came back to your cell phone."

Quiet descended on the room. A door slammed in the adjoining office. "I don't know what you're talking about."

"The phone records indicate that Abernathy called your cell phone a few minutes before he was murdered."

"That's preposterous," he said, a dull red creeping over his cheeks.

"Maybe so, but true. I'd say between my vehicle allegedly being seen, and your phone being called, we are in this rather deep."

"Goddamm it, Gillespie, if this is some sort of—"

"Call Pac Bell and find out for yourself if you doubt me. I'm only reporting what I've learned. Which is precisely what I was told to do."

He leaned forward, both palms on Torrance's desk, his fury contained. "This goes *nowhere,* do you understand, Gillespie? Abernathy called me on a case he was working on with the DEA. A big case with far-reaching implications. One I won't go into here and now."

"And who would I tell? The only people involved in this case are me, you, and him," I said, nodding in Torrance's direction. "At least I was involved. Now . . . ?" I shrugged.

"And if I leave you on the case, then what? I get to read about another of my officers killed?"

"What would you have me do? Sit at home on AL while someone else plays God with my life? Implicates me in a murder I didn't commit? I don't think so. Leave me on the case and let me work it my way."

He didn't say no. Instead he gave Torrance a cursory glance, then stormed out, slamming the door behind him.

"Jesus," I said, dropping into a chair.

Torrance stood, then sat on the edge of his desk, his arms crossed, regarding me with an intensity that was unnerving. "And at what point had you intended on telling me about Lombard's number showing up on the phone records?"

"Right around the same time I planned on telling you that the second call was to a Rosenkrantz, who works for the Drug Enforcement Agency, which apparently fits with what Lombard just said."

He looked even less pleased.

"Okay," I said. "Would you believe that's why I came here?" I attempted a smile filled with innocence and charm. His expression never wavered. "Fine. I had intended on telling you at lunch, but between your Greek goddess friend and your mysterious page, you cut out of there faster than I could regroup." When he raised his brows, I wished I could take the "Greek goddess" part back. "Okay. What it boils down to is that I'm sorry to blurt it out like that. But I was desperate. I didn't want to be placed on administrative leave."

"Never mind that he's right. You should be on AL."

"In everyone's opinion but mine, maybe."

"And perhaps the killer's. Or has it occurred to you that you might be flirting with danger?" His gaze was banked with anger.

"What, you're on his side now? Just because I didn't tell you about the damned phone records?"

"This has nothing to do with the phone records and everything to do with the appearance that someone out there is trying to set you up for murder. Or haven't you wondered about the source of that so-called anonymous tip?"

"Of course I have. What I want to know was how my vehicle description got thrown to the press like chum to sharks?"

"If you're thinking that Lombard was in on it, I can't blame you. I just don't see him being involved in this."

"Then how do you explain Abernathy calling him? And him denying it until I brought up my source?"

"I can't explain it. I do know that you've painted yourself into a corner. He's a dangerous enemy, not one to be trifled with."

"Then I guess I'm screwed either way."

"Apparently. Now was there a purpose to this visit? Or do you just like to watch the hairs on my head turn gray one by one?"

"Your concern is touching."

"So is your jealousy."

"Jealousy?" I said with a laugh. "Hardly."

"Do the words 'Greek goddess' ring a bell?"

"Purely facetious," I said, ignoring the wicked sparkle in his eye.

"This from the woman who thought it best that we date others to avoid ruining a good working relationship?"

"And I still think that way," I said, too chicken to admit otherwise. "So do me a favor, wipe that smirk off your face and pretend I never brought her up."

"Ten-four," he said with a mocking salute.

"I'm serious. Now if you can concentrate for a few seconds, I'd like to get back to this anonymous phone tip thing."

"Go on."

"I find it extremely odd that this tip came in after I'd located an eyewitness to the actual killing. Dellwood."

"The homeless man."

"I should have thought of this earlier, but then I didn't know that Lombard was going to be a wild card."

"Thought of what?"

"Taking Dellwood into protective custody."

"You want to go find him?" he said, grabbing his jacket.

"Yep."

We left via the outer office where the other IA sergeants sat working. Torrance grabbed two radios, one for each of us. As we headed out the door, he said, "I can't believe you did that to Lombard. Called him on the carpet about the phone call. You're either brilliant or a fool."

"Let's hope my brilliant foolishness doesn't get me killed."

11

"You drive," I told Torrance, figuring after the news segment, it would better to keep my car out of sight for the time being.

"You're letting me take control?" he asked, giving me one of his humor-laced looks.

"Don't get too excited. I just don't want Zim seeing me get into the Taurus. I can picture him putting two and two together, then calling out the SWAT team."

"It's not Zimmerman I'm worried about, even if he could form a couple of coherent thoughts," he said, backing out the car. The tires gave an echoing screech on the slick garage pavement as he pulled forward. "It's the unknown quantity. Who killed Abernathy, and why are you being thrust into the limelight because of it?"

"Answer the latter and we can solve the former."

A few minutes later, he turned onto the street where Abernathy had been killed.

"That's where Dellwood lives." I pointed between the two buildings and was heartened at the sight of his cardboard box shelter toward the back. At the same time, I was worried that it wouldn't last through the next rainstorm. I glanced up at the sky, blue and filled with wispy clouds of mare's tails, the harbinger of rains to come.

Torrance parked in front of Silva's Repair Garage, where a mechanic in greasy coveralls watched us from beneath the hood of a red Audi. We crossed the street at the corner when the light turned green, but only after waiting for the last car to run the opposing red. Signals seemed to be more of a warning device to many city drivers.

"You know anything about this guy?" Torrance asked.

"Other than what he told me? Not a thing." We entered the breezeway, and I called out. "Mr. Dellwood?"

No answer.

Our footsteps echoed down the narrow walkway. A gust of wind tore past us, bringing up the top of the cardboard lean-to and with it a view into what had been Dellwood's sanctuary. Empty.

I stopped, not wanting to look further, fearing that I might find signs of a struggle or even his death.

"He could be out," Torrance offered, his hand on my shoulder.

"Of course."

We approached. Looked in. There was nothing to indicate that anything out of the ordinary had occurred. No blood, no drag marks. Only an open bottle of whiskey on its side. It wouldn't have been so unusual. Except that it wasn't empty. As though it had tipped, spilled. And been left behind.

"He's probably gone off to find a meal," Torrance said.

"Dellwood was an alcoholic."

"Meaning?"

I couldn't force my gaze from the amber-colored liquid in the bottle. "Somehow I can't picture a guy who's living on the streets because he's so addicted to booze leaving behind what is tantamount to a morning's fix."

Torrance met my gaze. "Who knows about him?"

"Me, you, and Lombard."

"The captain is starting to look worse with each shift of the puzzle."

I was trying not to think about it. "We better start a canvas, see if anyone saw anything."

After a cursory search of the breezeway, we moved to the sidewalk and the street beyond. The wind picked up, whipping at my hair, and I pulled my jacket shut, warding off the chill. I thought of the nights Dellwood had spent here, forgotten by all, huddled in the cold, the fog, the rain, nothing but a bottle to keep him company. I wondered about his family. If they knew he was here, or why he was here. If he had a family.

Most of all I wondered if he would be there still, had I not become involved in Abernathy's homicide.

"It's not your fault," Torrance said, as though he were reading my mind.

"That remains to be seen, doesn't it?" I said, staring across the street. "I'll check at the garage. You start on this side."

I left before he could reply, heading straight for a mechanic, wearing blue coveralls, who stood watching me. "Inspector Gillespie," I said, showing him my star.

He wiped the grease from his hands on a faded red cloth, but didn't reply.

"I was wondering what you could tell me about the man who lives back there."

"Don't know if there's much to tell."

"You know him at all?"

"See him around. Bums a few quarters every now and then. Uses the phone," he said, indicating the same pay phone that Abernathy had used minutes before his death.

"How about today?"

"Yeah. Maybe an hour ago. Saw him walking to the store."

"He say anything to you?"

"Nah. Just walked past like he always does."

"How about any visitors in the past few days?"

He shrugged. "Can't say as if I ever seen anyone go over there. Except you."

"Thanks," I said. I checked a few businesses to the north of the repair shop that I thought would have a direct view of where Dellwood stayed, but no one saw anything. Back at the corner, Torrance met up with me.

"Find anything?" I asked.

"Nothing. How about you?"

"The mechanic thinks he saw Dellwood walking to the store this morning."

He looked at his watch. "I'll head over there. What about you?"

"The video store next to Silva's garage," I said. "They might have seen Dellwood if he was walking to the store."

"Worth a try," he said.

We parted, and a minute later I entered the dusty, poster-filled premises, where the same woman with the overprocessed blond hair sat behind the counter, this time watching a soap. Or she would have been had she not been waiting on a customer. He was renting the latest James Bond film.

While she rang him up, I took a moment to study the tapes on the "new releases" shelf, wondering what planet I'd been on the past few months—I didn't recognize the majority of titles I read. Couldn't say the last time I'd even been to a movie, come to think of it. Before my divorce? Talk about needing a life, I thought, picking up a video and reading the blurb on the back.

The customer left right about then, so I replaced the movie to speak to the woman, catching sight of the departing customer in the small monitor set to the side of the TV screen. In it, I could see him as he strode down the street.

"You wanna rent a tape?" she asked, eyeing me. "Oh, wait. You're that cop, aren't you?"

"Inspector Gillespie," I reminded her, then nodded at the monitor. "That thing working yet?"

"Yeah, right. And I got a ten-dollar-an-hour raise, too. What can I do for you?"

"I have a couple more questions for you, if you don't mind."

"Sure. It's a commercial break right now, so fire away."

"You familiar with a homeless man named Dellwood?"

"Dell? Sure. Nice guy. Drinks too much, but could be worse. Why? Something happen to him?"

"I'm not sure. Have you seen anyone unusual around where he's been staying? Seen him talking to anyone?"

"Can't say as I have. Come to think of it, I can't say when the last time I saw him was. Couple of days ago, maybe. No, wait. He was in last night just before closing, saying something about going to an AA meeting. He was gonna get sober and go visit his daughter. But don't ask me who or where. He didn't say."

"Thanks. If you see him, can you give him this?" I said, handing her my business card. "Tell him to call me right away? It's important."

"Sure."

"One more thing. Anyone else been here the past few days? Asking questions?"

"Nope. Just you."

"Thanks." I left, waiting on the corner for Torrance, watching the traffic drive past, horns honking, tires screeching. I thought of the monitor, and how for want of a tape a murder could have been solved, my name cleared.

Figured.

The wind picked up, the mare's tails giving way to a dark bank of clouds on the horizon, and I promised myself that as soon as I found Dellwood, I was putting him up somewhere.

Torrance returned. "You're not going to like this," he said.

"What did you find?"

"Your Mr. Dellwood was in maybe an hour or so ago and bought his usual bottle of whiskey," he said, naming the same brand sitting in the cardboard shelter.

Somehow I made it back to Torrance's car. "I should never have told Lombard," I said, unable to draw my gaze from the makeshift cardboard house as he pulled away.

"We don't yet know if Lombard's involved."

"Well, if he isn't, he's the weak link, somehow. Think about it," I said. "Everything points to him. The phone record, the press leak. Now Dellwood."

"Dellwood's disappearance isn't yet a confirmed fact. He could still turn up."

"Let's hope he does. Alive."

"What now?"

"Drive around until I find him, I guess." But even as I said it, I had a sick feeling, a knot in the pit of my stomach.

12

I hadn't been into the search more than an hour when my aunt phoned. "Kevin's acting up again. I need you to take him to school in the morning."

"Acting up, how?"

"You know. That talk of his mother again. I've been trying to distract him, but nothing seems to be working. Have you found her yet?"

"I'm still working on it," I said, since I didn't know exactly what I intended to do with that info. "I've hired Scolari to find her."

"Yes, I know. He came by to look at some old papers of your brother's."

"What papers?"

"Just some things in a shoe box. Receipts, that sort of thing. I told you she sent them to me after Sean died. Sam thought it might turn up a—what did he call it? Clue? No, that wasn't it, but whatever he called it, I was hoping he was right."

"I'm sure something will come of it," I said. "Tell Kevin I'll pick him up at seven-thirty."

"Be ready at seven-thirty, young man," I heard her say, followed by a muffled whiny response that I couldn't quite catch. Then, "He wants to leave earlier. Is seven-fifteen okay?"

"Perfect," I said, since that meant I wouldn't be as late to work. Not that it mattered that much. Traffic on the bridge would be a zoo no matter when I left.

I disconnected with her, then returned my attention to Torrance and our search for Dellwood. After hitting every homeless shelter and church within the area, we stopped momentarily at the top of a hill with a view of the bay below—not too far from where Crazy Mazy lived, and I wondered briefly how she was faring. I made a mental note to check on her welfare, feeling slightly guilty that I'd forgotten about her. Right now, though, I had more pressing matters, such as who was trying to frame me for a murder I didn't commit, and what had happened to the man who could clear my name?

"Now what?" I asked, frustrated that we'd failed to turn up so much as a hint of a lead, or a clue, as my aunt called it.

"Perhaps it's time to move on and assume the worst," Torrance said quietly.

I glanced over at him, dumbfounded and disheartened. He simply stared out into the distance, at the gray, churning water, his gaze narrowed against the ever-present offshore wind. "Don't say that."

"In light of my parallel investigation, what choice do we have?"

"Why do I have a feeling I don't want to hear this?"

He looked directly at me. "Hours before Abernathy was killed, we opened an IA on him."

"That's what Lombard was alluding to that night?"

"Yes. Abernathy was suspected of some illicit activity."

"Like what?"

"Money laundering, drug trafficking, possibly evidence theft, and evidence tampering."

"Jesus."

"He said he was being set up to take the fall, and implicated a number of other officers in other agencies. Said he'd give them to us for leniency."

Squeaky's words: *This is bigger than you and me.* I shivered in part from the blast of cold air, in part at the memory. I thought of the file I'd found in Jamison's desk drawer along with the gun. "Do you think this has anything to do with that cocaine shipment?"

"I don't know."

"Whom did he implicate?"

"That's the problem. He was killed before he could tell us. He was getting us the info that night."

Not sure I heard right, I said, perhaps too sarcastically, "That was before or *after* he was taken into custody?"

"He made a deal that I wasn't aware of until much later."

"With whom?"

"Lombard," he said, staring back out at the water.

"That's got to be why Abernathy called him from the pay phone." The events I witnessed that night came flooding back with an unexpected force. I was suffocating in the memories, unable to move or breathe. I pictured Lombard standing there, so calm while I related the events. That whole time he knew. Knew that it was his fault that Squeaky was murdered. His fault I was shot at. His fault that Abernathy, his star suspect, was dead.

His fault that Dellwood witnessed that death and was now missing. I prayed he'd wandered off, moved on to a new life. I didn't like that I couldn't guarantee it. And I hated the guilt that I felt. The guilt that told me I could have done something about this earlier if I had ignored Dellwood's plea to be left alone. If only I'd had the guts to go against Lombard and not tell him of Dellwood's existence. If only. That was a stupid game to play in this business. I knew better.

Anger surged through me. Gave me the strength to get past this. "Lombard's a goddamned son of a bitch," I said.

Torrance said nothing.

"Tell me there's been some mistake. That what you're saying isn't true."

Again, silence.

I looked away. Torrance reached out, took my chin in his hand, made me look at him. "What would you have me do?" he asked in that calm way of his.

"Change history."

"I can't, Kate." We stood like that, our gazes locked. The relentless wind blew around us, wrapping us in an invisible cocoon for an eternal instant. I closed my eyes and felt his thumb stroke the curve of my cheek. "I wouldn't," he said, so soft, just before he let me go, and I wondered if I'd imagined the moment.

A motorcycle raced past. In the distance I heard the wail of a siren. "We should get back," I said, and we headed to the car.

We didn't speak on our return to the Hall. Me, I didn't know how I'd face Lombard, knowing what I now knew. "Drop me off here," I said suddenly, not too far from the Hall, and within walking distance of decent coffee. "I'll walk the rest of the way."

He eyed me, then the coffee shop, as he pulled curbside. "I think it's time we changed tactics," he said. "You trust Andrews?"

"Yes."

"Who else?"

"Markowski and Shipley, of course."

"I think we should bring them into this. Be in my office in twenty."

All the more reason to stop for caffeine. I ordered my latte, then strolled back to the office, which was deserted. With the exception of Zim, I figured the others were up with Torrance, getting briefed. Andrews would understand why I hadn't gone directly to him, not after IA was involved. I wondered, though, what Shipley and Markowski would think, then decided it didn't matter. I still had other things to accomplish. I was not about to give up on finding Dellwood, and since I had five minutes before I was due in Torrance's office, I ran a background on Dellwood, including a criminal history check. His only crime that I could see was a number of arrests in the Central Valley for 647 (f) PC, public intoxication. He had undoubtedly hit bottom and migrated to the city for God only knew what reason. With nothing left to do, and time running out, I headed for Torrance's office. Markowski and Shipley were already present.

Torrance indicated I should sit, and I did.

He shut the door, then crossed the room to a white board, where he picked up a red dry erase marker, pulling off the top. No one used chalk anymore, and I couldn't wait for the days when dry erase markers became obsolete—probably not until they discovered the odor caused cancer or something. In the meantime, we had to suffer the smell.

"Let's get started," Torrance said. "I've informed Andrews, since he couldn't be here." He looked at Shipley and Markowski. "I'm not sure what you've heard, guessed, or deduced from what has been going on. Some of it unfortunately has been erroneously caused by the various factions in this department working against each other instead of together."

Markowski said, "Another case of those who need to know being determined by those who don't have a clue."

Shipley smiled. Torrance raised a brow, something I interpreted as meaning "Precisely," even though he said nothing, just went about drawing two vertical lines on the board, the pen squeaking with each stroke. Two lines for three columns, I figured. There were two murders, and I wondered what the third column was for.

"At this point," he said, "we have two unsolved homicides that may or may not be connected. The time of death in each is significant, as you'll soon see.

"The first is the homicide of an informant. Squeaky Kincaid," he said, writing Squeaky's name at the top of the board to the left of the first vertical line.

"Squeaky's dead?" Markowski asked. "When?"

"I'll get to that in a minute," Torrance said. He wrote Abernathy's name at the top of the second column. "You know about the suspected hit-and-run. What you're probably not aware of are the circumstances of the first homicide, in which an eyewitness saw Abernathy shoot Squeaky Kincaid about fifteen minutes before Abernathy was run down."

"Wasn't there a missing person's report on him?" Markowski asked. And then he looked at me as though he suddenly remembered who it was I was supposed to meet that night. "Holy shit. You were the eyewitness?"

"She was," Torrance said. "Which is why my office is investigating."

That caught the attention of both Markowski and Shipley. "Why?" Shipley asked.

I answered. "When Abernathy shot him, Squeaky was unarmed."

Markowski's face seemed to pale at my words as the implications of that night hit him—his indirect role in what took place.

Shipley started to say something, but Torrance stopped him with a wave of his hand. "Depending on whom you talk to, you'll come up with a different theory on the who and why of Abernathy's hit-and-run—one of them being that Gillespie committed it."

Markowski said, "Why the hell would she?"

I kept waiting for Torrance to say, "She wouldn't." Instead, he wrote my name over the third column in block letters. "That's why I've asked you here. To assist in the investigation," he said, tapping the pen by my name as he spoke, leaving several red dots that seemed to taunt me like drops of blood.

I kept thinking that this was an omen, that somehow I had become an unwilling participant, unable to control my own destiny. And then I realized it was this kind of thinking that would hurt me. I had worked too hard to get here. There were still those officers waiting to see me fail, waiting to say, "I told you so" about women in law enforcement, and especially women in Homicide. Lombard was one of them, even though he didn't dare say anything to me directly.

I was better than that, and I would not let them win, I thought, returning my attention to what Markowski was saying.

"Someone's investigating Gillespie?" he asked.

Torrance would not meet my gaze, something I found disturbing. I decided to ignore it for the moment. I trusted that Torrance would inform me of the particulars at the proper time. "Our office is investigating what Gillespie witnessed and the connection it may or may not have to Abernathy's case."

Shipley said, "So what is it you want from us?"

Torrance looked up at the board as though that held all the answers. "We're operating on a time constraint. Both Squeaky Kincaid and Abernathy alluded to something going down sometime in the next few days involving officers on the take. My office has not been able to discover what it was, but Lombard assured me that from the little he learned, he feels this is bigger than the scandal at LAPD's Rampart division. Lombard believes Abernathy was killed to keep him quiet about whatever it was. His theory? Figure out what Abernathy was involved in, it will lead you to his murderer."

"Sounds simple enough," Markowski said.

Shipley eyed the board. "I still don't see why Gillespie's name is up there."

"Gillespie is the link," Torrance said.

"The unwilling link," I corrected. "I suppose the easiest way is to start at the beginning from when Rocky and I were supposed to meet up with Squeaky." Markowski shifted in his chair, looking distinctly uncomfortable. He'd get over it, and so I plunged on, relating the details from the call Squeaky made that disrupted my life, to the twenty-two and the drug case file I found in Jamison's desk, on up to the moment Torrance wrote my name on the board as the link to the murders. Torrance stood to one side, his face the usual impassive mask, while Shipley and Markowski were having difficulty keeping their jaws from dropping at half of what I said. In the space of fifteen minutes, I had taken one man's life, Abernathy's, and forever changed their perceptions of him and what he stood for.

At my conclusion, Shipley said, "And you have no idea who may have killed him or what he was going to reveal about which officers were on the take?"

"It's gotta be Jamison," Markowski said.

Shipley nodded.

"We don't know that," I replied. "It's true he seems the logical suspect—"

"Logical?" Markowski said. "Why the hell else wouldn't he tell you about that multiagency cocaine case file until you confronted him?"

"Another of those misguided need-to-know reasons, I assume."

"And what about the twenty-two he had in his desk?"

"I don't know," I said. "Maybe just evidence from another case."

Shipley was nodding at Markowski's questions. "What about Lombard's number showing up on the pay phone?"

I repeated what Lombard had told me.

"That," Torrance said, "among other things, is what I'd like you two to check into. Along with the names Gillespie found in Jamison's case file. One is a DEA agent by the name of Rosenkrantz, who was also called from the same phone. The other is a guy by the name of Stilwell. I'd like to know if he's affiliated with any agency. At this point, we'll assume that Lombard and Jamison are running their own parallel drug investigation. It may or may not be related. And because of Lombard's number showing up, our investigation remains under the table—at least until we know who—if anyone—in Narcotics is involved."

"And naturally," Markowski said, "if they're dirty, they're not to be counted on. If they're legit, well, we all know how much confidence I have in anyone over the rank of . . . lieutenant," he said, eyeing Torrance, probably hoping he hadn't noticed the hesitation. Markowski's sentiments on the brass mirrored that of a number of officers who failed to trust anyone with rank, a fact of life in many departments.

Torrance, however, seemed to ignore the implication. "Since we don't know whom we can trust," he said, "I've handpicked you and the few people I can rely on in my office. Lombard will have to be brought in eventually. Right now I'm buying time, a commodity we have little of. If everything we have heard is to be believed, there is something going down in three days' time, and I'd rather not be surprised."

"Why the hell would anyone schedule something for then?" Markowski said. "The goddamned boat festival or whatever it's called is going on."

I looked at him in surprise, unable to believe it had not occurred to me earlier.

"What?" he said.

"The Parade of Boats," I said. "If you were going to smuggle in a gazillion pounds of cocaine and not want the authorities to notice, what better cover than something like that? There'll be more boats in the bay than the Coast Guard could possibly deal with in a lifetime, much less one afternoon."

"Son of a bitch," Shipley said. "They're gonna deliver a ton of coke under our very noses."

"Under everyone's noses," Markowski said. "Every tourist in the state will be parked by the bay, and every news crew within shouting distance will be covering it."

"You have a copy of Jamison's file?" Shipley asked.

"No. When I asked him about it, he said he knew

nothing about it, and when I brought up particulars, he acted as though the case had slipped his mind. I couldn't very well tell him I'd seen it in his desk."

"Yeah," Markowski said. "Probably not the thing to mention to a fellow officer you're supposed to trust. Just how did you get around it?"

"I told him that Abernathy had mentioned the case in passing. Whether he believed me or not, I don't know."

"You have a game plan?" Shipley asked Torrance.

"More of a wish list. We need to find Squeaky's body, and we need to find out who's receiving the incoming cocaine."

"Two needles in a city-sized haystack," Markowski said. "Maybe what we need to do is get the Coast Guard involved. Have them check out any boats that maybe aren't local. Or any local boats that feel the need to head out to sea just before the big parade."

"What about Foust?" I said.

The three looked at me.

I nodded at the board. "You were looking for connections. Squeaky was going to give me Foust. Abernathy killed Squeaky. Maybe Abernathy and Foust are connected. Foust has the money and the means to pull off something that size. And Squeaky alluded to something being big. A multi-million-dollar cocaine deal involving cops is pretty big in my opinion."

Torrance capped the pen. "Let's go with it. Markowski and Shipley, for the next few days, you'll be assigned here. I'll inform Andrews about what we're doing and he can come up with the usual excuses as to why you're not available without mentioning that you're working for me. No one will think twice about Gillespie, since she's been spending her time on the hit-and-run."

"What about Narcotics?" I asked.

"We'll have to come up with something there. Lombard will want to know and I can't keep him in the dark. Completely." Torrance tossed the marker onto his desk. "I think the easiest thing is to not mention that Shipley and Markowski are in the know. Better for everyone all the way around. And safer until we know whom we can trust."

We spent the remainder of our time going over a plan of action, and decided that it would be best if Shipley and Markowski worked the field, checking out the Foust angle and where he might be bringing in a shipment of cocaine. Torrance and I would continue with our separate investigations since they paralleled everything else. I figured that at last we were on a forward track, and about time, too. I was tired, mentally and physically. I wanted a break from all this. I'd needed my vacation and now, with everything that had happened, I felt very much as though I were balancing precariously on the edge of an endless black depth.

That night I went home thinking about Dellwood again. I turned on my computer, connected to the Internet, and ran his name in a search engine, while Dinky purred away at my feet. The only thing I knew about the Web was if a little hand symbol came up on my cursor, it was a link. Surprise of surprises. I received a hit on Dellwood's name. It appeared to be in relation to some article or exposé from a valley newspaper that had to do with the homeless. I printed out the screen and decided to contact the journalist who had written it, a Marty Weybret, sometime tomorrow. I didn't know if it would net me anything, but it was worth a try.

After fixing myself a peanut butter and jelly sandwich, followed by a glass of milk, I parked on the couch in front of the TV, the cat next to me. Too early for the news, too late to catch a sitcom, I flicked through a few channels, pausing only when I found a station without a commercial. I wasn't a big TV watcher; in fact I rarely turned it on unless I needed something to fall asleep to. Far from it, I ended up watching a grim movie of a young girl, maybe sixteen, on trial—if you could call it that—for being a witch in Salem.

The only thought I had after watching for several minutes was that the justice system had improved over the years. The girl was railroaded, so to speak, and all too soon dragged out, thrown to the ground, and covered with a board and stones. I turned off the TV in disgust, wondering what would happen if someone succeeded in pinning the rap for Abernathy's murder on me, if that was in fact what they were doing.

I went to bed that night worrying about Dellwood and hoping that my actions were not responsible for his disappearance. Not a particularly pleasant thought to drift to sleep on, and undoubtedly partly responsible for the disturbing dreams that flitted through my subconscious. I found myself in a courtroom that resembled a Picasso painting, none of the edges matching, everything off kilter, the colors garish. The judge's face was shadowed beneath a powdered wig. He slammed his gavel and asked if the jury had reached a verdict. I spun around to see twelve faceless men pointing their fingers at me. "Guilty!" they all shouted in unison.

I tried to speak, but no words came, and I felt myself being dragged down. The judge stood over me, his hands shaking from the weight of a large stone he held. "You must pay," he said, then dropped it on my chest.

I woke with a start. My heart pounded at the weight on my breast. Two eyes, iridescent green, stared at me from inches away.

Dinky.

I took a breath, waited for my pulse to slow.

"I hate you, cat," I said, and tried to roll over to go back to sleep. Dinky wasn't having any of it. He gave a loud meow that told me I had better let him out or else. I glanced at the clock. Once I looked, it was over for me. I'd never get back to sleep. I groaned. Quarter to five.

Throwing off the covers, I shuffled to the kitchen and opened the door. "See if I let you sleep inside again."

Dinky ignored the empty threat, scurrying out to destinations unknown.

I headed to the shower, turned it on, and leaned against the wall, waiting for the water to heat up. Well, if nothing else, I was getting a jumpstart on the day. Now if Kevin was on time, I would be a happier woman.

I was at my aunt's at precisely seven-fifteen, fully expecting Kevin to be late—his MO when it came to school. He usually had to be roused from bed and then pried from the breakfast table. Instead he was waiting on the porch, face scrubbed clean, hair neatly combed, and shirt and pants clearly pressed, albeit somewhat haphazardly. "Meeting a girl?" I asked.

"Ha ha," he said, climbing in and shutting the door.

"This have something to do with what you and Aunt Molly are fighting about?"

He ignored me.

I let it go. Kevin was at an age where it didn't matter what anyone said or did, it was never the right thing. Further attempts at conversation resulted in his turning the radio on, and then turning it up.

About a block from the school he suddenly tensed, and his hand went to the dash. "Can you let me off here?"

"Why?" I asked, suspicious, as I pulled to the curb.

"I just don't want people thinking I'm a baby, gotta be dropped off at school. That's why."

I looked around, didn't see his usual group of friends. A girl walked about fifteen feet ahead, and I glanced at Kevin to see if she was the cause, but couldn't tell. He got out, gave a quick "Thanks," then made a beeline past the girl to the school. This was not the norm for a boy who went to school just so he could play football, never mind that he brought home B's and C's without applying himself.

If it wasn't the girl, then who? Or what? I remained where I was, watching him as he approached the school. He didn't look right or left until he reached the steps, then it was a quick glance across the street toward a woman wearing a brown coat and white scarf. She took a step forward, then stopped when Kevin looked back at me and waved.

He raced up the steps as though that was his intent the entire time, but the woman seemed to watch Kevin, even after he disappeared into the building. There was no mistaking her interest in him, even without seeing her eyes behind her oversized dark glasses. I shifted into drive, then stopped in front of the school, smack in the dead center of the loading zone, and when a driver had the nerve to honk at me, I pulled my star from my belt and held it up to let him honk at that. I didn't care. I was going to find out who this woman was, and why she was there.

I got out, slammed the door, and crossed the street, going over several possibilities, one of them the movie *The Graduate,* where Mrs. Robinson has an affair with the much younger boy.

"Who are you?" I asked.

She looked taken aback, pushing up on her oversized sunglasses.

"Who are you?" I demanded, this time. "What are you doing here?"

"My son goes here."

"Your son?"

"Yes." She removed her sunglasses and looked directly at me. There was no doubt whom I was looking at, her eyes being the gray and feminine version of my nephew's. This was Kevin's mother, Cassandra White.

I would have far preferred Mrs. Robinson.

So many emotions ran through me in that moment, I couldn't identify any particular one, and I felt almost light-headed.

"I came to see him," she said.

"Kevin was to meet you here?"

"No," she replied all too quickly. "I-I just came here."

Fear started to surface from the roiling pit that was my stomach.

She fiddled with her glasses and I stared at her, trying to see into the woman my brother threw his life away for. She was a couple inches shorter than me. Her face was framed by collar-length dark curls. Her pouty lips held a certain allure. I imagined this must have been what drew Sean to her. There was something about her that reminded me of someone else I knew, but I couldn't place it, because each time I looked into her eyes, I saw Kevin's, and it was like a vise clamping around my heart. Yet despite their similarities, there were so many differences. Kevin's gaze still held the innocence of his youth. Hers carried with it the hardness of someone who used too many drugs. Someone who had seen life, and not necessarily the best side of it.

I took a step back, not knowing what to say or do, until I noticed Kevin eyeing us from the doorway of the school. When he saw me looking in his direction, he ducked back in, and right then I knew she'd set up this whole thing. This had to end, and now. "I don't know what you think you're doing here, but you have no business showing up out of the blue."

"Is it true that Lee Abernathy is dead?"

"Yes. Why?"

"Because I have every right to see my son."

I didn't try to interpret her twisted logic. "You have no rights. You gave them up twelve years ago when you abandoned him and my brother."

"I had to."

"Had to?" I said with scorn.

"They were trying to frame me."

"Who?"

"Your brother's partner."

Her statement caught me off guard. For once I didn't have a rejoinder.

"Look," she said. "I know it sounds unbelievable, but I swear, it's true."

"What is true?"

She crossed her arms over her chest and looked

away, her eyes glistening with what appeared to be tears.

My first instinct was to admit she was a good actor, crying on demand. Not bad. But deep down, a part of me wanted to hear her story. I wanted to know how she could just walk out of her son's life and leave my brother to die. "Well?" I prodded.

"I didn't kill Sean, if that's what you think," came her petulant reply. She wouldn't look at me. "I was out when it happened."

"Doing what?"

"Who knows? That was twelve years ago."

"Really? I recall exactly what I was doing right before they told me Sean died."

"Yeah? Well, we don't all have perfect lives. I was probably loaded. All I remember was that when I got home, one of the guys Sean worked with stopped me out front of my building, wanting to know where Sean was."

"Do you remember his name?"

She shrugged. "James? Jamis? I don't know."

"Jamison?"

"Him. I told him I thought Sean was working, and he said—he said they were worried about him. He stole some money and now he was going to kill himself."

While she bit at her bottom lip, I grew impatient at her theatrics. I held no sympathy for this woman. "Then what happened?" I asked when it was clear she wasn't going to continue.

"I ran home. They were lying. I knew it, because Sean had showed me the money the day before, when he was going to take it to IA. He said they were dirty, something about laundering money. Sean couldn't have taken it, because I—what I mean is that I left Kevin at the neighbor's, I ran up the stairs, and found Sean. He was sitting in a chair. His face was almost blue," she said in a near whisper. "The needle was in his arm. I didn't know what to do."

"Nine-one-one would have been nice."

"Oh, right," she said with a laugh. "Like that would have done any good. They were setting me up. Don't you see?"

"What I see is that you left him there to die."

"He was already dead," she yelled back, then started crying. "They found me. I pulled the needle from his arm, and they came in and found me holding it. His partner, Lee Abernathy, told me I'd killed him. But I didn't. I didn't."

She was sobbing, and I almost felt sorry for her. But twelve years of harboring hate and resentment for the woman was a hard habit to break.

"Why did you run away, then?"

"Abernathy told me my prints would be on the needle. They were going to arrest me. I didn't know what to do, so I grabbed the note and ran."

"Note?"

"His suicide note."

Her words stunned me. Several seconds passed and then the realization hit me that we were in full view of the school and Kevin, assuming he was still watching. Worried that he was, I drew Cassandra by her arm to a van parked nearby, using that to block anyone from seeing us. "Sean left a note? Where the hell is it?"

"Someplace safe," she said, wiping her nose on her sleeve. "He said he was sorry, but he didn't know any way out."

In the reports I'd read, there was never any mention of a note. I couldn't get that out of my mind, and a new anger surfaced. "You took the suicide note? I don't get it. There was a note *proving* it was suicide, and yet you still *left*?"

"Haven't you heard anything I've said?" she replied, her voice filled with a desperate plea. "They were going to pin me for Sean's murder. Don't you see? He was trying to get me off drugs. Why on earth would he be using them? Sean didn't kill himself. *They* did it."

My world started spinning. I heard her words, but they sounded a million miles away. I wanted desperately to believe her, but then that would mean Sean was murdered. I was confused. How does one take the news that one's brother didn't overdose, that he was murdered? After twelve years, I'd resigned myself that his death was an accident at best. I'd gotten over my anger at him, redirected it at her, this woman, who must have surely gotten him hooked on drugs. For twelve years I was at peace—well, as much peace as I could get at the thought. But now I didn't know what to think.

I was a little nauseous, a little shaky. My heart seemed to thud at an abnormal pace. "Sean didn't kill himself?" I asked, just to be sure I'd heard right.

She shook her head.

"Then why the hell didn't you stick around?"

"I thought they were going to kill me like they did Sean. I had a son to think of. I thought if I took him with me, they'd kill him too, so I left him at the neighbor's. I wanted a better life for my son. I wanted to see him grow into a man." She sniffed as she dried her tears with her arm, the black from her mascara smearing on her jacket sleeve. “Giving up Kevin was the most selfless act I have ever committed. Abernathy would have killed me if I came back. And now that he’s dead, I intend on seeing *my* son,” she said, her gaze narrowed and directed at me. “And no one—not you or your aunt—is going to stop me.”

13

Cassandra wiped her eyes and gave me a look of sheer determination, like a lioness fighting for her cub. That fear I'd felt earlier returned in full force. Kevin was my nephew. We'd raised him, my aunt and I. Surely he wouldn't abandon us as his mother had abandoned him? Was that what I was afraid of?

Whatever it was, I wasn't about to let her march in there and walk off with him. "Kevin might be your son," I said. "But fifteen minutes before his school starts is no time to hold a goddamned family reunion."

"You can't keep me from him."

"I have no intention of holding my nephew hostage. All I'm asking is that you allow us time to introduce you back into his life."

Cassandra glanced up at the school, her face filled with a yearning that seemed real. "Fine," she said. "I'll wait. But I won't wait long."

She walked off, headed up the street. I hesitated. I didn't want to leave Kevin, and when she turned the corner, I was too late. I missed her, missed seeing what car she was in.

My safe little world had been rocked. Suddenly I didn't know where I stood. Kevin must have had some phone contact with her, and I wondered if they'd ever met in person before, or was this to be their first time? I wanted to run into the school and ask Kevin if he was going to leave us.

But I knew better than that. I was not going to make him choose sides. What I could do was make sure that Cassandra didn't do anything stupid or rash. I went into the attendance office, noting that Kevin was nowhere to be seen, and asked the woman working there to let me know if Kevin did not show up to any of his classes. I gave her my cell phone number. After that I called work and left a message that I'd be late, then parked down the street and watched the school while going over a number of possibilities and scenarios in my mind—the first and foremost being that if Cassandra White took Kevin from us, I'd kill her.

The sheer potency of that thought scared me. Yet it was that very thought I kept returning to, and I knew I needed to maintain a level of professional detachment in order to think clearly. And to stay out of jail. I was not willing to forgive Cassandra in the space of a day. I needed someone to watch over Kevin who didn't harbor a decade's worth of hate and blame for his mother.

I called Scolari.

When I told him what took place, he dropped what he was doing and came right out.

"I'm not taking you away from something important, I hope," I asked when he got there.

"Hardly," he said, buttoning up his brown sport coat. "What I'm working on isn't that big of a deal. At least not to me."

"What's that?"

"Typical PI crap. Man thinks his wife's having an affair. Wants photos. Like that's gonna solve all his problems. These guys come in, slap down the fee—

which ain't cheap—and I feel like telling 'em they're lucky to have a wife. Go home, make it work before it's too late."

"Like they'd listen."

"Yeah," he said, looking away for an instant, no doubt thinking about his own late wife and the mistakes he'd made in his marriage. "So," he said with a nod toward the school. "What sorta car was Cassandra driving?"

"Who the hell knows?" Scolari raised his brows and I calmed myself and said, "I didn't follow her. I was afraid to leave Kevin."

"Anything else I should know?"

At first I hesitated, not sure I wanted to reveal all that she'd alleged. But then I realized I wanted Scolari's opinion. I told him about her belief that Abernathy and Jamison were responsible for my brother's death.

"Holy shit," he said. "I need to think about that one for a while."

"Yeah, you and me both."

"I'll keep an eye out. Let you know if she shows back up."

"Thanks. I owe you big time."

I left for the city feeling much more secure. He was thorough. Kevin would be safe.

For now.

But what about tomorrow? And the next day?

Maybe I should have called a lawyer instead for a stay-away order. But what would that do to Kevin if he learned we were keeping him from his mother? Somehow I doubted he'd see that it was for his own good. This was bound to end up a tangled legal mess. Visitation dates, shared holidays, and all the crap that goes with a messy divorce.

She did not deserve to see him, I thought as I fought my way through traffic on the Bay Bridge.

After leaving a message for my aunt to call me, I managed to put Cassandra from my mind for the time being. Scolari would not let anything happen to Kevin. When I reached the Hall of Justice parking garage, I had almost convinced myself that things would be okay—until I started to think about everything the woman had told me.

Could it be true? That my brother was murdered and she'd waited all this time to see Kevin because of Abernathy? Parts of it fit. Not once in the years after his death had I ever been able to reconcile the brother I knew with a lifestyle that included drugs. But then, neither had I *ever* been able to picture him with a woman such as Cassandra. Back then, I was busy with the academy. My father died a year later, and I had no idea about the process my aunt had taken to procure guardianship of Kevin. Would it hold up in court now that his mother had resurfaced?

I decided that knowledge was our best defense. Abernathy and Jamison had told me and everyone else that it was Cassandra who had taken Sean's life, instilling her lifestyle into Sean. But in light of Abernathy's murder, and my uncertainty about Jamison's involvement, I knew I couldn't walk up to Jamison and ask what he thought.

But there was something I could do, and that was dig up the old IA case. Read it, find out if there was any truth to what Cassandra had said.

And there was one man I knew who would help me with it, no holds barred. Mike Torrance.

I headed for his office, nodding at a few uniformed officers who stepped off the elevator as I stepped on.

The doors closed, and my anxiety level rose. What if Cassandra was right? What if all these years I'd overlooked information that could have cleared my brother's past? Given him back the honor of his name?

The elevator opened and I stepped off, turned the corner, and walked to the Management Control office, my footsteps echoing down the corridors. I entered the secretary's office, and Torrance saw me, waved me in. I shut his door.

"What's wrong?" he asked, forgoing his usual light banter.

I took a breath, not sure where to begin, and hating that I was so transparent that Torrance could read right into me. "My brother. What do you know about his case?"

His gaze narrowed. "Meaning what?"

"Meaning I ran into my nephew's mother today. Cassandra White. She was at Kevin's school, trying to see him, and said Sean was murdered and she was framed for it." I told him the details that Cassandra had related to me. They didn't seem real. If anything, even more far-fetched than when she'd told me.

"Did she mention why she came out of the woodwork now?"

"Because she'd heard that Abernathy was dead."

Torrance was quiet for several moments. I wondered what he thought of it all. I soon found out. "What she's saying goes against everything I've ever heard about the case."

"I still want to see the file."

"It's probably in archives," he said, picking up the phone. He called the clerk in charge and asked him to send up the file. "Do you want to wait?"

"I have a couple of calls to make. Can you let me know when it arrives?"

He nodded.

In my office, I reviewed my voice mail, all messages that could hold, since none had anything to do with my present caseload of one. I called my aunt again, still not home. After that, I left a message for Dr. Higgins, telling her in no uncertain terms how glad I was that we'd taken her advice and searched for Kevin's mother, and by the way, now that the woman showed up out of the blue, trying to arrange clandestine meetings with her son, was there any last-minute advice? I slammed the phone at the end of that recording, then pulled out the Internet printout I'd made last night on the journalist Weybret, who'd covered the story on Dellwood and the homeless. I called information, got the number of the *Sentinel,* the newspaper he had written it for, then phoned that.

A woman answered. "Mr. Weybret is not in at the moment."

"Is there a convenient time I can call him back? Or another number where I can reach him?"

"I'm sorry, who did you say was calling?"

"Inspector Gillespie, San Francisco PD, Homicide detail."

"You might try him at his hotel. He's staying near the Moscone Center right there in your city." She gave me both his hotel number and his cell phone number.

I tried his cell phone first, but apparently his phone wasn't on, then I left a message on his hotel's voice mail.

Shipley and Zim walked in a moment later, each holding a coffee cup and a manila folder.

Zim tossed his folder onto his desk. "You find that witness you were looking for?" he asked me.

"What witness?"

"The wino."

"How'd you know about him?"

"Heard it around."

Act normal. No reason to run up and strangle Lombard right off. I had bigger fish to fry, so to speak. Like Cassandra White. What the hell was I going to do about her?

"What about that lady?" he asked suddenly, as though he had read my mind.

"What lady?"

I almost laughed when he replied, "The one who called nine-one-one about the hit-and-run. The talk going around is that maybe she was the one who was driving the car they talked about on the news." Once again, another aspect of the case I had yet to hear about, not to mention a subject just as bad as Cassandra suddenly showing up. And about as funny.

I chose my words with care. "We don't even know if that's a legitimate lead, yet. Unless, of course, you've heard something I haven't?" I said in as casual a tone as I could muster. "Your source give a better vehicle description this time? Get a license plate?"

"Dark Ford was what we heard," Shipley said.

"No plate," Zim said, going about his business. He gave no indication that his questions were anything out of the ordinary. Polite interest, nothing more. Even so, I gave an inward sigh of relief when he left the room directly thereafter.

Shipley, however, took a leisurely sip from his coffee mug, white with the scrawling of a house and tree made by his four-year-old. He contemplated the steam rising up. "That's what's going around, Gillespie."

"Going around?" I gave a tired laugh. It was all I had energy for after what I'd been through this morning.

He looked me directly in the eye, his gaze filled with concern. "Just thought you'd want to know," he said quietly. "You wanna talk. I'm here."

My phone rang. "Thanks," I told him, then answered on the second ring. "Gillespie. Homicide detail."

"I have your case."

"I'll be right there." I cradled the phone and stood. "I'll be in IA if anyone's looking for me," I told Shipley, then left for Torrance's office before someone else waylaid me with something I didn't want to know.

Two thick black binders lay on Torrance's vacated desk.

I stood in his office and stared at them for innumerable seconds, not sure I'd like what I found.

"Why do you want to do this?" he asked. He leaned against the doorframe that separated his office from his secretary's.

Since I hadn't seen him enter, I didn't know how long he'd been watching me. "I couldn't live with myself if there were something in there I should see."

"From what I understand, your father looked over the entire thing."

This was something I hadn't heard. "Who told you that?"

"Lombard."

I mulled that over. My father had never talked about the case to me, had downright refused. As I eyed the binders, I thought I knew the source of his pain. I didn't need to open the books to see the evidence would be overwhelmingly against Sean. My father would have thoroughly read, reread, and checked out every lead to clear his firstborn's name. "Maybe he missed something," I said, but not very convincingly.

Torrance didn't reply right away. He stepped in, closing his secretary's door. Crossing the room, he stopped at the windows that separated his office from the rest of IA. He pulled the blinds closed and turned to face me. "Would you like to use my office while I'm gone?"

"Sure," I said, while he grabbed his suit jacket.

He paused on his way out, his gaze holding mine, missing none of my inner turmoil. Behind him I heard the other IA inspectors going about their work, phones ringing, voices droning on.

"If you need anything . . ." he said.

"I'll call."

He gave me a nod, glanced at the IA files, then left, shutting the door with a soft and ominous click.

I sat at his desk, running my hand over the cheap vinyl that housed my brother's life and death. My damp palms left marks on the covers, marks that evaporated as quickly as my brother's life had seemed to.

I knew why I hesitated. To open it and read that he was in fact guilty would forever tarnish my last memories of him. I'd been able to compartmentalize most of what I'd heard, choosing, hoping that some mistake had been made. Steeling myself for what I might find, I opened the first volume.

I read, unaware of time passing, turning pages that told of a dark side of a man I thought I knew, but now wasn't so sure. Apparently this wasn't my brother's first IA. The case I held kept referring to an earlier file, one in which Sean had been investigated for sexual intercourse with a minor, one Cassandra White, a runaway from Redwood City, who reported the incident while giving birth to my nephew. He claimed not to have known she was underage, and said they'd slept together only once.

That was not where the problem had arisen, I soon discovered. This IA centered on the theft of some drug-buy money, allegedly stolen by Sean. The information came from a confidential informant listed in the report as a CI, with no name given.

What I found particularly interesting were the names of the other involved parties. Abernathy, my brother's partner at the time, had been the officer initiating the investigation. George Jamison had also been named, but unlike my brother, Jamison had been cleared.

And he later became Abernathy's partner.

I leaned back in my chair, looking up at the ceiling, wondering at the significance of this. Was Jamison cleared because of his involvement with Abernathy? Was he involved in Squeaky's murder? Or Abernathy's hit-and-run?

And what of the allegations that Abernathy was going to give up the names of others who were involved in this recent scandal? Was Jamison one of the names? Was that why Abernathy was killed?

I returned my attention to the report at hand, my mind filled with dozens of questions, questions that multiplied a thousandfold at the name of the IA supervisor, a lieutenant at the time, who approved the final report of my brother's guilt in the theft of the money.

Lombard.

I don't know why it hadn't occurred to me before. Lombard had been in charge of IA back then, the position that Torrance now held.

I didn't know what that meant at the moment, wasn't sure I wanted to delve that deeply. My brother was dead, and nothing I found out from these reports would bring him back.

My eyes were blurry by the time I finished scanning the first binder. No wonder my father refused to discuss the case. The humiliation he must have felt, his son being investigated by the very department my father had worked at for over thirty years. Such a far cry from the day Sean graduated from the SFPD academy, my father watching him, dressed in his own SFPD class A uniform, chest swelled with pride, eyes brimming with tears of joy.

He shed no tears at Sean's funeral.

He didn't need to. I'd shed enough for both of us.

I closed the binder, unable to read further, my emotions in a tumble. Instead I sat there and stared at the wall, while my thoughts swirled in a number of different directions, trying to make sense of what I'd read, knowing if I were to find anything useful, I'd have to reread it again and again. I don't know how long I sat there, once finished.

"Kate?"

I looked up to see Torrance watching me. I hadn't even seen him enter. He took a step toward me.

"I'm okay. I just need a minute to myself," I said, standing. I left before he could say anything else. I sensed he wanted to offer comfort, but the sort of comfort he could give right there in his public office and the sort I needed were two different things.

Somehow I made it to the ladies' room without running into anyone. I stood before the mirror, going over my emotions, trying to sort out what I was feeling. I realized it was anger. Anger at my brother for putting me in this position. For shattering my illusions of his innate goodness. For having the gall to die. And anger at myself for daring to believe that Cassandra might be telling the truth. That maybe Sean was not to blame.

Dwelling on my brother's death was not going to help my current caseload, namely discovering who had killed Abernathy and who was trying to set me up for the crime.

Attaining an outer calm, I left for my office. Gypsy stopped me the moment I walked in. "You have a visitor," she said, nodding to a man seated in the row of chairs opposite her desk. He was dressed in a charcoal gray suit with a pale yellow shirt, no tie. Brown hair, blue eyes, I put him in his forties, and tried to figure out who I knew or was expecting that fit his description. I came up with a total blank until Gypsy said, "Marty Weybret."

"Mr. Weybret," I said, surprised to see him, but glad for the distraction. I held out my hand. He stood and shook it.

"I hope I'm not here at a bad time," he said. "I was in town for a convention, and frankly, a little curious as to why out of the blue, the local cops might be trying to get ahold of me."

I gave him a reassuring smile. "Nothing too serious," I said—at least as far as he was concerned— then led him into the main Homicide office. I offered him the seat next to my desk, then sat myself. "You wrote an exposé of sorts on the homeless a few years back. I saw it on the Internet. One of your case studies was a guy named William Dellwood? You don't happen to remember him, do you?"

"Yes, I remember him."

"Well, I happen to be looking for him. He's a witness to a homicide and has suddenly turned up missing."

"I'm not sure how I can help."

"I was hoping you could provide some background

information. Does he have any family in the area? Anyone he might contact if he needed a place to stay?"

"Sacramento area. A town called Galt."

"Galt?"

"Yes. I think he has a daughter there. I interviewed her on the story." He looked at his watch. "If you like, I can call my secretary first thing in the morning, and have her look up my notes."

"I'd appreciate that." I took a card from the holder on my desk and gave it to him. "If I'm not in, leave it on my voice mail."

"I will."

We stood and shook hands again. "I appreciate you coming out here on your own."

"I'd say anytime," he replied with a smile, "but I'm not always so conveniently located."

No sooner had he left than Shipley came bursting into the office. He made a beeline for the radios.

"What's up?" I asked as he took two from the charger.

"Got a body that just washed up on the beach."

"Got a name yet?" I asked, immediately thinking of Dellwood.

He tucked one radio in his pocket, held on to the other, then retrieved his notebook from his desk. It seemed an eternity before he finally answered.

"Yeah," he said, looking me square in the face. "Timothy Kincaid. Goes by the moniker of Squeaky."

14

I couldn't believe it. Finally the break I'd been looking for. "Squeaky Kincaid?"

"Yeah, you know him?"

For a second I was taken aback, and then I saw Shipley give a faint nod in the direction of Gypsy's office, where I heard Zimmerman chatting away. "He's a snitch I've used in the past," I said.

"I'll let you know what I find out."

He took off, probably to meet up with Markowski, and I thought at last we were getting somewhere. Squeaky was found and this crap about my car being seen at Abernathy's hit-and-run would finally go away. With Shipley taking control of Squeaky's homicide, they'd do ballistics, find out Abernathy shot him, and my life and my credibility could get back to normal. I called Torrance to tell him.

"I've been made aware of it," he said. "Lombard's ordering an immediate autopsy. I expect we'll know more tonight, once the preliminary results are in. In the meantime, why don't you go home, get some rest?"

"Yeah, sure." Like I'd be able to sleep until I knew what was found.

I hung up and realized I hadn't yet heard from my

aunt—not that I should be concerned. Scolari was on the case. I called her, and she answered.

"Where's Kevin?" I asked.

"Still at school, of course. Why?"

"Didn't you get my message?"

"Well, yes, you said that Sam was with him. Do you think that's really necessary? What if Kevin finds out?"

"And what if she decides to take off with him?"

"Well, he wouldn't go with her."

"That's just it. I don't know. And I'd rather not take a chance."

"You need to have more confidence in the boy."

"It's not him I'm worried about," I said, looking up as Gypsy stepped in and waved at me.

"Phone call," she mouthed.

"Look, Aunt Molly, I have to go."

"Try not to worry, dear."

"Right." I hung up, and Gypsy transferred the call through. It was a nurse at MEH letting me know that Mazy was able to talk. It was after two, and technically, even though I was on duty and ordered not to work on her case unless I was off duty, I still hadn't had lunch. I couldn't do anything on my case until Squeaky's autopsy was complete. Scolari was watching Kevin, so why not?

I headed to the hospital and spoke with the nurse in charge, Juli, according to her name tag. "Mrs. Maze is alert," she said. "Whether or not she's recovered all mental acuity, however, I can't be sure. She tends to, er, ramble, to put it politely."

"That would be about normal for her," I said, following her into Mazy's room.

"Mrs. Maze?" Juli said softly. "There's a policewoman to see you."

Mrs. Maze turned her bruised and pale face in our direction. Her white hair was matted to the side of her head, the area above her right ear shaved, silver staples visible within the stubble of hair that remained. "Ah, Inspector. I was wondering when you would finally get here."

Moving into the room, I seated myself in the chair next to her bed. "How are you doing?" I asked, though to me it was patently obvious.

"Oh, not bad. My head hurts. But I'm so glad you came by. I've been meaning to call you about that darned refrigerator truck. They keep it parked behind my house, running all hours of the night."

"Yes, I know. You were telling me about it not too long ago. But what I'd really like to know is if you saw who did this to you."

"Heavens, child. That's what I've been trying to tell you. It happened right after that sausage place was broken into again. I don't think he got anything that first time, because he was in and out of there so quickly. What he could possibly have wanted in there, I have no idea. They don't even make good sausage. But then you know it's a front."

"A front?" I repeated, then wished I hadn't.

"Democrats," she whispered. "Their headquarters. Did I tell you that they were after my campaign secrets?"

I nodded.

"Well," she continued. "I immediately locked up everything sent to me from Republican headquarters—I have a box in my pantry, you know, marked 'Recipes' so no one would think to look there—and then went out to investigate."

"You should have called us first, Mrs. Maze."

"And let them get away?"

"Much better than you getting hurt."

"Be that as it may, Inspector, I would have never seen who broke into the Democrats' secret headquarters if I hadn't looked out. And the last time, the police didn't believe me, but that was part of their cover-up, because they know I'm on to them."

"Mrs. Maze. What I'm really interested in is how you got hurt."

"You think I'm crazy, don't you. Just like the rest of them."

I didn't answer.

"Your brother didn't think so. He's the one who told me to write 'Recipes' on my lockbox. That way no one would look inside."

"He did?"

"Yes. The last time he came out. It's been years, now. I don't know what ever happened to him. He was investigating it for me. Such a clever young man. I told him he should get a haircut, but he said it was part of his disguise."

I smiled. How very like Sean to go along with Mrs. Maze, despite her delusions. "About your injuries?"

She sighed. "That's what I'm trying to tell you. It was right after that man climbed out of the window carrying a duffel bag and sped off in that car. I think it was black, but it's so dark back there, I couldn't tell. And I couldn't see the license plate. Someone else was driving it, though. They both had long hair. Shoulder-length, I think. You can't even tell if someone's a man or a woman anymore. And then the men came running out, and hopped right into that noisy refrigerator delivery truck, and off they went. And that's when I fell."

"You fell?"

"Well, of course I fell. Dry rot. The planter box I was standing on to spy over the fence. All my prized miniature roses. Ruined." She looked away and brushed at a tear.

"Someone thought you were attacked. In retaliation."

For several seconds she said nothing, just stared out the window. Finally, "Retaliation? For what?"

"The gang stabbing. They found a bunch of graffiti painted on your fence and house."

"Good heavens. It's those hoodlums again. Did I tell you I found them throwing bottles at my fence the other day?"

"Yes, ma'am."

"Why their parents let them dress in those awful clothes, I'll never understand. My father would have taken a switch to me if I stepped out of the house like that. What's the world coming to? And how am I ever going to fix my planter?"

She began crying, something in all my years I'd never seen her do. Crazy Mazy yelled, shook her finger, chastised, and most of all defended the Republicans against the Democrats. But she didn't cry.

I sat there helpless, unsure what to do or say, when Nurse Juli walked in, calmly and efficiently taking control. "Now, now, Mrs. Maze. You can't have visitors while you're upset. And it's time to take your medicine. This will help you relax."

I bid her good-bye, but I doubt Mrs. Maze heard me, instead going on about her garden. "Ruined. My poor roses." She dabbed at her eyes with a tissue, then said, "Heavens. You don't think *they* had anything to do with it?"

"Who?" her nurse asked.

"The Democrats," Mazy replied. I had to admit I was heartened as I stepped into the hallway and heard her add, "They know I'm on to them."

It was after five by the time I made it home. I was tired, hungry, and had a killer headache from sucking in exhaust fumes during the crawl through traffic. I checked my answering machine, listened to Scolari say all was well and he was following Kevin to football practice. After heating a frozen fettuccine Alfredo in the microwave, I sat in front of the television and ate while watching the news, but lost my appetite when they showed the press conference with the mayor and police chief, and Lombard in the background.

They were still looking for the dark-colored sedan, believing the driver might have been a woman, with the usual disclaimer that she was wanted for questioning only, and not really a suspect. There was even a tip line with a reward offered, ten thousand dollars. I wanted to call up and ask if they'd put it in my account if I turned myself in, since I was the obvious person they were trying to set up.

I left my uneaten dinner on the coffee table and switched the channel, wondering what the other news stations were reporting, but there was a knock on the door. Not expecting anyone, I went to the kitchen and pulled aside the curtain to find Torrance standing on my porch, looking a little James Bond–ish in a London Fog raincoat. He carried a large, heavy-looking box.

I opened the door, curious, and I'll admit a bit hopeful. There should be a law against anyone looking that good. "Fancy meeting you here."

"It's not how I would have chosen to do this."

"Do what?" I asked, hopes dashed and curiosity replaced by concern.

"The preliminary report is in on this Squeaky Kincaid."

"And?"

"May I come in?"

I stood aside, and he entered, setting the box on the kitchen table. He turned to me but said nothing, his dark gaze, normally so neutral, never giving anything away, now troubled.

"I'm not going to like this, am I?"

"No."

Suddenly I felt cold. "I'm going to make some tea."

He let me go about my business, pouring water into the teakettle, setting it on the burner. When I'd delayed enough, he crossed the kitchen, put his hand on my shoulder, and said, "Stop."

I looked at him, wishing I'd had the sense to become a teacher or an accountant.

"I'm sorry, Kate."

"For what?" Though I knew. For everything. Torrance rarely apologized. He rarely called me by my first name. I glanced at the box, the lid taped shut, wondering what was inside.

"The estimated time of death on your victim is a minimum of twenty-four hours ago, not the three days that you alleged."

"You're wrong," I said, backing into the counter, wrapping my arms about my middle. "I saw him shot. There's no way he could have survived."

"I'm only repeating what was told to me by the pathologist."

"Well, then the pathologist is wrong. There's been a mistake."

"I'm sorry."

I stared at the box on the kitchen table, unable to meet his gaze, knowing what was coming next.

"In light of the preliminary autopsy results, and the suspect vehicle description at Abernathy's hit-and-run, Captain Lombard has ordered that you be placed on administrative leave pending the outcome of this investigation."

Several seconds passed while the TV droned on in the living room. I had to remind myself that some of the people I worked for were idiots. They could get years of dedicated service from someone, and then suddenly that person was deemed guilty until proven innocent. "So now what?" I finally said, distinctly aware of Torrance's discomfort, but at the moment not caring. "You need my badge?" He didn't answer. "My duty weapon?"

"Yes," he said quietly.

I hesitated. There was only one reason they would take my handgun, and that was for ballistics testing. "Fine." I strode over to the kitchen table, opened my purse, and removed my gun. "All yours."

I wasn't worried. They'd do the same to Abernathy's weapon. The tests would show that his weapon had fired the fatal shots—assuming they found it and that he hadn't ditched it before he was killed.

"Do you have another weapon?"

"In my locker at work."

"You need a weapon. I have one in the car."

"I'll manage," I said, feeling particularly ungracious at the moment, and not hesitating for a second to let him know.

He removed the magazine, emptied the round from the chamber, then placed the ammo and magazine in separate manila envelopes that he pulled from the cardboard box he'd brought in with him. Next he pulled out a plastic strip to thread through the barrel and open chamber.

"Ever the efficient IA investigator," I said.

He stopped what he was doing to look at me, and I was surprised by the flicker of emotions that crossed his face. "This is not a duty I enjoy."

"Do you think I'm guilty?" I asked, unable to keep the accusation from my voice.

He finished securing and packing the gun, placing it in an envelope as well, then placing that in a gun box that he removed from the cardboard carton he'd brought in. That done, he held my gaze, his turning into unreadable obsidian. "My opinion in this apparently doesn't count," he said.

Doesn't count? With me or with them? Knowing Torrance, it was both. And he was right. I couldn't think clearly right now, I was too angry, so it didn't matter what he thought.

I held the door open for him, indicating he should leave. He did so after a searching look that I refused to acknowledge. Despite that he was a political pawn, as was I, I still wanted to lash out at him. I did so by kicking the kitchen door shut as I listened to his footsteps receding down the steps.

Behind me my teakettle whistled, and I turned off the burner, leaving the water untouched. Tea was the last thing I wanted. Opening the fridge, I pulled out a beer, twisted off the cap, and took a drink, then eyed the box that Torrance had left behind.

The man was an enigma to be sure, but one thing I knew about him. When it came to his job, there was not a single thing he said or did that was not weighed or calculated in some manner.

And here was the box he'd left behind.

I opened it and found the binders that contained my brother's IA investigation.

Torrance had done this once before, brought me a case to read on my own, discover what I needed to know. The circumstances were different then. My partner, Scolari at the time, had been investigated by IA for the alleged murder of his wife. And though Torrance was in charge of that investigation, he offered his silent support of my belief in Scolari's innocence by bringing me the IA files.

None of this had anything to do with my brother's case, of course—the only similarity being that Torrance took it upon himself to bring this particular case for my perusal. And once again came the thought that Torrance did nothing without weighing all the risks, all the factors. Which meant, in my opinion, that Cassandra's reemergence coupled with Abernathy's death were enough of a coincidence to bear looking into.

She said my brother wouldn't have killed himself. That he didn't use drugs. I wanted to believe that this was true more than anything. But I didn't trust her motives.

Abernathy was about to reveal several cops who were on the take, big time, in order to get himself off, when he was suddenly killed after murdering a snitch—the same snitch who had called me just hours before to report that he could get me Foust and that this was *"bigger than you and me."*

Abernathy had been my brother's partner twelve years ago.

I opened the files and began to read again the reports that painted such a dark picture of my brother. And as

I delved further into the mire of facts, the similarities of my brother's case to my present situation struck me hard.

We were both investigated by IA for serious crimes after bringing allegations against Abernathy. Granted, Abernathy was dead when I brought up my allegations, but that indicated—in my opinion—that there was at the very least one other person involved in whatever crimes he had committed.

The question now was this: Was it someone from within the department or without?

I decided to reread my brother's IA with the belief that Cassandra was telling the truth. That my brother was innocent, even murdered for what he knew. With that in mind, I paid closer attention to the peripheral reports, copies of which were in the second binder, and not really part of the main investigation, but included because of an arrest, or a location mentioned that proved my brother was or was not present at a certain time. After endless reading, with nothing standing out, I began to wonder if anything would click, make sense, when a name popped out. Antonio Foust.

Foust had been arrested on some drug charges and had offered up some confidential information in exchange for a lighter sentence. The information? That my brother had stolen some drug-buy money to pay off his underage girlfriend so that she wouldn't testify against him. Ten thousand dollars. The money was never recovered, and the case was cleared by "accidental overdose" of the suspect.

End of report.

I felt deflated, angry, helpless. How could they clear it? How could they assume he had taken the money if it wasn't recovered? There was no mention of suicide, undoubtedly because the alleged note was taken by Cassandra when she fled. Had she taken the money as well? I remember her hesitation when she told me of some missing money.

Was there something I had overlooked in the reports? Some clue that would set it all straight? I decided to start at the beginning again, and opened the first binder to review the main report. I read about two paragraphs when someone started pounding on my door. I glanced up to see a large silhouette behind the yellow curtain, too large to be Torrance.

Getting up, I pulled the curtain aside and saw Scolari standing there, looking far more like Columbo than any James Bond, his overcoat rumpled and stained. I yanked open the door. "What the hell are you doing here? Why aren't you watching Kevin?"

"Your aunt relieved me."

"What?"

"She showed up at practice and said she could take it from there, that she didn't want Kevin to suspect anything. Which he undoubtedly would have had he noticed me watching him all night."

"Well, I don't care what she says, I want you to get back over there and keep an eye on him."

He tapped out a cigarette, then dug in his pocket for a lighter. "Only one problem. Torrance hired me."

"For what?" I asked, crossing my arms, suspicious to say the least.

"To watch over you. Said you were unarmed, someone might be trying to set you up. Sorta like what happened to your brother. I brought you the thirty-eight I keep in my trunk. The one I used to keep in my ankle holster." He opened his jacket and showed me the butt of said gun sticking out of his waistband. With his nine-millimeter in the shoulder holster, he looked like a walking arsenal.

"Jesus." I stood aside and waved him in with as sarcastic a flourish as I could manage in so small a space. "And no smoking in here."

"Yeah, yeah. You and the rest of California. All nuts."

"I eat red meat with the best of them."

He stepped in, cigarette unlit, hanging from his mouth. "Now what? You want me to sleep on the couch?"

"No, I want to get my jacket and make sure Kevin makes it home."

"Think you might be giving this Cassandra a bit too much credit."

"Something's up with her," I called out from the living room. I grabbed the hooded jacket I'd thrown over the back of my armchair. The phone rang as I headed for the kitchen. I picked up and gave a curt "Hello."

"Kate?" came my aunt's frantic voice. "Kevin took off."

My heart pounded. "What do you mean, took off?"

"One minute he was here at practice, the next he wasn't. I was watching him the whole time. The coach thinks he switched jerseys with another boy so we wouldn't notice."

"Jesus, Aunt Molly—" I stopped myself from berating her for dismissing Scolari. I covered the mouthpiece. "Did Kevin use the restroom while you were out there?"

"Yeah," Scolari replied. "Him and another boy went in, carrying their helmets."

"Wearing them when they came out?"

"Didn't notice. That was when your aunt showed up."

I heard my aunt crying on the other end of the line. "Don't worry, we'll find him."

"I'm so sorry, Kate. I should have listened."

"We'll find him," I said again. "Now listen carefully. I want you to go home and stay there in case he calls. You have my pager number and cell phone. If you hear anything, call me immediately." I disconnected. "Might as well earn your money, Scolari."

"Where to?"

"To look for Cassandra." I took the thirty-eight he handed me and tucked it in my own waistband. "I'll drive."

15

All my fears were realized. Cassandra had come to take Kevin from us, and he'd left. Gone with her. I thought of what Dr. Higgins had said—wondered what I would have done at thirteen if my own mother had suddenly shown up out of the blue. I used to imagine what she was like, pretend she'd gotten amnesia, forgotten we'd existed, then suddenly her memory was restored, and she'd appear at our door.

But she never did. Over the years I'd tucked that dream away, dismissing it as a silly child's fantasy. My father had refused to talk about her. He refused to talk about a lot of things, and we had all deferred to his wishes.

Now, as I drove, I thought about what it must be like for Kevin, the wondering, the not knowing. I remembered it all, and I knew with a certainty that at thirteen, I would very likely have done the same thing as Kevin.

But I was no longer a child, and if my mother suddenly showed up on my doorstep, amnesia or not, I'd be hard-pressed not to slam the door in her face.

Dr. Higgins would undoubtedly have something to say about that.

Personally I didn't care, and I put her from my mind.

The first place we headed was to the football field in case someone overlooked something, such as my nephew. The coach was still there. He was a tall man, broad-shouldered, definitely ex-linebacker material, dressed in gray sweats, working with several kids on drills, apparently while waiting for their parents to arrive.

Scolari and I were walking across the field when my cell phone rang. I nearly dropped it in my hurried attempt to answer.

"Aunt Kate?"

"Kevin. Where are you?"

"I'm with my mom. She told me to call you so you wouldn't worry."

"You need to come home."

He didn't reply. The background noise was loud and white, as though he was on a pay phone near a freeway.

"Tell me where you are."

"No. You'll only make me come back."

"Back? Where are you going?"

"I don't know. But it's only for a little while. She just wants to visit. I promise."

I took a frustrated breath. What was I supposed to do? Hey, Kev, the newspaper clippings were true—we suspect your mother of dealing drugs, maybe supplying the heroin that killed your father? A week ago, before I saw Abernathy murder Squeaky, I might have done so without hesitation. But after reading the IA, and listening to Cassandra's side of the story, I wasn't so sure. Yet neither was I ready to let her play Suzie Homemaker with my only nephew. I had reasons not to trust her. Twelve years of reasons.

Beside me, Scolari cleared his throat to indicate the coach, who was fast approaching. I didn't want him in on this conversation. Kevin's past and maternal parentage was something we'd kept from everyone. Unfortunately, hindsight being crystal-clear, Kevin had been given the watered-down version, and now was not the time to explain it in any great detail. "Look, Kev. There're things you don't know. Things I can't go into right now. But you need to really listen to me and tell me where you are. Okay?"

"I'm safe, Aunt Kate. My mom won't let anything happen to me. I'll call you. Bye."

"Kev? Kevin?"

Dial tone.

"Dammit."

"Miss Gillespie?" The coach eyed me with the sort of patience reminiscent of one who is used to dealing with a number of manic, sports-crazed parents.

My being there now was a moot point. I knew where Kevin was. Sort of. But I was still upset that he'd so easily been spirited away. "Hi." I forced a smile. "I understand you think my nephew switched jerseys with another kid?"

"That's the only way he could've left without me seeing," the coach said. "I know he seemed distracted, didn't have his mind on the ball all night. One of my other kids said his mom was picking him up early. Keith Greene. So when I saw a kid wearing number thirty-two running out to the car, I didn't think anything of it."

"Did you see what sort of car he got into?"

"Didn't pay that much attention, truthfully." He shrugged and nodded toward my car parked at the curb. "Something like that. Midsized sedan, maybe black."

"Thanks." I gave him my card with all the pertinent

numbers on it. "Call immediately if you hear from him."

"Something I should know about?"

"His mother decided to make an impromptu visit," I said. "She left before we could . . . make visitation arrangements."

He nodded. Put that way, Kevin's situation fit in with just about every other kid from a typical broken home.

"Son of a bitch," I said when we were back in the car. I started it, then leaned back in my seat, not sure where to direct my anger. At Scolari for letting my aunt so easily talk him off his assignment. At my aunt for being so naïve. At the coach for not doing his coachly duty and watching the boys more closely. Or at myself for underestimating Cassandra's determination to get to her son.

"You wanna clue me in?" Scolari asked.

"Kevin said Cassandra is taking him somewhere for a 'visit.' "

"Let's check her apartment."

"I'm beginning to wish I never hired you to find her."

"Don't think it woulda made much difference."

I signaled and pulled away from the curb. "Why is that?"

"Apparently she stayed pretty much in touch with your aunt throughout the years. Mailed her things."

"What sort of things?" I asked, wondering if Sean's suicide note was among them.

"A shoe box full of papers from the woman, papers I didn't bother to go through. Didn't need to. It wasn't too hard to track her. She had her address all along. Granted it was a P.O. box, but still."

"Well, what's done is done," I said, signaling for a left turn. "Now all I want is to find Kevin, bring him home, and make sure this never happens again."

For the remainder of the trip, Scolari and I discussed my brother's IA and Foust's name being mentioned. Scolari opted to play devil's advocate, speculating that if Foust's statement was true, it didn't mean much of anything, other than that he was one of several witnesses.

I, on the other hand, opted for the other side. "Everything points to Foust lying. Look what we know about him from past cases. He didn't think twice about setting up Paolini," I said. Foust had worked for Paolini, a mob boss, and had attempted to pin a couple murders on him. Foust's involvement in the murders was discovered, a warrant was issued, but he had yet to be arrested. "He could very well have set up my brother twelve years ago to take the blame for the missing drug-buy money."

"And Abernathy?"

"Right there in the thick of things," I said, recalling in vivid detail the night he murdered Squeaky.

They saw me.

I reminded him of Squeaky's call, his promise to give me Foust, his urgency to meet with me.

Scolari said, "You think Foust is trying to set you up to take the blame for the murder? Maybe to take the attention off until after this big cocaine shipment arrives? And, what, Lombard is playing right into his hands? Or is he one of the involved, too?"

"I don't know. But Foust is probably behind this in some way. If he was involved from the beginning, from when my brother died and Cassandra fled, then you can damned well bet he's still got his nose in this."

16

It took us about an hour and a half to get to Heron, a small Delta town off Highway 12, not too far from Rio Vista and the Sacramento River. En route, I told Scolari about the IA file on my brother, and what Cassandra had alleged about my brother's death.

"What's your take on it?" Scolari asked.

"I'm not sure. I've thought one way for so many years, it's hard to shift gears. Right now I don't know what I want to think. I mean, Christ. What if what she says is true? What if Sean was murdered?"

"Holy shit."

"To say the least," I said, turning onto Main Street. Cassandra lived in a not so nice area, judging by the number of yard cars and broken windows. The duplex she lived in was just off the highway, white stucco with black trim. Her car was nowhere to be found, but all the lights were on in her apartment. We got out and walked the perimeter, listening in, hearing nothing but a neighbor's television. Scolari took one side of her door, I the other.

"What'dya think?" he asked softly. "Knock or kick it in?"

I looked at the door, my heart speeding up a notch at the sight of the splintered frame. I drew my borrowed thirty-eight, pointing at the damage.

"Christ." Scolari pulled his semi-auto from his holster.

"Police," he shouted. Old habits die hard.

He kicked the door open with his foot. It swung easily on the already damaged frame.

I followed him in. Then froze at the destruction I saw. "Kevin?" I finally managed, eyeing the bedroom just beyond the carnage of what used to be a living room.

There was no answer.

Please don't let Kevin be here.

We moved in, shoes crunching on broken glass, our weapons pointed as we systematically searched, first the living room and the kitchenette.

Scolari stepped over a small bookcase that had been toppled, paperbacks strewn about the living room floor. The bathroom was to my left, and I gave it a check, quickly clearing it as Scolari moved past me into the bedroom. "Jesus," he said.

Something inside me snapped. "No."

I jumped over the bookshelf and tried to push past him into the bedroom.

He grabbed me, stopping me short. "It's not him, Kate," he said. "It's not him."

"I need to see."

He nodded, then stood aside.

A man, mid-fifties, maybe, was sprawled on the floor. A small entrance wound on his forehead belied the pool of blood soaked into the beige carpet beneath him. He had been wearing boxer shorts at the time of his death, and so I had no trouble discerning the early signs of lividity from where I stood, the settling of blood.

My knees went weak. But not at the sight before me.

It was a strange mixture. Relief and fear. Relief the body was not that of my nephew. Fear that Kevin was out there and I wouldn't be able to help him if he needed me.

"God, Kevin. Where are you?" I whispered.

"We'll find him, Kate."

I used Scolari's phone to keep mine clear in case Kevin tried to reach me. The Heron PD dispatcher asked for our descriptions, said the officers would be right there, and told us to wait out in front. I disconnected and we moved out, picking our way over the debris, careful not to disturb any more evidence than we already had.

Scolari hesitated in the midst of the living room. "It'd be kinda nice to know what they were after. What the hell would she or that poor schmuck in there have that someone would want?"

"Information about a twelve-year old murder?" I replied, eyeing the countless numbers of papers scattered across the living room floor, and terribly tempted to scoop them all up, shake out the bits of broken glass, and read each one. Unfortunately I'd be contaminating a murder scene. Couldn't have that. But then I'd already contaminated it to some extent, just by walking in. So looking, in my opinion, couldn't hurt. As long as I didn't touch.

Scolari watched, an amused expression on his face, as I leaned over, reading what was on the floor, what was within sight as I continued on my way "out."

The muffled ring of the telephone brought me to a standstill. I looked at Scolari. He shrugged. "Can't hurt. If you can find it," he said.

I listened carefully, and the next ring seemed to originate beneath a slashed cushion from the couch about a foot from where I stood. I kicked at the cushion with my foot and located the phone. It had a speaker feature, and I stepped carefully, pressed the button, and said, "Hello?"

"Look, bitch," came a deep voice. "I'm tired of waiting. Bring me the goddamned money you stole."

"Or what?" I asked, keeping my own voice soft, hoping I sounded like Cassandra, and wondering who the hell was on the other line.

"Or I'm going after the boy just like I did your old man. You hear me?"

His words sent a chill through my heart. I prayed he wasn't talking about Kevin. My instincts told me he was. "Leave him out of it."

He laughed, a sick guttural sound. "Feeling suddenly maternal, are we? A bit late, don't you think?" And then he hung up.

Had there been a chair left intact, I would have thrown it against the wall. I wanted to find Kevin. Now. Prints be damned, I hit *69 on the phone. A recording came on, saying it could not reconnect the call. Which meant the caller could be out of the area or on a cell phone.

"What the hell is going on?" Scolari mused aloud.

"I don't know," I said, wondering what we could possibly find in this mess that would lead me to my nephew. *Please let there be something.* I looked at the freezer contents dumped on the scarred linoleum floor, then up to the refrigerator, realizing that whoever did this had been looking for—and hadn't found—this so-called stolen money. And that's when I saw a slip of paper held to the refrigerator door with a small magnet, a plastic strawberry to be exact. I don't know why it caught my eye, or what made me take a closer look, but as I approached it and the writing took focus, I tried to keep my panic at bay.

"Tony Foust," it read. The number beneath it was a San Francisco prefix with the word "pager" written after it.

"Look at this," I told Scolari.

He eyed the note. "Tony. Antonio? What connection would she have with Foust? Drug supplier?"

"I can't see Foust wasting his time with a two-bit addict like Cassandra, can you?"

"I see your point. But what, then?"

Our attention was distracted when the cops arrived just then, their uniform shoulder patches emblazoned with a heron in flight, the city's claim to fame. We showed them our identification cards, mine current and Scolari's showing he was retired. I skipped over the fact I was on AL, and explained to them that my nephew was with Cassandra and I was worried about his safety. We needed to leave, immediately. He said he couldn't let us, that he'd have to wait for his supervisor to arrive. Unfortunately his supervisor was even more stubborn and insisted we convene to the station for questioning. We followed in my car. Scolari drove. Before we went in we tucked our weapons beneath the front seat. Scolari figured they'd probably want to see them. And if they wanted to be real assholes, insist on holding them for ballistics to make sure we weren't the shooters. Great.

Frustrated, and scared for Kevin, I telephoned Torrance, the escorting officer allowing me to make a call when we got there. His phone rang several times. "Answer, answer."

He finally picked up.

"Kevin may be in trouble," I said. "There's been a murder. We're being questioned at Heron PD."

"Slow down. Start from the beginning."

I did. From the brief mention of Foust's name in the IA report mentioning the ten thousand dollars my brother allegedly stole, to Kevin's disappearance with Cassandra, to the murder of the man in her apartment, and finally to the conversation I'd just had on the telephone with the unknown caller who also mentioned some stolen money.

"You're thinking it was Foust, talking about money stolen twelve years ago?"

"It's as good a guess as any," I said. "Maybe Cassandra hid it until the time was right. Abernathy is killed, she comes out of the closet and Foust decides it's payback time. You don't steal from the mob and get away with it, even twelve years later. Now he's saying he wants the money, or he's going after the boy."

"As in Kevin."

"Who else?" I said, unable to keep my fears about Kevin from my voice. "Cassandra shows up out of the blue, Kevin takes off with her, there's a murder, and then this guy calls to threaten her?"

"Okay. What are your plans?"

"To find Kevin. Only we're sort of being detained."

"I'll get something out on her Vehicle right away. I'll see if I can't get you out of there."

"I want a missing person's report on Kevin."

"I'll take care of it. Give me your aunt's number."

I did. Disconnecting, I stared out into the darkness, frustrated, scared, especially when they separated us. Just as we would have done were it our investigation. The knowledge didn't make it any easier to bear. I was left alone in a small interview room, the walls scuffed, the table scarred with graffiti. It was not the sort of room I would have taken a fellow investigator to—

which made me wonder what exactly they thought my part in all this was.

All too soon, it was endless questions, multiple repetitions of why we were there, what department we worked for, as each new investigator arrived. And each time I repeated my statement, I stressed the importance of finding my nephew. No one seemed to care.

Eventually another detective came in, short, dark hair, stocky build, maybe forty, wearing a brown suit, white shirt, his yellow tie pulled loose from the collar. He smiled.

"Can I get anything for you?" he asked, as if this were a casual visit."

"Coffee would be nice. A latte would be better."

"Latte? You're one of *those* kind of coffee drinkers?"

"I hate coffee, a necessary evil in this job. Lattes make the stuff bearable to drink."

"Coffee I can do, the latte thing, I'm afraid you're out of luck." He stepped out and called to some unseen person, asking for two cups of coffee. "It'll just take a sec," he said, sitting opposite from me. He put his yellow legal pad on the table beside him, then scooted his chair so that we faced each other, no table between us—which could be good or bad, depending on how you looked at it. A table acted as a barrier, and any good investigator wanting a confession didn't put one between them.

"Can you tell me how long this will take?" I asked. "My nephew is missing—"

"Trust me, we're doing everything we can to wrap this up. But you of all people should know—"

"Look, Detective . . ."

"Conners."

"The person in that apartment is already dead. I

don't think he can get much deader. Someone called and threatened my nephew's life—"

"All the more reason you cooperate, Inspector Gillespie. Maybe we can help—"

He stopped when a blond uniformed policewoman brought in two Styrofoam cups of coffee, then left without a word, shutting the door behind her. I heard it click, eyed the keyhole in the doorknob, and wondered if we were locked in.

The detective sipped at his coffee.

I picked mine up but didn't drink. "What is it you want to know that I haven't already told you and at least five other officers five different times?"

"Why you just happened to show up at a dead guy's apartment?"

I took a breath, telling myself that I'd already lost my temper with these people and that tactic hadn't worked. "As I said before, I went there to look for my nephew. His mother lives there. At least I assumed she does. I've never been there before, and I've never seen that man before."

"But you walked in without a warrant?"

I paused, wondering if this guy had heard one word I'd told him. "I was—am *still* worried for my nephew's safety. I thought he might have been taken there. When I saw the split doorframe, we went in. It's called *exigent circumstances,*" I said, unable to keep the sarcasm from my voice.

"Thank you for the lesson in police science, Inspector." He jotted something down on his pad, probably the word "bitch," but I didn't care. "Now tell me again about this phone call you mentioned *receiving,* while you were there?" This said in a tone indicating his displeasure.

I gave him the details of the phone conversation.

"And the caller did *not* mention your nephew by name?"

"No."

"Then he could have been talking about someone else?"

"I doubt it. Which is why, if you don't mind, I need to get the hell out of here."

"We'll need some prints for elimination."

"Am I under arrest?"

"No, Inspector."

"Then get my goddamned prints from the FBI, or my department. I don't care. Just let me go find my nephew."

He stood, taking his notebook with him. "It'll be just a few more minutes."

He left, shutting the door behind him, again with a click. I checked, and sure enough, it was locked. My jaw clenched, I paced the room, spouting off every swearword I knew. I heard keys outside, and suddenly the door opened.

An officer poked her head in, not one of the detectives, but the young blond who brought in the coffee. "Someone to see you," she said.

I looked past her and saw Torrance, wearing jeans and a black T-shirt, and over that his leather jacket. Tired-looking, unshaved, and easily the best thing I'd seen all night. Or was it morning yet? I'd lost track.

"Open another can of worms?" he asked.

I nodded, too tired to come up with a suitable retort. "Any word on Kevin?"

"No. I filed the missing person's report."

"Thanks."

"You okay?"

"Never better. My nephew's missing, I'm holed up

in this godforsaken interview room, and nobody around here seems to give a rat's ass."

He reached out and brushed a strand of hair from my face. He didn't say anything, just stood there and looked at me.

After a moment there was a knock even though the door was open. It was Detective Conners, who for some reason wouldn't look Torrance in the eye. "I appreciate your help in this, Inspector," Conners told me. "We're, uh, sorry if we delayed you, but this is a homicide."

I glanced at Torrance, who angled his head toward the door, indicating I should leave. I walked out. Torrance followed, ignoring the detective completely. Scolari was waiting for us in the hallway.

We walked past an open door, and a man behind a desk called out, "Lieutenant?"

Torrance stopped.

"My apologies."

"Thank you, Captain," Torrance said, then moved on.

"That was our mistake," Scolari said, glancing back at the captain. "We were talking to the wrong end of the food chain. If we'd started at the top instead of with a lowly detective, we might've gotten out sooner."

The three of us stepped from the building into the sunlight. Torrance slipped on his sunglasses. Went with the image. And the unshaven face. Scolari and I squinted in the light.

"I'll follow you," Torrance said. "Where to?"

"My aunt's, I guess."

He nodded and headed to his car. Scolari and I walked to mine. I tossed him the keys. "You feel like driving?"

"Sure."

A minute later we were following Torrance onto the freeway. "I suppose I should have thanked him," I said.

"I wouldn't worry about it."

We both lapsed into silence. I was having trouble keeping my eyes open, but each time I closed them, I saw my nephew's face, then the splintered doorframe. "I blew it," I said after a while. "I should have opened a missing person's case on Kevin the moment I found out he took off."

"On what grounds? He took off with his mother, for Chrissakes."

I gave Scolari a penetrating look.

"Okay," he said. "So she's not June Cleaver on *Leave It to Beaver*. And you can second-guess yourself till kingdom come. Right now you're wasting your energy on something that can't be helped."

"I know," I said, leaning against the window. "Where would you take a kid if you didn't want to be found?"

"I guess that depends on why. I mean, was it just the long-lost relative thing? Or was there something else on her mind?"

"She told me that now that Abernathy was dead, she wanted to see Kevin."

"I'm putting my money on long-lost relative theory."

"Meaning what?"

"She regrets not seeing her son for years, decides now is the time."

"I'm not taking any chances. The odds suck."

My aunt was standing on the porch, watching for us when we got there. Scolari parked in the driveway, Torrance at the curb.

I gave her a reassuring hug, but could tell she hadn't slept a bit. "Hear anything?" I asked. I didn't want to give her the opportunity to ask me what I'd been up to. She'd raised me. She knew when I was lying.

"Nothing. But the two detectives who came by assured me they were working on it."

"What detectives?" I asked.

"I don't remember their names. But one of them had long brown hair in a ponytail. I think he used to work with you."

Jamison? I glanced at Torrance, whose face remained impassive, whether for my sake or my aunt's, I didn't know. He said, "I'll make some calls. See what I can find out." He went out to his car, his rolling office.

I asked my aunt to see Cassandra's papers. Casual. Not wanting to alarm her that any of us were worried.

"Oh, those old things?" She led us to the back bedroom, which she used for sewing, and pulled a shoe box from the top shelf of the closet. "I don't know what good they'll do, but here you go."

I took the box, curious, and I'll admit a bit apprehensive. I was holding a piece of my brother's history, a part of which I wasn't sure I wanted to know.

Aunt Molly left us to sort through the contents while she made a pot of tea. I dumped the box on the white chenille bedspread, my eye catching on what appeared to be a savings passbook. "The missing money?" I told Scolari, opening it.

"That'd be novel. Hiding it in a bank," he said, turning his attention from the papers he was looking through to the tiny book I held.

Inside I found the account number, and the account name, which I read aloud. "C. K. Gillespie, in trust for Kevin Gillespie."

"They were married?"

"Not that I knew of," I replied, noting the only entry

was for sixty dollars, made a good month before my brother's death. "Maybe she did it for the look of legitimacy."

I put the book aside, scanned a couple of the letters Cassandra had written to my aunt, asking about Kevin's health, how he was doing in school, that sort of thing. The letters were spaced years apart, not exactly the dedicated mother. But then even this much correspondence surprised me. She hadn't forgotten about Kevin as I had always thought, and I had to grudgingly give her credit for her effort—not enough to wipe out twelve years' worth of abandonment, however.

"You find anything?" I asked Scolari.

"Not much more than the first time," he said, examining a pink torn paper. "Can't imagine why your aunt kept half this stuff. Look at this. A receipt for casings."

"Casings? For what?" My brother had been a gun enthusiast, so I assumed it had something to do with that.

"Your guess is as good as mine," he said, handing the invoice to me. It was a copy of the original on carbonless paper for one hundred casings, but no purchase amount. The company's name had been torn off the top, possibly when it was pulled from the receipt book. What remained was a San Francisco zip code, nothing more.

I tossed it into the shoe box. It landed face down. Something was written on the back in pencil in block printing. All capitals. The way cops write.

I stared at it, not quite believing what I saw.

Sean's suicide note.

17

As I read the note, I tried to justify and analyze the implications of what it meant, not just to me, but to Kevin, my aunt, even the department. At least Cassandra had the foresight to mail the note to my aunt. I only wished I'd known about its existence years ago.

For the second time in as many days, I had to reconsider, reformulate my beliefs. From accidental overdose to Cassandra's shocking suggestion of murder, and now this, suicide.

How was I supposed to feel? Elated that my brother wasn't a drug addict? Relieved that he wasn't murdered? Thank heaven it was only a suicide?

This proved one thing and one thing only. We never really buried the dead.

I read the note again.

San,
Take this and know I did all I could. This was the only way. I'm sorry. Make sure Kevin is taken care of.

S

I took a breath and handed the note to Scolari.

"Jesus," he said, reading it. He flipped it over, eyed

the receipt it was written on, then read it again. "San short for Cassandra?"

"I would think so." I wasn't sure what I thought of the nickname, something that implied they were closer than I wanted them to be, I suppose.

"Ya think this is legit?"

"Yes," I said. In my heart I believed it was written by Sean. It certainly appeared to be his handwriting, the flourishing *S* pretty much the way he signed things, though why he would scrawl so hasty a note on the back of a receipt was beyond me. And that's what made me look at it again.

Torrance walked in then, and I showed him what we'd found. He said, "A suicide note doesn't exactly tie in with Cassandra's theory that he was murdered, does it?"

"No," I said, turning it back over. "Unless there's more to it than we're seeing."

"Such as the receipt for the casings?"

"If this was something he wanted found, what better way to do it than write a suicide note on it?"

"He never factored in that it would get stuffed in a box for all these years."

"Of course not. He'd be thinking like a cop. He knew it would get examined and booked into evidence at the very least. To that end, we have to assume that it has something to do with his IA. A key to prove whatever it was he was trying to prove at the time."

Scolari said, "That some dirty cops were skimming drug-buy money."

I looked at the writing again, my heart aching that these were my brother's final words. "Or maybe we're reading too much into it. Maybe it's simply his last attempt to make sure his son is taken care of." And here I'd gone and lost his son.

We stared at the pink slip of paper, and Torrance suggested that we all try to get in a nap. He was right. At the moment, we were basically prisoners waiting for Kevin's call. I don't think I slept much, but I tried, waking with a start each time I heard a noise. I don't know how much later it was when the phone rang. I jumped from the bed and ran down the hall.

My aunt answered it from the living room. "Kevin?" I heard her say. Scolari and Torrance were standing next to her. "It's Kevin," she told me. "He wants to talk to you."

How she remained so calm was beyond me. I grabbed the phone. "Kev? Where are you?"

"Up in . . ." he whispered.

"Where?" I asked, motioning for everyone to be quiet. I could barely hear him.

"Tahoe. At Grandpa's cabin."

"Are you okay?"

"I'm scared. Cassandra said my dad used to bring her here. She knew about the key hidden under the stone."

I gripped the phone tighter. "Is Cassandra there with you?"

"She just went outside. I think she's in trouble."

"Why?" I asked, resisting the urge to call him honey, knowing full well they were both in trouble.

"She has this pager, and she called the number and was talking to some guy named Tony. I think he thinks she took his money, and she sounded scared, too. She told me to call you."

Foust. *Please, God, keep Kevin safe.* "Okay, listen, honey," I said, unable to withhold the endearment. "The man your mother was talking to is dangerous. I'm calling the police to send them to you. It should only take them a couple minutes. You stay with the police until I get there, okay? Do *not* go anywhere."

"Okay," he said softly. I wasn't sure, but it sounded like he was crying.

"If anyone shows up and it's not the police, and it's not me, call nine-one-one."

"I will."

I didn't want to hang up, but I knew every second with him on the phone kept me that many seconds from reaching his side. "I love you, Kevin."

"I love you, too, Aunt Kate."

"I'm calling the sheriff's office now, so I have to hang up."

"Okay," he said, his voice cracking, making me wish I could reach through the phone and hug him.

I disconnected and called the operator to have her switch me to the 911 dispatcher in Placer County. I briefed the dispatcher on the information, referenced the murder in Cassandra's apartment to make her understand the gravity of the situation, gave her the address of the cabin, and disconnected after leaving my cell phone number with her, and receiving her assurance that they would not leave the cabin without Kevin.

I looked over at Aunt Molly. She seemed so frail. Much smaller than I remembered and no longer the seeming pillar of strength that I had always believed her to be. I wondered if anyone knew how much she'd given up—again—to raise Kevin. She'd done the same for Sean and me, put her life on hold to raise someone else's kids.

When she saw me looking at her, she put on a brave smile, and in that space of a moment I knew that I would not be half the woman I was, had she not been there for me, guiding me, whether I liked her direction or not. Her belief in the goodness of mankind made her a wonderful woman to be around, but it also made her vulnerable. To that end, I knew that until we found out who had come by her house looking for Kevin, it wasn't safe for her to stay there.

I took Torrance aside. "Have you found out anything about the officers who were here?"

"I tried contacting Lombard to see if it might be Jamison. Can't get ahold of them."

"Did they know about Kevin running off with Cassandra?"

"Lombard was with me when you called about Kevin. Perhaps he was simply trying to help. Especially after the murder in Cassandra's apartment. That's not exactly information I could withhold from him."

"Where was Jamison?"

"I don't know. I filed the missing person's report, then took care of getting you the hell out of Dodge, so to speak."

Scolari cleared his throat. "I'll take your aunt to my place, while you two check the cabin," he said. "I think you need someone who's, uh, not retired, in case you stumble across any more homicides."

I glanced at Torrance. He nodded in agreement, and I could tell he wasn't too happy, probably from the administrative viewpoint, the IA viewpoint. I was already a suspect in Abernathy's murder. It didn't help matters that I seemed to be leaving a trail of bodies in my wake.

"We can take my car," Torrance said. "You might want to sleep."

I gave Scolari my keys, since his truck was at my

apartment, then I hugged my aunt and told her I'd get in touch with her the moment I heard anything.

Her blue eyes pooled with unshed tears, but she smiled as she looked up at me. "You be careful," she said.

"I will," I told her, keeping all traces of emotion from my face. She'd always been there for me, the one constant in my life. But it seemed as though she'd aged suddenly, and I wasn't about to let her know that I was worried beyond belief.

We took off, Scolari and my aunt waving at us. At the car I asked Torrance, "Mind if I drive?"

"The idea is to get there. You're too tired and too emotionally involved."

"If he were your nephew, how fast would you drive?"

"About a hundred."

It was said with such calm authority, the sort he was always so good at. The sort I didn't have time for right now. But I saw his point. I walked to the passenger side of the car. Dark clouds cast a pall over the sky, and I shivered in the chill air. "Pretend he's your nephew," I said.

He offered something close to a smile, something that on him I didn't see quite enough of. Once we hit I–80 toward Sacramento, he drove at a calm eighty-plus miles per hour.

I stared ahead, my mind spinning a million scenarios of what was happening up there, none of them good. I'd been a cop for too long, seen too much evil in the world. Even so, I still wanted the proverbial happy ending.

We were approaching the city of Fairfield when Torrance said, "I'd like to solve this damned case and shove it down the mayor's throat." He looked over at me, then back at the road, as usual his face betraying no sign of emotion.

My gut feeling was that he was none too pleased with me when back at my apartment I'd asked him if he thought I was guilty of Abernathy's murder. But his statement about the mayor was, to me, telling, and probably the most comforting thing anyone had said to me in days. The least I could do was be completely open with him. "There is one angle I think we need to look at. I think the murder in Cassandra's apartment may be tied to my brother's IA."

"That's a rather broad stretch, don't you think?"

"Yes, but there are too many links to be ignored."

"Such as?"

I counted them off my fingers while I spoke. "Cassandra. Foust. Stolen money—"

"I still think ten thousand dollars is too small an amount to kill a person over, after some twelve years."

"To you and me, maybe. But we're talking the mob here. Their interest rates aren't as competitive as your local savings and loan."

"I'll agree with that, but why then involve Cassandra now? Scolari had no difficulty locating her in, what, a few hours' time? A dedicated gangster wouldn't need twelve years."

"Okay, I'll admit it's somewhat of a weak link right now, but you have to admit it's there. The fact that Cassandra and Foust's names were mentioned in my brother's IA, and then again now, is too coincidental to be ignored, no matter how seemingly insignificant Foust's involvement was in my brother's case."

"Exactly how was he listed?"

"More of an involved party, a snitch passing on

some information about my brother stealing ten thousand dollars in drug-buy money. You and I both know that's bull. Foust has never been involved in something that wasn't twisted deeper than anyone else realized. I'll lay odds he's behind that big cocaine shipment they're expecting in tomorrow. Back when my brother was alive, Foust played the peon, because that suited his needs at the time. Just the fact he has so neatly eluded capture since a murder warrant was issued for him tells us that he has some degree of sophistication. And look at the guy who was going to turn him in. Squeaky said he was giving me Foust, and he ends up dead. My brother was going to turn in someone for money laundering, and he ends up dead. I see a perfect connection. I just can't figure out the why of it yet."

"And now it appears that someone's trying to pin you for Abernathy's murder?"

"It appears that way. Foust, I'll bet. That seems to be his MO. But that's the least of my worries right now. Someone threatened my nephew's life."

"Foust?"

"I don't know his voice. But I'd lay odds on it. The dead guy in Cassandra's apartment looked like a hit. Definitely Foust's style."

"You said the apartment was trashed."

"Systematically trashed. Whoever was in there was looking for something. Maybe a clue to the missing money—never mind that they were sending a very clear message. I think he fully expected Cassandra to walk in there, find that mess, and then her dead boyfriend or whoever the hell he was. That much was plain when I answered her phone."

We discussed that angle for several minutes, then lapsed into silence. I may have dozed off, but woke completely around the town of Auburn, when I realized the police still hadn't called about Kevin. A moment later, when I looked for my phone on the seat, I knew why. Wrong car. Crap. "You don't happen to have a phone and a spare thirty-eight lying around, do you?"

He pulled his phone from his pocket. "Where's your gun?"

"Under the seat in my car."

"Would have been a nice thing to know before we started out." Playing the father figure.

"Yeah, well, I had my mind on other things," I said, punching in double zero and asking the operator to put me through to Placer County. A dispatcher answered, unfortunately not the same one. Which meant I had to reexplain everything.

"This is Inspector Gillespie, SFPD," I said. "I'm calling about my nephew. Your agency was doing a mutual aid, checking on his welfare?"

"Oh, yes, Inspector. Hold on."

She went off the line, then came back a couple minutes later. "I checked with the deputy who's still at the cabin. Everything's fine. He's waiting there for you."

"Thanks," I said.

I decided to call the cabin. There was no answer, and I disconnected, feeling uneasy. I called the sheriff's office again. The dispatcher explained that the previous shift had taken my call. She was unfamiliar with the situation. I told her I wanted to speak with my nephew, that he was supposed to be brought to their department.

"I'll see if I can contact the deputy," she said.

"Can you have him call me?"

"I'll try."

A few more minutes passed. Outside, the flora

changed from low-lying scrub and oaks to pine. A few patches of white began to appear the higher we drove. It started to sprinkle, the tiny drops hitting the windshield, drops that soon turned into minute crystals of snow. "You didn't happen to listen to the weather report, did you?" I asked. I sure as hell hadn't paid attention.

"Rain expected for the Bay Area."

"You have chains?"

"None."

"Let's hope it holds off until we get there."

The deputy never called back. I telephoned the department, and they said they were having radio difficulties, but not to worry. My anxiety grew the farther we drove. I tapped my foot. No doubt about it. Had I been driving, we'd be pushing light speed. Torrance seemed to have no problem breaking every speed law without my help, so I bit my tongue instead of telling him to drive faster.

The snow fell in earnest right about the time we hit Truckee, a gentle whiteness covering the manmade scars on earth. Ten more minutes and we'd be at my father's small cabin near the outskirts of Lake Tahoe. I gave Torrance directions. He had no trouble finding it. I, however, grew more nervous the closer we drew, expecting forensic teams to be crawling over the place and crime-scene tape barring our way as we turned down the long, snow-covered drive. I couldn't erase the vision of the dead man in Cassandra's apartment with a single bullet wound to his head, lying in a pool of blood. But mostly I couldn't erase my initial fear that it was Kevin lying there, and the guilt that followed. The guilt that he would not be in danger if not for me. How could I have been so blind, to drive off to work and leave him at school?

No sun broke through the clouds at day's end, and the forest that surrounded the cabin deepened into endless shadows. Ours was a small place compared to some of the other homes in the immediate area, maybe eight hundred square feet, with a corrugated metal roof and a stone chimney that blocked what I always considered a quaint dormer window. I saw only one vehicle through the falling snow as we neared, not the multitude I had feared. The Jeep with the shield on the doors obviously belonged to the waiting deputy, who stepped out of the cabin at our arrival. I panicked when I realized there was no other vehicle—one that might have belonged to Cassandra.

Torrance barely eased to a stop before I was out the door, running up the drive, my footsteps crunching in the thin layer of snow. I shouted Kevin's name.

The deputy watched me with a wary expression as I slid across the icy path toward him. He zipped his drab green uniform coat against the crisp air. "I take it you're Inspector Gillespie? SFPD?"

"Yes," I said, slowing before I broke my neck. "My nephew. Where is he?"

"Don't exactly know, ma'am," he said.

My heart stopped.

"I tried calling you," he continued, "but my phone's been on the blink these past few days. Hasn't worked since they installed it, and I couldn't find a phone in the cabin."

"Where are they then?" I heard myself ask, feeling as if I were standing in the midst of a long tunnel, my voice echoing from far away.

"Don't exactly know," he replied, pausing to pull on his gloves. "Place was empty when I got here."

18

The snow came down faster, shrouding everything around us, swirling in macabre shapes. My imagination took control of my sanity. I didn't wait for the deputy's answer. "No," I said. "I told him to stay here, no matter what."

"I'm sorry, ma'am."

I moved past him into the cabin. The air inside felt as frigid as the outside. "Kevin?" I called out. He wouldn't have left the doors open, I thought wildly, moving faster, going through the rooms, opening closets and cupboards. Anyplace he might hide. I was hit with the recollection of when he was four and he couldn't find my aunt or me. We'd come in from the garden calling his name, only to find him hiding under the covers of his bed. Before that I'd always taken his presence for granted. But when I saw him huddling beneath his sheets, crying, his vulnerability frightened me. He had been so innocent, believing us when we'd told him we'd never let anything happen to him. And now, once more, I couldn't find him. "Kevin?"

I looked around, saw a set of keys on the kitchen table. Cassandra's? Then where was her car?

I heard a scuffling sound above me. My pulse quickened as I raced into the living room, just past the hearth. "Kev?" I shouted again.

Torrance entcred, and the deputy behind him. I ignored them, dragging a yellow vinyl kitchen chair into the hallway. I stood on it and knocked on the ceiling. The brass ring that normally hung down had been unscrewed, the cracks of the trap door to the loft barely noticeable from the rest of the exposed wood planks that matched the paneling on the walls.

"Aunt Kate?" came his voice, muffled.

"Open the door, Kevin."

He did, and I pulled it down, exposing a ladder hung on springs that reached to the floor when fully extended. It led to the loft, never meant to be a real room, but my father had gutted the attic, made it into one anyway. The single window faced away from the front, hidden by the chimney, and most people never realized it was anything more than a fake dormer. My brother and I had slept up there, and then years later, Kevin, when my aunt and I brought him.

He descended, and I wrapped him in a hug.

"You're squishing me," he said after several seconds.

"I'm sorry. I just can't believe you're here."

"Why?"

"Never mind."

I let him go, then turned to the deputy. "Thanks for staying."

"No problem," he said. "You want me to stick around till you get out of here?"

Torrance said, "It probably wouldn't hurt."

The deputy pulled out his radio, to notify his dispatcher of our arrival, but she asked him to clear to assist CHP with an injury accident that had occurred about a mile up the road.

He eyed Torrance, who said, "We'll probably be fine. We'll be leaving shortly anyway."

"I'd make it real short," the deputy said. "Before the roads close up. Snowing pretty hard right now," he said, looking out the window at the snow swirling down from the sky. "Expect we'll get several more accidents before the night is through."

He took off, but I barely noticed, my attention riveted on my nephew. His face was pale, and he was shivering. I needed to find out what had happened, but the last thing I wanted to do was scare him any further. I glanced up at the ceiling.

"You take off the handle to the loft door?"

He nodded, digging it out of his pocket and handing it to me.

"Smart kid," I said, tossing it onto the dinette table next to the keys. That was when I noticed the telephone wasn't on the wall in the kitchen. "Where's the phone?" I asked. Then, in an attempt to bring a sense of normalcy to the chaos our lives had become, I added, "And why's it so cold in here?"

"They must have taken the phone, because it was there when I called you," Kevin said. "Maybe they left the doors open when they took off."

"Who?" I asked in as casual a voice as I could muster. I drew him to the couch, and we both sat. Torrance moved about the cabin, eyeing the windows, the doors, the general layout of the place.

"Cassandra and the two men who were here."

Torrance stopped his perusal. "What men?" he asked.

"I never saw them before."

"Were they young? Old?" I asked, immediately thinking of Lombard and Jamison. After all, if they showed up at my aunt's, why not here?

"I don't know," Kevin said. "I was hiding. But one of them might have been that guy my mom was talking to on the phone. Tony."

"What makes you think it was the same guy, Kev?"

" 'Cause a couple hours after she calls this Tony guy from the number on her pager, she looks at me and goes, 'Do you think he could find me just from talking to him on the telephone?' and I go, 'If he has Caller ID, maybe,' and she gets all scared. And . . . she starts crying," he said, his own dark eyes glistening with tears.

I wanted to take him into my arms, hold him tight, and curse Cassandra. Instead I said, "And then what happened?"

"She, like, asks if there's any good hiding places in here, and before I can answer, she goes, 'You gotta hide. Now. I'm going outside, I don't even want to know where you are.' And I go, 'Why?' and she goes, 'I can't tell you. But you gotta call your Aunt Kate. And then you gotta hide. And you don't come out till your aunt gets here. You don't come out for no one. Don't trust anybody, especially not the cops. You hear?' "

Kevin brushed at his eyes. His gaze kept straying to the window as though he expected his mother to return any moment. "It's my fault," he said. "I know I shouldn't have left practice, but I wanted to meet her so she could tell me about my dad."

"You can't blame yourself for that," I said, wondering what profound and deep advice his wretched psychologist would give him. I thought of a few things I'd like to tell her—"You're fired" being one of the nicer comments.

"Yeah, but if she hadn't brought me here, that man wouldn't have come."

"He would have caught up to her somewhere else." Now was not the time to tell Kevin he was grounded for life. "What happened next?"

"I called you, and then I hid up in the loft. And then I heard a car drive up, and the front door slam," he said, eyeing the door. He looked away, swallowed; this time the tears were spilling down his cheeks. "I couldn't hear everything at first, but then she started screaming that she was alone. It sounded like someone was hitting her. And they came inside, and the one guy goes to the other guy, 'Search the place,' and I can hear them walking around, and she tells them she came up by herself, and the guy goes, 'You want what happened to your old man to happen to the kid?' and she goes, 'I'll tell you where the money is.' " He wrapped his arms about his middle, and I waited for him to continue. Finally he said, "She goes, 'It's in the city, right under your nose. But if you think I'm gonna tell you where, so you can kill me, you're outta your mind.'

"And then they leave."

"And you were up in the loft the whole time? You didn't see their car?"

He nodded.

"Even when the deputy got here?"

He shook his head. "She told me not to trust the cops. She squeezed my shoulder, like she was worried. I didn't know what to do."

"You did the right thing," I said, giving him a quick hug.

Torrance and I exchanged glances. "I left something in the car," he said. And then he took off out the front door.

Kevin and I sat there for a few minutes in silence. I held him and he let me. But after a while, I wondered what Torrance was up to.

"I need a glass of water," I said. "You want one?"

"No." He followed me into the kitchen anyway. I filled a glass and drank, looking out the window. The snow came down faster, and through it I saw Torrance sitting in his car talking on the cell phone. When he finished, instead of getting out, he draped his arms over the steering wheel, then rested his head, not moving for several seconds. Like he was admitting defeat—something I'd never seen him do. But then he got out, stood in the falling snow, looking every inch like the Torrance I knew. Surveying the area. He tromped around, undoubtedly getting the lay of the land. How best to protect us. I decided that what I'd seen in the car was my imagination.

I lost track of time, but eventually he returned, banging on the door. I opened it. The sight of him standing there, carrying a bundle of firewood in his arms, seemed so rustic, especially with the day's growth of beard. So out of place with who I believed he was. It caught me by surprise—much more so than the blast of cold air that blew in with him.

"This stuff's getting heavy," he said.

"Sorry." I moved aside, and he wiped his feet on the mat and walked past me. I pushed the front door closed against the wind. "I just didn't expect you to go out and gather wood."

Kevin asked, "We are going home now, right?"

"We should have followed the deputy out. It's snowing too hard to leave, even if we did have chains," he said, depositing the wood on the hearth. "Of course, that works both ways. No one in, no one out. And it's too damned cold in here."

He was right. Now that Kevin was safe, the cold was definitely more noticeable. "I'll get some coats from the closet," I said, heading into the hallway. I grabbed one of my father's Pendleton jackets for Torrance and a wool sweater for myself. Kevin already wore one. When Torrance finished stacking the wood, I tossed the jacket to him. "I vote for some hot chocolate, chili, and a fire."

"You have hot chocolate and chili?" Torrance asked.

"We can check. Kev, how about you start putting some wood in the fireplace, and see if you can find something to watch on TV. Torrance and I will try to rustle up some dinner."

"Okay."

We went into the kitchen, opening cupboards and making a great show of hunting for something appetizing. The moment I heard the television, I asked about the call.

"Mathis is taking care of it. He's running her as a missing person, endangered, listing Foust as the possible suspect."

I thought about the way he looked in the car. "Something else going on?"

He glanced at Kevin. "Nothing I can go into right now."

There were several seconds of awkward silence. I decided to fill it. "As much as I hate to say it, I have to admire her for protecting Kevin."

"I would have admired her more for not bringing him here in the first place," Torrance said quietly, moving up several notches in my opinion. He glanced out the window. Night had fallen. "Even if the snow stops, the roads might be too icy in the dark."

"I'm not thrilled about staying here," I said.

"Cassandra, I mean my mom, has chains."

Torrance and I both looked up to see Kevin watching us.

"Does she?" I replied, wondering how much of our conversation he'd overheard.

"She bought them on the way up when it started snowing, and I helped her put them on myself. We could leave now."

I glanced at the keys on the table. "Where's her car?"

"She hid it in the neighbor's lean-to. She said that way no one would know we were here."

"I think we should wait until it clears," Torrance said.

I watched Kevin's face, the disappointment and fear he tried to hide. "Find anything good on TV?" I asked him

"No."

"Want to help us make dinner?"

"Okay," he said quickly.

After going through the contents of the cupboards we came up with a can of corn, string beans, chicken soup, and chili. We dumped it all in one pot and at Kevin's suggestion, christened it Chile Chicken Vegetable Stew. It wasn't half bad, and I was pleased to see Kevin go for seconds. An appetite in a thirteen-year-old boy is a good thing, I figured, getting up to clear the dishes when we had all finished. Kevin rinsed the plates, and then we all settled on the couch to watch a little TV. Torrance offered to do the dishes—in the dark, I noticed, and suspected that what he was really doing was keeping an eye out the kitchen window, something he couldn't do with the lights on.

Soon after, Kev started to nod off.

"Hey, bud," I said. He lifted his head and valiantly tried to appear awake. "Why don't you climb up the ladder and grab a little sleep?"

"I'm okay," he said. "What if it stops snowing and we have to leave?"

"I promise I'll wake you. Now scoot. We have a long drive ahead of us."

He rubbed at his eyes, sat there for a second while his sleepy mind processed what I'd told him, then he rose and headed up the ladder to the loft.

Only then did Torrance come out from his self-appointed kitchen post. I shut off the TV and watched the snow falling outside the front window. It didn't seem all that deep. More drifts from the wind than anything else. "You think it'll stop tonight?"

"Maybe. It doesn't seem as heavy as it was earlier."

He stirred the embers in the hearth, then stood there watching as the fire jumped to life for a brief moment. The effect on his chiseled features was surreal—dark, with a flickering glimpse of red-gold light, what I imagined his soul must be like.

He remained there for a long time, just staring at the glowing coals, and I wondered what went on in his head at a moment like this. It was the first time all night his gaze hadn't been fixed out the window. Knowing him, anything on his mind had something to do with the case. Logistics. When we would leave. Whose car we would take if the roads were icy.

I didn't know what to say, since he wouldn't meet my gaze, so I got up and moved to the front window. I stared out, barely registering the blue cast to the white blanket of snow that covered everything in sight, the few flakes that floated down from the sky. I only noticed the intense cold radiating from the pane of glass before me.

And the sudden heat behind me.

"Kate," Torrance whispered, the warmth of his

breath a caress on my neck, light enough to send a shiver down my spine. "We need to talk."

He was so close that I was at once afraid to turn for fear he'd kiss me, afraid not to for fear he'd move away. I knew Torrance. He'd crossed every boundary he'd placed on himself, every line by taking this step.

I turned, surprised to see his look of apology—or was it sympathy?

"Talk about what?" I asked, backing into the cold window behind me. In a single step he closed the distance. Pressed himself against me. Denim to denim.

His mouth came down on mine, his whiskers scraping me with the force of his kiss. He reached up, grasping my hair, holding tight, while his other hand caressed my back, my shoulder, then my breast. His fingers splayed against it, his thumb teasing at me. Trapped between the icy windowpane and his unyielding stance, I couldn't have moved, even had I wanted to.

Not that it mattered. I doubted he'd go too far with Kevin upstairs—asleep or not. For the moment, though, I let my imagination wander along with his hand.

He trailed his finger down to my waist in a languorous caress. "Do you have any idea what I'd like to do to you, Kate?" he asked as he touched the button of my jeans, hesitating. "Have you ever made love without making a sound?"

I shook my head, my pulse rushing through my veins.

"That night we were in your bathroom," he whispered, "when Reid and the others were waiting in your living room. I wanted to take you right there . . . Could you have done it? Without making a sound?"

I closed my eyes and didn't answer.

"Could you do it now?" he asked, his mouth against mine.

My breath caught at the mental image, and he kissed me again, this time slow, deep. Then all at once he stopped, simply held me, my head against his chest, his arms protectively around me. His heartbeat matched mine, quick with suppressed desire.

I would never have guessed it could beat faster. But suddenly it did and he held me like a vise. He never showed fear on the outside, but now I knew he felt it. Human after all, I thought in a panic, as he calmly said, "Someone's out there."

He turned slightly, affording me a view outside. All seemed quiet. Nothing but snow and trees.

"To the left," he said. "Near my car."

I saw only the serene beauty of a Currier and Ives print—a view that turned deathly cold as a dark shadow moved toward us like a wraith across the snow.

19

Torrance drew his gun and moved me from his side. Away from the window. "We have to get out of here."

"Cassandra's car," I said, eyeing her keys on the kitchen table.

"If we can get to her car before he gets to us."

I crouched down, below window level, retrieved the keys, shoved them in my jeans pocket. I grabbed our jackets from the couch, tossed Torrance his, shrugged into mine, then crept to the ladder. "I need to wake Kevin," I said, backing toward the loft, eyeing the front door and the kitchen door, the only two exits, within ten feet of each other. Both easily seen by the intruder. "We'll never get him down in time."

He glanced at me, his expression telling me he'd come to the same conclusion. "Hell, it worked for Kevin, maybe it'll work for us."

I started up the loft, Torrance behind me, taking aim at the exit while I climbed.

Kevin was curled on one of two twin beds that took up most of the space. A moonbeam from the small window above him fell across his bed, lighting him in a soft blue glow. I shook him gently, whispered his name, put my hand over his mouth.

His eyes opened wide. His breath caught.

Torrance appeared. "Help me close this."

We pulled up on the ladder, closed the trap door. The springs hummed in vibration. I grabbed one, Torrance the other. Stilled them. Then we slid back toward the wall. Kevin's shoes were at the foot of his bed. I handed them to him.

He put them on and then his jacket, scurried into my embrace, his gaze glued to Torrance's gun directed at the floor. The trap door. I wanted to comfort him. Calm his fears. I didn't know if I could get past my own. Afraid for his life, I tried to hear over the pounding pulse in my head.

Trapped. No other thoughts came to mind.

I took a breath. Deep, slow.

I thought I heard a noise near the front. The kitchen door opening? The quiet of it unnerved me. Foust had entered my apartment in the past, picked the lock as though it were a toy.

I closed my eyes, hugged Kevin more tightly at the sound of footsteps below us. I felt his fear all over again. Thought of him hiding helpless while his mother was kidnapped. Now this.

Several minutes passed. The rustic wooden floor below clued us to the intruder's movements. The kitchen to the living room. Slow, methodical. Searching. From there to the bathroom. Finally the bedroom. And then the quickening pace. Retracing. Realizing we weren't there. The front door opened. I heard him on the porch. Pictured him standing there. Looking around to see if we'd fled.

Now leave, I prayed. *Leave.*

But he didn't leave. He came back in, his footsteps heavy. No longer concerned he might be heard. Again, from room to room.

"I know you're in here," he shouted.

Kevin flinched but remained silent.

I glanced at Torrance. Could just make out his face in the dark. His gaze remained fixed on the trap door, barely visible. His aim steady, he didn't move.

I heard the crunching of snow. Several minutes passed. No one moved. No one dared. Each second felt like an eternity.

And then the heavy footfall on the porch. Careless. Hurried. The front door slammed into the wall as he entered. Kevin shifted uneasily. Another crash. Heavy. And another. The sound of tearing, ripping.

The destruction of Cassandra's apartment invaded my thoughts.

Hidden money.

The dead man. Executed.

I buried my face in Kevin's hair. Held him tight. Memorized the feel of him. The scent of him. The warmth of his tears on my hand.

I breathed in again. Then froze.

The odor of gasoline?

My gaze flew to the closed trap door. The edges—once hardly distinguishable—lit up. A molten, orange rectangular line.

"Jesus Christ," Torrance said.

Smoke seeped through. Kevin hugged me more tightly. I had to save my nephew. Please God.

Torrance and I looked around. Both of us eyed the useless window. The decorative diamond panes.

I stood on the bed and peeked out. The chimney, to my right, shielded the dormer from the front of the house. Our only saving grace. Beneath the window the corrugated tin roof sloped sharply toward the ground where the snow shimmered as the flames grew. "Knot some sheets, Kev," I said, grabbing a blanket. "Mike, help me break the glass."

I held the blanket over the window. Torrance smashed at the panes with the butt of his gun. The sweat on his brow was from the growing heat, I told myself. But when his gaze met mine, I knew otherwise.

Cold air rushed into the window. And more smoke. I dropped the blanket over the base of the frame. Torrance holstered his weapon, then looked out. "Okay," he said. "Let's go."

Kevin had taken two sheets, knotted both together, and tied one to the foot of the bed. Torrance went first. The moment he hit the bottom and drew his gun, I motioned for Kevin to begin his descent. When he was safely on the ground I followed, my palms burning as I let the sheet slip through my hands. A few feet from the ground I let go, landing in slush.

A halo of yellow-orange emanated from the cabin. I wondered how long until someone saw it and called the fire department. At this hour and this time of the year it could go unnoticed. Most of the surrounding cabins were occupied only during the summer.

"The trees," I said, nodding to the back of the house. It was our only safe bet. Try to make it to the woods, then to Cassandra's car.

"I'll cover you," Torrance said.

Kevin hesitated. "Aren't you coming with us?"

"Soon," Torrance said.

"Do what I do," I told Kevin, tugging on his jacket. I led, keeping close to the cabin, ducking as I passed each window, to avoid silhouetting myself. Kevin did the same. At the corner, I stopped and Kevin bumped into me. There was about ten feet of open space from the back of the cabin to the first tree. About ten more feet to the next. I looked to my left, down the rear of the cabin, saw flames shooting out the bedroom window. But no sign of a suspect.

Now or never, I thought, grabbing Kevin's hand. We ran—waded, actually—through a foot or more of snow in some areas, mere inches in others. Torrance remained near the chimney, his weapon aimed toward the front. I glanced behind us, saw no threat, then dragged Kevin to the next tree, leaving a clear trail. If the suspect came back here, he'd know immediately where we were.

It was a chance we had to take. Kevin and I crouched behind a line of shrubs, covered in a mantle of white.

I glanced over the top. Torrance edged his way against the cabin toward us. Flames shot up from the roof. Something crashed in the front. Torrance spun toward the sound. His view blocked by the cabin, he couldn't see on the opposite side.

But I could.

My heart hit my sternum. A man dressed all in black sidled against the wall, parallel to Torrance. The edge of the man's weapon reflected the light from the burning structure. Square, semi-auto.

I knew Torrance wouldn't clear the cabin without checking around the corner. He still might not see the threat. To call out risked Kevin's safety. To remain silent risked Torrance's. And there was no guarantee he'd hear me over the raging fire.

Turn around, Torrance. Turn. Turn. See me.

When he didn't, I dug beneath the manzanitas, forcing my frozen fingers through the snow. Felt the prickly spines of a pinecone. Too big, too light. I foraged again, this time coming up with a marble-sized stone.

"What are you doing?" Kevin whispered.

I pointed out the man. "I need to warn Torrance."

He took the rock from me, his hand shaking. "You throw like a girl," he said, looking through the branches.

His father had always said the same.

Kevin stood to the left of a wide cedar, out of sight of the suspect.

I held my breath as he drew his hand over his shoulder. He threw, then dropped to the ground. The rock landed squarely against Torrance's back.

Torrance whipped around, his gun thrust forward. Saw me.

I signaled for him to stop. Made a shooting motion and nodded to my right.

Torrance stilled. A few more steps, he'd be out in the open. Vulnerable.

He pointed at me, then Kevin, then in the direction of Cassandra's car. Sharp, staccato movements. Do this or else.

Had Kevin not been there, I would have defied his orders. Torrance moved back and out. See the enemy before being seen. Slicing the pie, the SWAT guys called it.

"Come on, Kev. We need to go."

"But—" He looked at Torrance.

"Now." I grabbed his sleeve and yanked him forward. "Move it."

We crawled through the underbrush. Hands numb, pant legs soaked. I looked back.

I saw the suspect clearly now. Ten feet from Torrance, hidden by the corner of the building. Torrance held his position. Steadfast.

The suspect stopped. Saw our trail. Immediately he started in that direction. I took a deep breath. Good for Torrance. Bad for us.

"Faster, Kev."

A deafening explosion cracked the night. Echoed sharply against the mountain. Another shot, another echo rocked through the trees.

Adrenaline sent me scrambling forward, dragging Kevin with me. I didn't dare turn. Saw Cassandra's car, a blue Mercury, parked in the neighbor's lean-to. Left front fender dented, side mirror hanging. I hoped it ran better than it looked.

Just a few more feet. And then we were there.

I dug for the keys. My frozen hands barely functioned. Shoved the key in the driver's door lock. Turned.

The lock popped up. I reached in, unlocked the back. "Get in," I told Kevin.

I glanced up, saw someone running toward the road. Toward us. He seemed tall. I didn't know who. Prayed it was Torrance. I jumped in, tried to get the key in the ignition. I couldn't see. Missed. Tried again. Turned. The engine chugged. *Start, goddamm it. Start.*

It chugged again. Slowly came to life. I shifted to drive. Fought against the rush, the urge to floor the gas pedal. The tire chains caught. We moved forward.

"It's your friend!" Kevin yelled.

"Unlock the door," I said.

Kevin reached over the seat. Unlocked the front passenger door. Torrance slid against the car with a thump. He grabbed the handle, yanked the door open. I slowed but didn't stop, afraid to lose traction. He jumped in, yelled, "Go! Go!"

I drove as fast as the chains allowed. From the corner of my eye, I caught a glimpse of my father's cabin. Engulfed in flames. A pickup, high like a four-wheel-drive, was parked farther up at the edge of the property. We passed it and I saw a man limping toward it. Short, square-headed, definitely not Foust. He saw us, fired off a shot.

"Get down," I shouted.

Kevin ducked. Torrance opened his window, returned fire.

I headed for the main road. My teeth chattered, whether from the rough ride on tire chains or the cold, I didn't know. Didn't care. I drove around a bend and down a hill, accelerating until I felt the back end slide out. Then I eased off, my eye on the rearview mirror. So far no headlights. I felt for the seatbelt, found it, pulled it over my lap. I couldn't hook it, but Torrance reached over and secured it for me. "Thanks."

"Buckle up," he told Kevin, his voice as calm as if we were simply coming from a ski trip. "And then stay down," he added, returning his focus and his pistol to the rear.

I heard Kevin's seatbelt click. Felt minutely better. Even more so when I saw Cassandra had a full tank of gas. Other than the cosmetic damage on the left side, her car appeared to be in fair shape. Mechanically, I didn't know. Nor did I have time to worry about it.

"Anything?" I asked Torrance, who kept watch behind us.

"Not yet."

"Maybe you got him?"

"Let's not count on it," he said, taking out his cell phone. He called the operator, had them hook him up to the sheriff's office. When seconds counted, 911 on a cellular did not always provide the best odds. Valuable minutes wasted while the phone rang, then queued you on hold forever, because forty different people were calling about the same thing.

Torrance reported the shooting to the dispatcher, gave our current location, direction, and the suspect vehicle description, then his cell number. The call finished, he told me, "They're sending a car to escort us. ETA ten at the most."

"Thank God," I said. I wanted this over with. I wanted to go home.

I turned onto the main highway and thought I heard sirens. Soon red and blue strobes flashed up ahead in the distance. Grew closer and brighter. I hoped they were for us, but then saw they were fire trucks. Too late for my father's cabin. A lifetime of memories. Gone.

I wasn't about to stop, but pulled closer to the side, slowing as they passed us, before they turned onto the road we'd just come from.

"Can I get up?" Kevin asked a couple minutes later.

I glanced at the rearview mirror, nearly useless from the vibration of driving on chains. "No," I said, catching sight of what seemed like bobbing headlights. The reflection jiggled too much. I could see Torrance watching it, trying to determine friend or foe. I looked to the hanging left side mirror, cracked and useless. I glanced over my shoulder at the approaching vehicle. Whoever it was switched on their brights.

"Tell me that's our deputy," I said, turning back to the road.

"Christ. It's a pickup." A heartbeat later, "Floor it."

"I'm pushing fifty with chains."

"He's doing seventy."

I pressed down on the gas. Headlights flooded our

interior as the vehicle neared. I could feel the chains slipping on the surface.

Suddenly there was a loud pop from behind. *A tire?* I thought, glancing back. The rear windshield, clear one moment, looked like Jack Frost had touched it, turned it to ice. Then it fell, completely disappeared. Cold air rushed in. Kevin screamed.

The pickup sped closer, swerved at us. Tried to force us from the road. I stabbed at the gas, looked forward, saw the guardrails too late. The curve in the road. We were going too fast. Too straight. I hit the brake. Went into a skid. Chains screeching, the tail end of our car swung around. Struck the rail. Skittered backward along its length. Metal scraped against metal. We slid to a stop facing the opposite direction. Saw the truck coming at us. It swerved. Slammed into the guardrail, metal twisting, plastic flying. Its headlights, twin beams, shot across the precipice as the truck hovered for an instant, then fell into the inky black.

No one moved for several seconds. Torrance's arm was braced against my abdomen.

"Kev?" I said.

"Yeah?" His voice was shaky. Weak.

"You okay?"

"Yeah."

Torrance dropped his arm. We both looked at the gaping hole in the guardrail. I closed my eyes, said a quick thank-you, then took inventory of our situation. The engine had stalled, and it took me twice to get it started. Torrance picked up his semi-auto from the floorboard. As he rose, we saw a vehicle approaching. We both tensed.

It slowed, and an instant later blinded us with a spotlight, then the flashing red and blue three-sixties, a welcome beacon in the night. I leaned back in my seat, took a breath, and wanted to cry. "It's okay, Kevin. You can get up now."

Kevin rose slowly and I reached back, held on to his hand.

Torrance holstered his gun, got out, and met the two uniformed deputies. He pointed to the break in the guardrail, then stood back as the deputies, weapons and flashlights in hand, proceeded to the point of impact. Finally they called Torrance over, and he signaled for me to follow. I had to exit via the passenger door. Before I did, I leaned over my seat, kissed Kevin on the cheek, and brushed some flecks of glass from his hair. "You stay here."

He nodded, and I scrambled over the center console and out the door.

"Careful," one of the deputies said. "Kinda icy out here." He was taller than Torrance, maybe about the same age, brown hair and bushy mustache. I picked my way carefully until I reached them. They had gathered in front of an intact part of the guardrail.

The younger deputy, shorter by a good half foot, held out his hand. I took it, and he guided me over a small ditch. He smiled, his ruddy cheeks dimpling. "Have to say you were pretty lucky, Inspector. Can't say the same for your suspect, though." Both deputies shined their Streamlights into the precipice. My gaze followed, taking in snow, rocks, the crumpled mass of what used to be the black pickup maybe twenty yards down, its fall stopped by a mammoth-sized granite boulder jutting from the cliff. The suspect had been thrown, perhaps might even have survived if the granite hadn't been there. But he'd landed on said boulder, and the truck on him. I knew, because I saw his legs sticking out, bent in unnatural angles beneath the wreckage. Whether he was still connected to those legs, I didn't know, nor did I care.

"I'm assuming you've notified CHP?" Torrance asked.

"Yes, sir," the younger deputy said. He looked over at our car, saw its condition. "You all want to wait in our unit, get out of the cold, feel free. I got a thermos of coffee in there. Piping hot."

"Sounds good," I said. "I'll get Kevin." I didn't want him to see the wreck. He'd been through enough, with more to come once the Highway Patrol arrived to take statements.

Torrance accompanied me. We looked at Cassandra's car. Involved in a fatal accident, we couldn't move it. But I guessed the entire left side was crunched now, not just the front fender. Whether it was still drivable remained to be seen. The left rear tire was flat. Kevin watched us approach, his frightened gaze taking in our every move. His hair sparkled with diamond dust from the broken safety glass of the shot-out window.

I helped Kevin from the car, had him close his eyes, lean over, and shake his hair. That done, we walked to the deputies' vehicle. I told him to sit inside while I spoke with the officers.

The CHP arrived, took our statements, measured, photographed. Kevin had fallen asleep, but they woke him, asked what happened, then let him sleep. Just when we thought we were done, detectives from Placer County came out to investigate the arson and shooting at my father's cabin. We showed them the windshield. Told them we thought it had been shot out. Perhaps the bullet ricocheted off the glass, since there was no sign of it entering the vehicle's cab. It was well past dawn when we finished, and we were left with the task of finding the best way home.

I didn't want to wait for a ride. The deputies, on since twenty-two-hundred hours, were due for relief, and the Highway Patrol had a cage in their unit, leaving nowhere to ride. I looked at Cassandra's car. "It made it this far," I said. "I vote we fix it and get the hell out of here."

"Assuming she has an adequate spare," Torrance said. The harbinger of doom.

Thinking positive myself, I removed the keys from the ignition to check. Unlocked and opened the trunk. Inside was a duffel bag of clothes—Cassandra's, I assumed—Kevin's backpack from school, and the empty tire chain case. I moved those aside, lifted the carpet that covered the compartment where the spare was stored. Or should have been. I took a step back in disbelief.

Torrance must have sensed something. He approached, took one look into the trunk, and said, "Son of a bitch."

Never before had I *ever* seen that much money in one place.

20

I wanted to kill Cassandra. Figuratively, of course, but had she been standing in front of me at that moment, I would have been hard-pressed not to jump on her, hit some sense into her at the very least. Then kill her. How could she endanger my nephew like this? Her son, for God's sake? What the hell was she thinking?

What the hell was I thinking? I slammed the trunk shut as one of the CHP officers approached. People had killed for this. Would do so again. Now was not the time to test the will of anyone who might be tempted at the sight of what must surely be hundreds of thousands of dollars.

I glanced at Torrance. His face remained impassive as he headed the officer off at the side of the car. "Apparently we don't have a spare," he told him. "We need to return the vehicle to San Francisco. Evidence in a current investigation." Sounded good to me.

"You want me to call a tow truck?" the officer asked, eyeing the flat.

Torrance looked to me. I didn't like the idea of trusting the vehicle to some tow company. Not when we needed an armored car driver. I shook my head. Torrance said, "The rim appears okay. Is there someone we can call this early to bring us a new tire? Someplace that takes a credit card?"

"Pike's Garage," he said. He checked the tire size. "I'll call it in for you. He's got the best mobile service in these parts. Don't think you're gonna get that rear windshield taken care of, though."

"Thanks," Torrance said.

The officer walked back to his unit. I moved to Torrance's side and said under my breath, "You think using stolen money for that tire's probably not a good idea?"

"Funny, Inspector." He reached out, put his arm around my shoulder. I looked up at him. When his gaze met mine, his expression turned serious, the sparkle of humor in his eyes replaced by a dark passion. I recalled our kiss the night before. The way he touched me . . . But we weren't alone, and the Highway Patrol officer exited his vehicle and walked toward us. Torrance gave me what could only be described as a reassuring pat on the back, sort of defusing the situation for everyone involved, including the officers and deputies who had paused to glance our way. For once I wanted to say, *Screw them. Screw them all. Let's focus on us.* But then I saw Kevin stirring in the backseat of the deputies' Jeep and wondered if he'd seen us. Torrance, as usual, was right. We had other more important matters at hand, my nephew the most important, the mystery of the money in the trunk the most pressing. My sex life was not even remotely close to the top ten.

Someday I was going to change that. Right now I wanted to get home. Safely. It was at least an hour before we were finally on our way, a new tire, no chains, and a much smoother ride. By then I was yawning profusely, and sex was no longer on my wish list. What I wanted was a good strong latte. Double at the least. We stopped at a little place in Truckee. Torrance, being armed, remained with the car and told me to get him a double mocha with almond, no whipped cream. Kevin was out like a light in the back. I went in, got some donuts and milk for Kev along with our drinks, and somehow managed to get it all to the car without spilling. I handed Torrance the drink carrier. He handed me my cup after I started the car.

I sipped, found it not too hot, and was surprised at the rich balance of chocolate, espresso, and almond flavoring. "I'm in heaven," I said, taking another drink.

"Good latte?" he asked.

"No. I think I got your mocha. I don't suppose you'd want to trade?"

He took a sip of his. "They must have made two by mistake."

"I can't believe I've been drinking lattes all this time. This is good. Maybe better than sex."

Torrance laughed. "I don't know what's in your mocha, but I want some."

"Sorry, all mine. Maybe you should concentrate on playing guard. Let me drive."

"Anytime," he said. He didn't look at me, but his answering grin told me he wasn't talking about the car.

I ignored him, felt my cheeks heat up, and hoped he didn't notice. Even so, I couldn't help thinking that maybe when we got back, maybe when this money was booked into evidence, and Cassandra found and questioned, and Abernathy's murder solved, we might take some time for ourselves.

Then again, who was I kidding? Torrance and I had

been this route before. Granted, I was the one who had broken things off before they went too far, i.e., before we slept together. But it wasn't as if he was knocking down my door to win me back. If circumstances and opportunity hadn't thrown us together, would things have gone this far?

As I angled out of the parking space, I told myself I should ask him. Of all the men I knew, he'd give me a direct answer. Then I heard Kevin make a noise, almost a whimpering sound. We'd cleaned out the broken glass, and I hoped we hadn't missed any. "Kev?"

Torrance checked on him. "Still sleeping. Probably having a bad dream."

I glanced at Torrance, saw the lines around his eyes, the dark circles. He looked tired and worried, but I detected something more. A burden he carried, one he couldn't or wouldn't share. I realized there was so much about him I didn't know. So much I wanted to learn. Other than the fact he lived somewhere in Marin, he was a total enigma. He wasn't married, but I didn't know if he ever had been. Did he have kids? Hobbies? What did he do when he left work?

I wanted to know. I wanted to be invited into his world, just for a moment. I wanted to know if the Greek goddess was anything to him. I wanted to know if I stood a chance. I decided to plunge right in before I lost my nerve.

"Mind if I ask you something?"

"No."

"That girl you were with last week . . ." I let the question hang.

"A good friend." I waited for him to clarify, perhaps add the "nothing more" sort of thing. But he didn't.

"Do you think—"

"I think a lot of things, Kate." This last was said with a quiet conviction. He reached out, ran the backs of his fingers across my cheek. "Especially when it comes to you."

My breath caught at his touch. I thought about the way he said my name. I wanted to hear him say it again and again.

I wanted him to kiss me again and again.

I wanted to get the hell out of this car.

I pulled onto the freeway, ending that particular conversation, mostly because hearing was nearly impossible over the blast of the heater to offset the rush of air that roared in where the rear windshield used to be. But I couldn't quit thinking about it, and the remaining three-hour drive back to the city took almost forever.

We decided to stop off at Scolari's first, check on my aunt, and leave Kevin with them before heading to the Hall, but we didn't get far. Once we neared the Bay Bridge, traffic came to a stop. At first I figured accident, but then my glance strayed out toward the water and the multitude of boats, big and small, many with decorations and flags whipping in the steady wind.

"Parade of Boats," I said, nodding to our right. "Any word on whether Markowski or Shipley found anything?"

"Good question," Torrance said. He took out his cell phone and called his office, only to have an indecipherable one-sided conversation, I assumed to keep Kevin somewhat in the dark. We were almost to the bridge, a twenty-minute stop-and-go venture, when he ended it.

“Anything?” I asked, quietly.

“Apparently they’re setting up out at one of the piers, now. I’m having Mathis send a couple radio cars to meet us at Scolari’s to bring this in. They’ll escort us to the Hall to book the money,” he said, looking in the mirror to see if Kevin was listening.

A boxwood hedge lined Scolari’s driveway where his black pickup was parked. I pulled in behind it, looking up to see Scolari watching me from his front window. I waved, and my aunt came bursting out the door, Scolari after her. They descended the staircase, and headed our way.

Kevin got out, and my aunt ran up to him, sweeping him into a bear hug. I started to follow, but stopped when Torrance put his hand on my arm. “A moment, Kate?”

“Sure,” I said, curious and, I admit, hopeful. He didn’t immediately respond, as though gathering up the courage.

“There’s something I need to talk to you about. Something that . . .” He paused when he saw Scolari speaking to my aunt and Kevin. They both nodded, then headed up the steps to the apartment, my aunt looking over her shoulder at me. Torrance watched Scolari, his expression guarded.

“Gillespie,” Scolari called out as he approached, his voice sharp, his gaze stern. The ridiculous thought came to mind that Scolari was trying to get between us, keep us apart. And Torrance knew it.

“I better see what he wants,” I said, hesitating.

Torrance gave a slight nod. Apparently whatever he had to say wasn’t that important after all.

I exited the car, my disappointment vanishing at

Scolari's urgent tone. "Tell me you know about the warrant."

"Warrant?" I asked.

He drew me away from the Mercury. "They came and took your car last night. Evidence in a crime."

"What are you talking about?" I said, confused at his demeanor. From the corner of my eye I saw Torrance get out and stand next to Cassandra's vehicle. I don't know why this bothered me, but my instincts told me there was something terribly wrong with this entire picture.

"Torrance didn't tell you, did he?"

"Tell me what?" I asked, feeling a slight panic. I immediately tried to dismiss it as a result of sleep deprivation, coupled with too much caffeine.

"Jesus Christ," Scolari said. He looked over at Torrance. "You want me to do the honors? Or you want to stick the knife in yourself?"

"Can someone clue me in to what is going on here?" I asked.

Several tense seconds of silence followed as both men eyed each other, Torrance's gaze dark, forbidding, while Scolari's was filled with rage. Finally Torrance said quietly, "I will tell her."

"I'll wait for you on the steps," Scolari informed me. He headed to the staircase, leaning against the rail, his arms crossed, his stance indicating very clearly that he was not letting me out of his sight.

Torrance looked away, and I was suddenly reminded of the night before when he stared into the fire lost in thought. Before I could comprehend the connection, he said, "Lombard is under pressure to make an arrest in Abernathy's case. The sketch artist came up with a composite of the driver at the hit-and-run."

"What do you mean?" I asked. "Where'd they find a witness?"

"They located Dellwood."

"Who did?"

"Your newspaperman. Knew where his daughter lived. Jamison went out with him, picked him up."

I felt relief. That Dellwood was safe, and that Jamison had found him. If that was true, then Jamison couldn't be guilty, could he?

"The sketch looked like you, Kate."

I stared dumbfounded, not sure I heard him right. And then the significance of what he told me hit like a jackhammer to my gut. I glanced over at Scolari. His narrowed gaze was pinned on Torrance. I folded my arms across my chest, wondering if the cold from Tahoe had finally caught up to me. Here I was standing in the bright sun and I couldn't get warm. "Are you telling me there's a warrant for my arrest?"

"Not yet."

"Not yet? What the hell is that supposed to mean?"

"They picked up your car last night after a CHP officer reported pulling you over after Abernathy was hit. He saw the sketch on the news, the dent in your car, figured it was you."

"That's ridiculous."

"Were you pulled over?"

"Yes, but—"

"Why didn't you mention it?

"It seemed insignificant."

"Insignificant?"

"At the time, yes. I needed to get home, check on Kevin."

"They found a bullet lodged in the front grill. This Dellwood insists that Abernathy shot at the vehicle."

I stared at Torrance, angry, confused, afraid he didn't believe me. "Is that what you think?"

"Lombard believes there are too many coincidences to be ignored. He feels you had motive and opportunity. The fact your movements can't be accounted for prior to Abernathy's death . . ."

His voice trailed off, and I knew he was talking about Squeaky's homicide. The fact he was found days after, the time not matching up. Did they blame me for that murder, too?

I glanced up at Scolari's apartment, saw my aunt watching me from the window. I wondered how much she had heard or deduced from being with Scolari and watching the news. I felt sick. I tried to speak but couldn't find the words.

And then it struck me. His mood last night—thinking about me. Right. Thinking about how he was going to arrest me when the warrant came out.

I turned my back on Scolari and kept my voice low. "You goddamned son of a bitch. When did you plan to tell me? After you'd read me my rights? Or after you got what you wanted? You knew about this last night. You kissed me and you knew about this."

"Kate—"

"No," I said, shaking my head. "I can't believe what a fool I was to think it meant anything." He reached out, but I brushed his hand from my face, unable to contain my anger or my hurt. "They're setting me up to take a murder rap, and you didn't think it was important enough to tell me? Is there anything else you forgot to mention? Such as, Oh, I'm seeing someone else, she's just a friend, but let me kiss you, because you're conveniently present. What am I? Just a suspect?"

"Stop it, Kate."

Two radio cars pulled up, and the stress of the past few days finally caught up to me. Trying to find Kevin, being shot at, my father's cabin burning to the ground. I choked back a sob, turning away, hating that Torrance was seeing me like this, refusing to let the uniformed officers see me like this. Torrance held up his hand, signaling for them to wait by their cars, then moved around me until he was face-to-face with me once more. I wouldn't meet his gaze, and he took my chin, forcing me to look at him.

"Are they here for me?" I asked, unable to contain my sarcasm.

"I didn't want it to come to this," he said, his grip on my chin tightening when I tried to dislodge his hand. "I didn't want you to find out this way."

My stomach knotted. This was how my brother felt, why he'd killed himself, I thought, swallowing past the lump in my throat. I was going to be arrested.

"They're here because of the money, Kate," he said, reading me. "Will you listen now?"

I didn't answer, and he let go. He stared at me a few moments, then turned and walked away.

"You should have told me."

He stopped, his back to me. His shoulders fell. Slowly he turned, his gaze hard, closed. "At what point? While your nephew was missing? After we found him, and he'd just seen his mother kidnapped? Or maybe while we were sliding into the guardrail and over a cliff?"

How could I answer that? "So what do I do now?"

"Allow me the goddamned courtesy of calling you and letting you know if it comes to be. Until then," he said, slipping on his sunglasses, "anything you want." He turned on his heel and walked away.

Case dismissed, relationship over.

How was it that I had such crappy luck with men? The bad, I had no problem latching on to—Reid was a perfect example of that. But when it came to the good—men like Torrance—I always managed to screw it up somehow.

Always? Who the hell was I kidding? Torrance was a once-in-a-lifetime kind of guy. Certainly not a man who lost his temper easily, yet I somehow had a knack for making him do it at the worst possible times. He was better off with someone who wouldn't question him. Someone who wouldn't second-guess his motives and actions. Someone like his Greek goddess.

Through a blur of unshed tears, I watched him speak to the officers, then get into Cassandra's car and drive away.

"Good going, Gillespie," I whispered as the cars disappeared from sight.

Scolari came up to me, put his arm around me, and said, "Maybe I shoulda stayed out of it."

"Maybe I should've been a bookkeeper."

"Yeah. Right."

Together we headed up the steps. My aunt met us, looking worried. "Is everything okay?"

"Fine," I said. "We just have some things to work out about the case."

"Can't someone else work it? You've been through so much. They should let someone else work the case," she said. In my aunt's world, things should be handled that way. Simply.

Scolari said, "That, unfortunately, is part of the problem. They've got a bunch of—"

He stopped at my look. My aunt had enough to worry about without being told what we thought of some of my coworkers' pedigrees. "You have any food in this place?" I asked him. "We haven't had lunch yet."

"Yeah, in the kitchen."

I looked around Scolari's apartment, surprised at how neat everything was. "You hire a maid?"

"Your aunt got bored," he said, looking slightly embarrassed. He eyed Kevin sprawled on the couch watching a rerun of *Star Trek.* "Maybe we better talk on the balcony."

Aunt Molly said, "I know right where everything is. I'll fix something and bring it to you."

I followed Scolari out the sliding door, taking a seat in one of two green plastic chairs separated by a low glass-topped table, sporting an overflowing ashtray in the center, a pack of Marlboros, a lighter, and an empty Budweiser bottle beside it.

Scolari moved the ashtray to the floor, then took a cigarette from the pack. "Your aunt wouldn't let me smoke in the house," he said, lighting it. He blew a plume of smoke, watched it fade, then said, "You always take off without your gun and phone? I called you, your aunt's hip started ringing. She was sitting on it."

"I already got the lecture from Torrance. I was in a panic over Kevin. I wasn't thinking."

"Did he happen to mention if you panic, you're a goner?"

"Not in so many words."

"Fine. The gun's in the top drawer of my dresser. So's your phone. Lucky for you I got both out before they towed off your car. Now ya mind telling me what the hell happened up there?"

I told him the facts, starting with finding Kevin up in

the loft, but skipping the more intimate details between Torrance and me. If Scolari guessed anything he gave no indication, but I doubted he was fooled for a second. Not after my little exchange with Torrance out front just a few minutes ago.

My aunt brought us sandwiches and ice water. When she left, Scolari said, "Who do you think is setting you up?"

"Good question. Does the sketch really look like me?"

He shrugged. "Hell, Kate. You know how those things work. 'Meant to eliminate, not identify,' " he said, repeating the mantra we'd told numerous witnesses over the years. "Let's just say you can't be eliminated as a suspect. At least not by the drawing. Andrews faxed a copy to me at my office last night. On the QT. He spoke with the sketch artist. Got worried when she showed it to him."

"Andrews?"

"Yep."

I took a bite of my sandwich, couldn't really taste it, not surprising under the circumstances. Tuna, I realized after looking. "What did he have to say?"

"Same crap. Lombard announcing that they're gonna make an arrest soon. Got new evidence. A new eyewitness."

The food stuck in my throat. I washed it down with the ice water. "Dellwood."

"Which, frankly, they wouldn't have had, had you not done your job so well."

"It was my case."

"Yeah, well, your case is looking pretty sucky right now. I suggested to Andrews that this Dellwood was an alcoholic. Saw you in an intoxicated state when you questioned him, probably. No wonder the goddamned thing resembled you. Either that or someone got to him first. Paid him off somehow. For all we know, Jamison or Lombard did it."

"Why not just eliminate Dellwood like someone did Abernathy?"

"I don't know. I haven't figured that part out yet."

Scolari bit into his sandwich, then finished it in two more bites. I stared out into the distance, watched a seagull, wings outspread, gliding against a clear blue sky. "Does Andrews think I did this?"

"No, but he had a few choice things to say about Lombard."

I smiled, thinking about that.

Scolari drained his water glass, then eyed my sandwich. "You gonna finish that?"

"All yours. What I really need is a shower and a nap."

"We're not going anywhere. You can sleep in my bed. You might want to turn the ringer off on the phone."

I rose. "Do me a favor. Keep a close watch on Kevin."

"Trust me. I won't let him out of my sight."

"Wake me if anything comes up."

"Yeah. Sure."

I remember very little after my shower. Scolari gave me an old T-shirt, and I threw that on, turned off the phone, then crashed on his bed. His pillow was soft and smelled slightly of cigarette smoke, and my last thought before I drifted off was that someone ought to get this guy some pictures for his walls.

I slept solidly until Scolari woke me. "The kid's hungry," he said. "You wanna go with us to get an early dinner?"

I was having trouble concentrating. The lighting seemed wrong somehow. The room had been shaded when I came in. But now the sunlight angled in through the mini blinds, hit the edge of the bed. I wondered if I was dreaming. "Yeah. If I had something to wear."

"Your aunt washed and dried your clothes," he said, nodding to my jeans and shirt neatly folded.

"How long did I sleep?"

"Four hours, maybe?" He leaned against the doorframe, then said, "Torrance called."

I glanced at the bedside phone, suddenly very wide awake, and hoped his call wasn't about the case. But I knew better. I'd questioned his integrity and I didn't think that was something he'd forgive too easily—if at all. Suddenly I became aware of how much I hurt—beyond the ache in my heart. Every muscle in my body screamed. Crashing into interstate guardrails will do that to you. "What'd he want?"

"He says they got an ID on the dirtbag's car that drove off the cliff. The pickup is registered to one of Foust's businesses. You'll never guess who the guy was."

"Who?"

"Someone named Rosenkrantz. Works for DEA."

"Squeaky was right. This is bigger than you and me."

"I'll say. Every DEA bigwig, along with the FBI and every other agency you can think of, are about to descend on our fair city, and they ain't coming to watch no boat parade. Apparently this Rosenkrantz had a Beretta on him. Torrance figures he probably offed the guy in Cassandra's apartment. Tentatively ID'd the vic as a someone named Frank Kincaid."

"Kincaid?"

He nodded.

"As in Squeaky Kincaid?"

"As in maybe Cassandra was shacking up with Squeaky's old man. Oh, yeah. Found a nine-millimeter casing, and a neighbor gave a description that fits Rosenkrantz. You know she had over a half-million dollars in her trunk?"

I was still on the Frank Kincaid thing, my mind slowly coming to life. "That call at the apartment. *Like I did your old man.* Squeaky's father is murdered. Squeaky's murdered. Squeaky's girlfriend says he's supposed to bring home the bacon. We find the bacon in the back of Cassandra's car. Foust comes looking for her . . ." I glanced at the window, watching the dust motes dance down to the bed. "It all connects. Abernathy killed Squeaky for the money that Cassandra has, and now Foust has Cassandra. End of story."

"Definitely explains his interest in her and why he sent one of his henchmen up to the cabin. You know what I'm thinking?"

"That the money in her trunk was supposed to be used as partial payment for this cocaine shipment that is supposed to be coming in?"

"Bingo."

I sighed, drawing my gaze from the window. "Well, it sure blows my theory about her hiding the ten thousand dollars in drug-buy money from when my brother overdosed."

"Maybe Foust set up that, like he's setting up you. I'll bet that entire half mil he's behind it."

"Maybe . . ." I said, trying to place the missing pieces, such as *how* Cassandra got the money in the first place.

"Why not? He goes back as far as Abernathy. You told me yourself that his name was mentioned in your brother's IA, witness to the missing drug-buy money. We've got the Abernathy-Foust connection. Maybe Abernathy's been working for Foust this whole time. Then when Squeaky calls you and says he's dropping the dime on him, Foust sends Abernathy to go get the money, but he gets caught by you, loses the money, and the game's up, so Foust has Abernathy eliminated. Maybe Foust indirectly blames you for losing his half mil. He certainly blames you for the two counts of murder standing over his head, and he figures it's payback time. Makes Lombard his patsy and sets you up to take the fall."

"What good does that do him?"

"A lot of good. That way if he goes to trial on the two counts of murder, the state's prime witness—you—ends up looking like crap. Suddenly the DA's cut-and-dried case on Foust ain't so tight after all." He stopped when he heard the phone ring out in the kitchen. "Hold on a sec." He crossed the room to answer the bedroom extension. "Yeah," he said. "She's awake now. In fact, she's right here next to me in the bed." Scolari, the king of tact.

He handed me the phone. "It's Torrance."

This is it, I thought. His promised call to inform me that a warrant had been issued for my arrest. I needed to figure out what to tell my aunt, Kevin. "Yes?" I said, trying to sound calmer than I felt.

"I just finished speaking to Lombard. Apparently Cassandra was able to get to a phone and call him. Foust is holding her hostage, until he gets his money."

I sat up. "Where?"

"City Meat and Sausage. Lombard thinks Foust was using it as a front. Jamison and Abernathy were working a case on it. Jamison's heading over there, too."

Something about the call bothered me. Like when you're trying to remember a word or someone's name, and it's hovering right on the tip of your tongue.

But before I could figure it out, he said, "I have to go. I thought you'd want to know what was going down."

And then he hung up.

21

I dropped the phone in the cradle, then sat there for a minute, trying to think what I was missing. Something so simple. Something that had nothing to do with my disappointment that Torrance's call was purely business.

"What was that all about?" Scolari asked.

"Torrance said Cassandra called Lombard. Lombard told Torrance that she's being held hostage at City Sausage and Meat for the half mil we found in her trunk. Foust has her."

"City Sausage? The dumpy little place right behind Crazy Mazy's house?"

"The same," I said. I doubted there was a person in the city who wasn't familiar with Harriet Maze. "She said it was a front for spies."

"She hasn't changed much, has she?"

"Back when we had that gang killing, she saw someone climbing in their window. I'll lay odds it was Squeaky. Markowski and I found him a few blocks away that night. And right after that, he calls to say he's giving me Foust." In my mind's eye, I saw Squeaky running down the alley, the glare of lights behind him. The truck lights? "That's got to be how they kept Squeaky's body from decomposing. Pick it up in their truck, instant refrigeration. Dump it in the ocean a couple days later, no one's the wiser. Water's cold, which also slows the decomposition. Throws a wrench in our entire investigation."

"You figured all this out from Torrance's call?"

"No," I said, fitting all the pieces together in my mind. "Crazy Mazy. She complained about that truck all the time."

"That'll go over well in court."

I caught a glimpse of Kevin slipping from the bathroom into the hallway. He looked at me, his face stricken.

Suddenly he took off.

"Kevin. Wait," I said. I shot out of bed, wearing nothing but Scolari's T-shirt. My scraped and bruised knees were stiff, I hurt all over, and all I could think was that Dr. Higgins was going to have a field day with this.

I grabbed my jeans and pulled them on to go after Kevin in an attempt to salvage what was left of his childhood.

My aunt stood at the window looking out, her hand over her chest. "I don't know what got into him. He just ran out the door."

I didn't answer, just ran after him, stopping midway down the steps. From there I had a good view of the street in both directions. He was nowhere in sight. "Kev?"

No answer. I looked up and down the street, hoping he was hiding nearby. "Kev?" I called out again. I heard a car start, then realized that the sound was coming from Scolari's driveway.

"Oh, shit," I said, jumping down the remaining six stairs, stubbing my left toe. "Kevin! No!"

Scolari's pickup backed from the drive, the shiny black paint scraping against the boxwood hedge. The right rear wheel ran off the curb, bouncing the shocks, as he came to an abrupt stop. And just as abruptly, the vehicle lurched forward, tires screeching as he turned quickly out of the drive, then sped southbound.

"Kevin!" I screamed. "You're grounded for life!"

I raced up the stairs, ignoring the pain in my toe and every other part of my body. Scolari was at the door in an instant. "Please say that wasn't my new truck I just saw heading down the street."

"We have to go after him."

"I'll borrow a car from the neighbor."

He took off. I ran into his room, took my phone from his drawer, and saw the Smith and Wesson next to it. I hesitated only a second, then shoved that in my waistband, scooped up my shoes, and flew out the door.

Aunt Molly followed me. "What should I do?"

"Stay here in case he comes back. If he does, call me."

Her hand went to her mouth, her eyes pooling. I gave her a quick hug. "He'll be okay. Don't worry." Like she wouldn't. And then I was down the stairs.

Scolari came out of the neighbor's apartment, holding a set of keys. "White Ford," he said.

My gaze followed his to a white Ford Fairlane parked in the neighbor's drive. "God, I hope it runs."

"Single owner," he said, as if that explained everything.

Scolari unlocked it, and we slid in. "Where to?" he asked.

"He went southbound. Christ. I didn't even know he could drive." We both stared down the street, then looked at each other. "Oh, God," I said. "He's going to rescue his mom."

"You think he could find City Sausage? He's a kid."

"A kid who stole your car. The only thing we didn't do was hand him a goddamned map."

"You don't suppose he knows how to work that satellite map system?"

"Great."

The Ford took a few moments to warm up, since the neighbor lady took it out only on Sundays for church. I called dispatch to have them put out an APB on Scolari's truck. And then it occurred to me that Scolari's cell phone was in it. I called it. No answer.

"Damm it." I tried calling Torrance. Got his voice mail.

"Maybe he didn't hear us talking. Maybe he's just taking it for a ride."

"Right. Can you drive any faster?" I asked, scanning the traffic. There wasn't a black pickup in sight. "I can't believe this is happening."

"Okay, worst-case scenario. He goes there. You think he's gonna get by SWAT, and negotiators, and about a gazillion uniforms on the perimeter? You don't think they're gonna let some kid in, do you?"

I gave one of those laughs, the sort that lodged in your throat on the verge of hysteria. I told myself I was being silly. Scolari was right. There would be a full-scale operation in progress. I was worrying for nothing.

When we got there, I found out how very wrong he was.

Scolari's pickup was parked about a half block past City Sausage. Kevin wasn't in it.

And there wasn't a cop in sight.

Scolari cut across the lanes, parking on the wrong side of the street next to Crazy Mazy's fence. We could see the whitewashed front of City Sausage. It didn't look open. Or even occupied. There were cars parked up and down the street, but they probably belonged to surrounding businesses.

"You sure Torrance gave you the right location?"

"This is what he said."

"Maybe they're gone."

"Maybe they're not here yet."

"We better check for the kid."

Scolari exited first, closing the door only partially. I did the same, then walked to the back of the car, meeting him at the fence line. He was about six inches taller than the fence and had to duck as we edged our way along it, stopping at the alley. City Sausage was directly across from us.

Scolari took a quick look into the alley. "Looks clear."

We both darted across to the corner of the building. Two large windows faced north to the street. He crouched, took a look. "I'm going to check the other side."

I glanced down the alley, saw the refrigerated truck there. "I'll take this side."

Scolari and I separated. I kept close to the building, ducking below the window that Crazy Mazy had seen someone climbing into. The side door was about five feet ahead, closed. Beyond that, City Sausage's truck. I thought about Squeaky and the plausibility of his body being picked up and stored within it.

I wondered what was in it now—I never expected anyone to be hiding behind it. I crept out, around the front of the truck, heard the static of a police radio, and ran straight into Torrance.

"You shouldn't be here, Gillespie," he said, his voice

like cold steel. I didn't need to see behind his mirrored glasses to know he wasn't pleased. "You're on AL."

"Kevin might be in there."

"What?"

"He overheard me telling Scolari. Stole his truck. We found it up the street. I think he's going to save his mom."

"So much for Plan B."

I didn't say anything, just waited for him to explain.

"Lombard's playing Lone Ranger," he said. "Ordered all radio cars out of the area. There wasn't time to go over his head."

"Oh, my God. Tell me you're kidding."

"I don't kid about the insane, I just investigate them."

"You were going in there by yourself."

"I was waiting for Mathis and the others to arrive. That was Plan B. Kevin's presence changes all that."

I bit at my lip. *Please God . . .*

"You armed?"

I lifted my oversized T-shirt, drew the Smith and Wesson from my waistband, and said, "There's something bothering me about this."

I saw his brows rise over the top of his glasses.

"Don't you find it odd that Cassandra would call Lombard of all people?"

"Explain."

"She doesn't trust cops. She's been hiding out for twelve years, thinking they were going to arrest her for Sean's overdose."

"Christ, Gillespie. You got any more bombshells you want to drop on me?"

"Not yet."

He took a breath, as if wrestling with the decision. "Scolari at the front?"

I nodded.

"Plan C. We go in."

I followed Torrance to the door. He reached over, opened it. We didn't hear anything, and it appeared dark at first in contrast to the light outside. Torrance took a quick look, then stepped back to the side. "I think it's a storage room. Let's hope it goes somewhere."

He took off his sunglasses, dropped them in his jacket pocket, then gripped his nine-millimeter in both hands as he pushed the door wider with his foot. "Don't play hero, Gillespie."

And then he entered.

I was right behind him. Saw only shadows at first and a wall about four feet in front of us. Five feet to our left, a door stood open on the same wall, fluorescent light spilling from the room beyond. It mirrored the door to our right. Open, light coming in.

Probably led to the same area. We could go either way.

He tapped my shoulder, pointed at the left door, then held his hand up in a stopping motion. He wanted me to look, stay put, until he checked the right.

I nodded, then headed to the left. My sight was starting to adjust, and my peripheral vision picked up buckets, mops and brooms, shelves with cleaning supplies. As I neared the door I saw it opened out, the hinges closest to me. It afforded me a perfect view between door and frame. And allowed me to stay shadowed.

I looked through. Saw a flash of blue and white, Kevin in his football jersey, crouched behind a stainless steel cabinet. He was holding a hammer, and I had this crazy picture of him standing up, throwing it, and getting shot. I wanted to call out to him, but didn't dare. There was only one thing I could do. Go out there and drag him back with me. I crouched down and edged toward Kevin. Beyond him on the other side of the counter, Lombard had his gun pointed at Foust. Foust stood with his hands behind his head, Jamison gripping them in one hand, patting him down with the other. Cassandra, nervous, hugged a small black handbag to her chest. She stood apart from them, her dark hair framing her bruised, pale face, so like Kevin's. And yet so unlike his.

In a rush it hit me. Squeaky's call that night. What I was missing. What was about to happen.

Lombard with the gun, his hand shaking. The Lone Ranger. Foust about to be arrested by Jamison. The suicide note—a receipt for casings. Sausage casings, I realized, not bullets. All the players together. Kevin hiding in their midst.

The last puzzle piece fell into place. And the world fell apart.

Torrance moved out on the opposite side. But everything happened too fast. Lombard stepped back. Cassandra pulled a small semi-auto from her bag, before I could call out. I had barely reconciled in my mind Squeaky's words to me the night he was killed. *My sister's in town. She'll give me a ride.* The headlights in the alley. Cassandra had driven him there. She'd seen him killed.

And now she was pointing her gun at the captain.

But Foust shouldered Jamison, then knocked the gun from Lombard's hand. It hit the concrete floor. Foust lunged for it. Cassandra raised her weapon to the ceiling. And fired.

Plaster and dust rained down.

Everyone stopped dead.

Everyone but me. I was not leaving Kevin unprotected. And Cassandra wasn't watching me. She aimed her gun at Foust.

"You move, Tony, and the next thing I shoot is you."

Foust slowly held his hands palms out. "You and I had a deal."

"Fuck you, Tony," she said. "You're going to hell. You and this goddamned cop," she said, using her pistol to indicate Lombard. "Now tell your flunky if I see him go for his gun, you're dead."

Lombard's face drained of color when he saw Jamison lift up his hands. "What are you doing? We came here to save you."

"You want me to lay it out for you?" she said. "You came here because I set this up. Me. All because my brother, Squeaky, calls me for a ride. He doesn't even have a clue who he ripped off until he shows me the money and tells me where he got it from. By then it was too late, they'd seen him. He figures he's gonna turn them in. But Abernathy came after him. Shot him down in cold blood right there in front of me, while I sat in my car."

"But Abernathy's dead," Lombard said. "You have nothing to worry about now."

"Oh, my God," she said. "You just don't get it, do you? It's *my* car they're looking for. Abernathy killed Sean. I watched him kill my brother. I'd already let twelve years go by, because I was scared he'd kill me, too. But you know what? Fate brought my brother here to steal the money. Fate made Abernathy cross the street after he killed him. Fate gave me the opportunity to set this up. I was not about to let it pass me by a second time."

"Why?" Lombard asked.

"Why? Because twelve years ago you were too stupid to figure out that Tony was using this place as a front. And the one good guy in my life, Sean, figures it out, but doesn't know his partner's involved. So when he brings the evidence to you, Captain Lombard, his partner and Tony set him up."

"I didn't know that then," Lombard said. "You have to believe me."

"Yeah," she said as I moved closer to Kevin, realizing that the man in that apartment must be her father—and wondering if she knew he was dead. "Well, that's your problem. Your problem that Lee Abernathy tells Sean to check out or he's killing me and my kid. You get it now, you dumbfuck?" she said, her gaze narrowing as she added, "*Check out* as in kill himself. You as good as stuck the needle in his arm. He never used heroin a day in his life. It scared him to death when he saw me doing it."

Cassandra hesitated, and I stopped where I was, just within arm's reach of Kevin, worried that if I moved, upset the balance, she might go off.

But she didn't seem to notice my presence as she continued. "A lot of good it did me. I've been clean for twelve years. And there's not a day goes by that I don't want it. But not Sean, you sick bastard. He was good. Just like my son."

Tears streamed down her face as she used her gun to point at Lombard in accusation, thrusting it forward with each word. "You let everyone think he killed himself. But he didn't. You hear me?" she said. "And now I got two bullets in here with names on them. Tony's and yours." She laughed, more of a hysterical choking sound. "You want to know the funny part? I don't know who I want to kill more. You two or me."

She looked down at the shiny silver semi-auto, then leveled it at Lombard's chest. I was nearly to Kevin, reached out and grasped his shirt. But Kevin saw Torrance with his gun and pushed at me and away from the cabinet, screaming, *"No! No! Don't kill her."* His voice reverberated on the walls, the concrete floor. Pierced my heart.

Torrance aimed.

He could have shot her. He should have. But he glanced at Kevin. I saw his hesitation. How do you tell a kid you were about to kill his mother?

Kevin scrambled around the cabinets, screaming.

His mother saw him. She threw her gun across the room, shouting, "Oh, God!"

And then Foust reached out and grabbed him.

I saw Kevin jerk back, the hammer he held falling, his shirt tightening in Foust's grasp. A flash of silver, and time fragmented in that one instant.

Cassandra started forward, sobbing. Foust pulled Kevin against him, using him as a shield. But he faced us, and started backing from the room, a knife at Kevin's throat. "Drop the guns or I kill him," Foust said to us.

Torrance remained steady. "Let him go," he said, though neither of us had a clear shot.

"I don't think so." He pressed the knife into Kevin's carotid. No one moved except Foust with Kevin, his young face pale and tear-streaked. Not making a sound.

"You're not taking my nephew."

"No?"

"No." I took a step forward. Scolari was undoubtedly covering the front door, but I couldn't chance it. Life meant nothing to Foust.

"What're you going to do, *Inspector* Gillespie? You're going down for Abernathy's murder, his hit-and-run. Why do you think I hid Squeaky's body? Your testimony won't mean shit when they get done with you."

"I didn't kill Abernathy."

"Yeah, well maybe the kid here doesn't quite understand his mother's pretty little speech. Maybe you should clarify it for him. Tell him who did."

If I could have put a bullet in Foust's brain right there, I would have. But adrenaline and fear made my hands unsteady.

He saw that and laughed. "You can't do it, can you? Hit me, hit the boy. Now drop your gun like a good little girl, and I'll think about letting him live."

I'd never try a fatal shot, not while he held Kevin. I lowered my gun toward the floor, thought of trajectories, angles. What would be fatal, what wouldn't. Saw Foust smile, like he won. And then I fired into the concrete about a foot in front of his right leg.

The shot ricocheted, as I knew it would, hitting him in the shin. Torrance dove, knocking Kevin to the ground. Foust was wide open. His gaze met mine, and I saw a look of defiance.

I raised the thirty-eight and fired. He jerked back. His knife clattered to the ground. And then I fired again.

That one was for Sean.

22

I vaguely remembered what happened after that. Jamison and Lombard, scrambling for the guns, drawing down on Foust. Foust on the concrete, facedown in a growing pool of blood that inched steadily toward a drain on the floor.

Scolari appeared, said something about the front doors being locked, and there was Torrance covering Cassandra, telling Scolari to take me and Kevin out—not wanting Kevin to see his mother arrested—Kevin cradling his arm against his chest, looking back at Cassandra, both of them crying.

"Let's go," Scolari said. "I think we better get Kevin to the hospital."

My heart constricted. I looked for bleeding, thinking I must have shot him after all.

Scolari saw my panic and said, "Busted arm."

He hustled us outside, and there in the alley, right behind Crazy Mazy's house, I took Kevin by his shoulders, examining every part of him.

"Maybe we should call an ambulance."

Kevin shook his head and pulled away, then winced at the pain his movement caused. "It's okay. I did it when I fell."

"No, it's not okay. And you're grounded for life."

"She's my mom. I couldn't just let something happen to her."

I stopped and looked at him. Twelve years of anger at Cassandra came out at once, and I thought, *Screw Dr. Higgins and her psychoanalyst bullshit.* "I'm going to say this once, Kevin, so listen up. Your mother gave birth to you. She may have even cared about you. But you can't ever forget who raised you. Or who raised me and your father. Aunt Molly did. Not because someone asked her, or because you were dumped on her doorstep. She did it because she loves you more than life itself." I looked away, not wanting to cry, but knowing I couldn't stop. "And she's scared to death right now, worried that something terrible is going to happen to you."

I felt Kevin touch my arm, but I didn't turn.

"Aunt Kate? You think maybe we should call and tell her I'm okay?"

I nodded, trying to speak past the lump in my throat. "Yes, Kevin. I think we should."

They ended up putting pins in Kevin's arm, and Scolari picked up my aunt so she could be there for the surgery. When it was over, and Kevin was finally awake, we went into his room. He was groggy but alert, smiling when Scolari asked him how he was going to play football with a cast.

Kevin looked at me, then my aunt. I heard him say, "I love you, Aunt Molly." She started crying, and I backed out of the room, taking Scolari with me.

"You sure know how to lay a guilt trip," he said.

"Stuff it."

We walked to the waiting room, sitting side by side. A long silence ensued, and then Scolari said, "Nice piece of shooting. What made you think to do it that way?"

"Bowling pins," I said.

Scolari glanced at me.

"Haven't you ever shot bowling pins at the indoor range?"

"Tried. Could never hit the damned things."

"It's easy. You just aim in front of them. The ricochet takes care of the rest. I saw Foust's leg sticking out, and decided it was the only way to do it and . . ." I didn't want to relive the fear. The thought I might miss and hit Kevin.

"Yeah," he said. "What do you think they're gonna do about Abernathy's hit-and-run?"

We both looked at the door to Kevin's hospital room, and then I stared out the window, into the darkness, seeing Cassandra's car, the damage down the left side. I thought about the composite drawing. The sketch that could have been me. But was really her. "I guess that depends on the jury. Abernathy killed her brother trying to get the money back. In the heat of the moment, I suppose it can be argued that all she did was go after Squeaky's murderer—and run him down."

"You know what I think? I think she'll get in more trouble for pointing a weapon at Lombard."

Probably true, but I didn't answer because Torrance walked in just then.

He looked at us and said, "How's Kevin?"

"Fine," I said, standing. "He's visiting with my aunt right now."

He nodded.

Scolari said, "I think I'm going to get a cup of coffee. You want one, Gillespie?"

I shook my head, and he left.

Torrance strode to the window and looked out. I could see his reflection, the pain in his eyes. I wanted to go to him, but he started talking about the case.

"Lombard told me he's retiring. He blames himself for what happened today. And for Sean. That's why he and Jamison showed up at your aunt's, hoping to help find Kevin. It was Lombard who ordered Jamison not to talk about Abernathy's drug shipment case."

"And why was that?" I asked, crossing my arms, not ready to forgive Lombard for his part in all this.

"Because it was Jamison who suspected Abernathy and Rosenkrantz were dirty, and started pointing out the similarities in the case to one Sean had worked right before he died. Lombard figured Abernathy's murder was a hit, and he intended to minimize the danger to any other officers by keeping the entire investigation under wraps."

"And that's why he showed up today with Jamison?"

"Yes. He wanted to make up for the mistakes that cost Sean his life." Torrance looked at me, my reflection actually, in the glass. "Lombard asked me to talk to you about having a service for Sean. He wants it known that Foust was responsible. He wants to reopen the investigation."

"Lombard wants it off his chest," I said, surprised by the force of my anger. "What good does it do twelve years too late?"

"The choice is yours," he said softly. "But I thought you might like to do it for Kevin."

My glance strayed down the hall, to the open door, where my aunt hovered over his bed, stroking his hair. I hugged my arms about me, felt my eyes sting. "Yes," I said. "Tell him that would be nice."

Torrance moved from the window to stand before

me. He reached out, brushed a strand of hair from my face. "Are you okay?"

Somehow I knew he wasn't asking about the shooting.

"Yes. And you?"

There was a long moment of silence.

"I don't know," he finally said.

And then he walked away.

The department and the DEA ran parallel investigations into Rosenkrantz's and Foust's cocaine smuggling, finding that Abernathy was a key player, had been for a number of years. At the same time, a smaller, quicker investigation went on—that one involving my brother. His death was determined to be an on-duty homicide and the city started the proceedings to enlist death benefits for Kevin. A week later, the day of my brother's memorial, the fog shrouded the cemetery in a layer of mist. I didn't mind. It brought everything together, made it seem more personal than the affair the department made it into. I looked over at Kevin, his suit coat draped over his casted arm. He seemed in awe of the turnout, his gaze taking in the rows of uniformed officers standing at attention. My aunt held on to his good arm, lost in her own private thoughts. She, too, wanted this, believed it was good.

I went along, keeping my feelings to myself. My father should have been here. He was the one who needed to see this. The one who died with a broken heart, thinking his son had betrayed everything he stood for.

Suddenly the bagpipes started to play, their solemn tones conjuring up images of souls lost. My brother's soul. My father's soul. Tears welled up in my eyes, and I let them fall.

Kevin leaned into my aunt, and Scolari, on the other side of her, had his arm around her in support. I stared at my brother's headstone, completely lost. I closed my eyes, wondering how I was going to go on, be strong enough for what was left of my family. And then I felt a presence beside me. A warmth. I looked and saw Torrance.

He put his arm around me, and held me. Not saying a word. Just looking at me with complete understanding.

And in that moment, I knew that everything was going to be okay.

Valediction

We gather round
On hallowed ground
And bid our last farewell.

Cry for our fallen
As we hear the solemn
Bagpipes' haunting knell.

Each tear we shed
Not just for the dead,
But for those left behind this day.

We think of the past
And pray this is the last
That we hear the bagpipes play.

Oh, how we rue the day
That we hear the bagpipes play . . .

Robin Burcell 2001

The Joanna Brady Mysteries by New York Times Bestselling Author

An assassin's bullet shattered Joanna Brady's world, leaving her policeman husband to die in the Arizona desert. But the young widow fought back the only way she knew how: by bringing the killers to justice . . . and winning herself a job as Cochise County Sheriff.

DESERT HEAT
0-380-76545-4/$7.50 US/$9.99 Can

TOMBSTONE COURAGE
0-380-76546-2/$6.99 US/$9.99 Can

SHOOT/DON'T SHOOT
0-380-76548-9/$6.50 US/$8.50 Can

DEAD TO RIGHTS
0-380-72432-4/$7.50 US/$9.99 Can

SKELETON CANYON
0-380-72433-2/$7.50 US/$9.99 Can

RATTLESNAKE CROSSING
0-380-79247-8/$6.99 US/$8.99 Can

OUTLAW MOUNTAIN
0-380-79248-6/$6.99 US/$9.99 Can

DEVIL'S CLAW
0-380-79249-4/$7.50 US/$9.99 Can

PARADISE LOST
0-380-80469-7/$7.99 US/$10.99 Can

Available wherever books are sold or please call 1-800-331-3761 to order.

JB 0502